When I Saw You

Laura Branchflower

For Jordan

Content

Prologue

Arlington, VA

"I want you to understand this is between me and your mother," the man was saying as he paced back and forth in the center of the living room.

The twelve-year-old girl concentrated to hear him, the wails from her younger brother increasingly loud. Not that anything else he said mattered. He was leaving them behind. The Navy was sending him to San Diego, their mother had been talking about the move for months, and now he was telling them they weren't going.

"This has nothing to do with the two of you," he continued.

How could this have nothing to do with us? the girl wondered, no longer listening as he droned on. He was moving three thousand miles away. The movers just left with half their furniture.

"Why?" she asked, interrupting his monologue.

He looked at her in confusion. "Why? That's what I've been explaining to you. Your mother and I—"

"Why can't you make it work?" She could feel the pressure behind her eyes, but wouldn't let herself cry. She didn't want to cry.

"We've been trying, honey. We just can't—."

"Why can't you try harder?" Her eyes flew to her mother. "Do you want this too?"

Her mother's tear-filled eyes met hers from across the room. "Your father thinks—"

"What about what I think? Does it matter to either of you what I think?" She stood up. "This is our life too." She gestured with her hand towards her brother. "We don't want this to happen." She hated the desperation she could hear in her voice and knew her eyes were preparing to betray her.

"Calm down, sweetheart." Her father moved towards her.

"Don't touch me," she whispered, tears beginning to fall from her eyes. "I don't want you to touch me," she cried as he pulled her trembling body into his arms. "I don't want to be divorced, Daddy." She laid her cheek against the soft material of his sweatshirt, taking comfort in his familiar smell. "Don't you love me?"

"Oh, honey, of course I love you." His voice caught on the last word. "This has nothing to do with you."

Then why do I feel so awful? she wondered. If it had nothing to do with her, why did she feel her very existence was being redefined?

1

Fifteen years later...

"Mommy...Mommy...Mommy," Taylor Merrick said as she pulled on her mother's arm.

"Taylor, please." Lia Merrick's eyes remained on the legal document in her hand. "Can't you see I'm busy?"

"But, Mommy," Taylor continued, tugging harder, "you have to see this. Lizzie and Raymond have been turned into turtles and they're—"

"I can't right now. I have to finish reading these documents."

"I just want you to see this one part."

"Taylor, no!" She closed her eyes, instantly regretting her harsh tone. "I'm sorry." She turned to Taylor, running her hand down the girl's mane of dark brown hair. "I just can't right now."

"Why are you crying?" Taylor asked.

"I'm not." She wiped at the few stray tears beneath her eyes. "Go finish your show and let me finish reading this, and then we'll watch a show together, okay?"

"Okay." Taylor wrapped her small arms around her mother's waist, giving her a tight squeeze. "I love you, Mommy."

"I love you too," she whispered.

As soon as Taylor left the kitchen, Lia's eyes returned to the document. She was legally divorced. It felt surreal and yet there it was, in dark, bold letters. She was no longer Mrs. Ned Merrick.

She walked the short distance from the kitchen to her bedroom and lay down on the unmade bed, rolling onto her back and staring up at the ceiling. Ned was free to marry Candice. The thought made her stomach turn.

She must have fallen asleep because sometime later, Taylor was waking her up.

"Mommy, I'm hungry."

"What time is it?" She turned her head towards her alarm clock.

"I think it's eighty-two," Taylor answered.

"Eight twenty," she corrected, her eyes focusing in on the red digital display.

"I'm hungry," Taylor repeated.

"I know." She reached for the bedside lamp and turned a small knob, lighting up the room. "I must have fallen asleep."

"You must have," Taylor agreed. "Did you finish reading your paper?" She picked up the divorce papers from the bed.

Lia's eyes focused on the document in Taylor's hand. "No." She took the papers and set them on the nightstand next to the bed. "I'll finish them later. How about Chick-fil-A for dinner?"

"Yeah!" Taylor jumped into the air. "Can I play in the—"

"No, just the drive-thru. It's late." She slipped off the bed she used to share with her now ex-husband and looked down at her wrinkled suit, regretting not changing into something else before lying down. "Let me put on some jeans and I'll be ready."

"Okay. I'll get Maggie." Taylor ran off in search of her favorite doll.

Lia pulled open the middle drawer of her dresser, riffling through her clothes in search of a pair of jeans. She sighed, remembering she needed to do laundry. Taylor didn't have anything clean to wear to school the following day. She walked into the closet-sized adjoining bathroom and found some jeans lying over a wicker basket in the corner. After judging them clean enough to wear, she walked back into the bedroom and changed out of her suit.

She was in desperate need of new casual clothes, she thought as her eyes focused on the frayed knees of her jeans. But then again, she needed a lot of new everything.

Her eyes swept over her bedroom with its worn beige carpet and off-white walls, which, like the rest of the apartment, looked like they were decades from their prime. She pushed down the feeling of self-pity attempting to surface.

It could have been worse, she reminded herself. She could still be a twenty-eight-year-old living with her mother and stepfather, upsetting their lives. No. As old and decrepit as the apartment was, at least she had her own place and she was managing, albeit barely, to pay her own bills.

Lia pulled her long hair back in a ponytail and tried to remember the last time she changed its style. Too long ago, she decided when she couldn't immediately recall. She knew she was pretty with her light blue eyes, ivory skin, and dark hair, but she also knew she was dated.

She found Taylor lying on the carpet in the windowless family room, which, after several steam cleans, still looked soiled and stained. "Come on, Taylor."

"But I think Ross and Rachel got divorced," she said, pointing at the television screen. "Look, Ross is in bed with somebody else. He must be married to her now, right?"

Lia looked up at the ceiling. She needed to start monitoring Taylor's TV watching. "He must be," she agreed before pushing the off button on the remote. "We have to go if you want to eat."

"What are we going to do tomorrow?" Taylor asked moments later, preceding her mother out of the apartment.

"The same thing we did today." Lia closed and locked the door before taking Taylor's hand and leading her towards the stairs. "You're going to preschool and I'm going to work."

"Ohhh," Taylor whined. "I don't want to go to school. I hate school."

"You told me yesterday you liked school."

"Well, I don't." She held on to the rail with her free hand as they walked down a flight of stairs. "Can't I go to Grandma's?"

"No. You're five now, remember? Kindergarten is going to start in a couple of weeks and you can't miss school anymore." She continued to hold Taylor's hand as they walked out into the parking lot.

"Where did I park?" Her eyes scanned the parking lot in search of her two-and-a-half-year-old Honda, which Ned surprisingly let her keep. She recalled how happy they were the day they bought their first new car. It was Labor Day weekend and they were celebrating Ned's new position at Blackman and Associates. He'd been working for the district attorney's office in Fairfax County, Virginia, just outside of Washington, DC, since graduating from University of Virginia Law School two years prior, and the new job came with a substantial pay increase. Of course, if she knew then it also came with a woman who would steal her husband, she may not have been so happy.

"There it is." Taylor pointed to the blue Honda Accord across the parking lot.

"Good job, sweetie."

It was 10:00 p.m. when Lia finally closed Taylor's bedroom door. She needed to organize her life a little better, she decided. Taylor never seemed to go to bed before ten and getting her up and ready in the morning was becoming an increasingly difficult task.

As she headed towards the laundry room, balancing a basket of dirty clothes on her hip, her cell phone began to ring and she glanced at the display. She thought about not answering it, having no desire to talk to her now ex, but after a moment's hesitation she brought it to her ear.

"Did I wake you?" Ned asked.

"No. What do you need?"

"We never spoke logistics about Friday."

"We didn't?" She set the basket of clothes on the dryer and began sorting through them.

"Not that I recall."

"We agreed you would pick her up from my mother's at six thirty," she said, knowing he was lying. Ned remembered everything.

"Right, okay." There was a pause and she knew he was about to reveal the real reason for his call. "Did you get the papers today in the mail?"

"The divorce papers? Yes."

"Good. I'm not sure what's going on with your job search, but the rehabilitative alimony only goes on for another year."

"I'm aware of that, Ned," she said shortly.

"These temp jobs you're working for twelve dollars an hour aren't going to be enough."

A now familiar sinking feeling gripped her stomach. "I received my degree in May."

"May was three months ago, and you should have been looking for a job before you graduated. This area isn't even in a recession. I don't understand why you haven't found a real job yet."

"Remind me of how this is your business. You're not my husband anymore, remember?"

"But I am Taylor's father. I don't like her living in that dingy apartment."

"Well maybe you should have thought about that before you left her."

His sigh was audible. "Look, Lia, I'm sorry I hurt you, but we need to put this in the past. Candice is going to be a big part of Taylor's life, and—"

"Are we done?" she asked. "Because I have things to do and frankly, Ned, I don't want to waste any more of my time talking to you."

"Actually, there is one more thing. I want to keep Taylor overnight on Friday."

"We've been through this. Taylor is not spending the night with you while you're living with a woman you're not married to."

"Well, you see, that's the thing. That's why I'm asking. Candice and I got married yesterday."

Her grip on the phone tightened. "Then I guess she can. Is that all?"

"Yes. That's all."

"Goodbye, Ned." She slowly sunk to the floor.

❦

"Taylor, your waffle's getting cold," she called out the following morning. She poured herself a cup of coffee and leaned back against the counter, still feeling numb after the events of the previous evening.

"Can't you bring it in here?" Taylor called from the family room.

Lia was about to tell her she had to eat at the table, but stopped herself. Who cared where she ate her breakfast? "Here you go," she said moments later as she set a cut-up waffle and glass of milk on the coffee table in front of the couch. "Don't spill the milk," she called over her shoulder as she left the room.

"I won't. Mommy, you forgot my fork."

Lia went back to the kitchen and forced open the utensil drawer, which seemed to have come off its rollers. As she picked up a fork, she noticed an unheard voicemail from the evening before on her cell phone.

"Hello," an unfamiliar female voice began. "This message is for Lia Merrick. My name is Cecile Mann, and I'm in human resources at Zurtech in Reston. We received your resume last week and are interested in speaking with you and setting up an interview. Would you please call me at (703) 555-8910 at your earliest convenience? Again, my name is Cecile Mann and I'm in human resources at Zurtech."

"Thank you, God," Lia said looking up at the ceiling

⸺ ⸺

Lia felt a little nervous as she pulled her Honda into the massive parking lot at Zurtech's sprawling campus in Reston, Virginia, two weeks later.

After what she thought was a promising interview the previous week, she'd received a phone call Monday morning with the news that they were going with a different candidate.

"I do have another vacancy," Cecile Mann continued before the rejection took full root in Lia's mind. "We have an opening in our Marketing Department, and I think you would be perfect for the position. I know your resume indicated you are interested in finance, but would you consider a different direction, possibly?"

Lia assured her she would, admitting she was more interested in working for Zurtech in general than in any specific department. Now she was sitting in their parking lot, twenty minutes early for her 11:00 a.m. interview with the vice president of marketing, trying to preserve her confidence. Receiving the initial call from Cecile Mann the same day she received her divorce papers wasn't a coincidence. No, she was meant to work for Zurtech and this job was going to serve as the catalyst she needed to turn her life around. Not even Ned's recent nuptials could dampen her excitement at the prospect.

An international company with offices in fifty countries and one hundred thousand employees in North America alone, Zurtech was one of the largest computer technology companies in the world. Their Reston location, which housed over fifteen thousand employees, served as the corporate headquarters.

In a classic-cut black suit and a chic new shoulder-length haircut, Lia looked the part of a young corporate professional as she entered the lobby of building number five. After giving her name to security she was handed a badge and sent to a bank of elevators with instructions to go to the sixteenth floor and ask for Stan Hall.

Lia stepped off the elevator into a reception area, and a young woman sitting behind a desk looked up from her computer. "Good morning. May I help you?"

"Hi, good morning. I'm Lia Merrick. I have an appointment with Mr. Hall."

"Please have a seat," the receptionist said. "I'll let him know you're here."

"Thank you." Lia turned and almost collided with a tall, distinguished-looking man of about forty-five with sandy-colored hair, a lean build, and intense blue eyes.

"Lia, I presume?" he asked, touching her arm briefly to keep her from walking into him.

"I'm sorry. I didn't see—"

"It's fine," he said, smiling. "I'm Stan Hall." He held out his hand.

"Hi." She slipped her hand into his, feeling mortified she'd practically plowed him over.

"You're blushing," he said, his eyes alight with humor.

Lia forced herself to maintain his gaze. "It's a trait I curse daily."

He laughed aloud. "I've been looking forward to meeting you, Lia. Cecile couldn't stop raving about you. Let's go back to my office." He released her hand and led her through an expansive open space, filled with sleek gray-and-white work areas, to a corner office.

"After you," he said, pushing open his door.

Lia preceded him into his large office, her eyes taking in the modern furniture. Floor-to-ceiling windows offered an unobstructed view of the woods surrounding the campus.

"Have a seat." He indicated a conference table to their left with the toss of his hand.

Lia lowered herself into one of the eight high-back leather chairs, her eyes continuing their perusal of his office. "This is nice."

He followed her gaze to the two abstract paintings on the wall behind his desk. "Are you into art?"

"I like it," she said. "I don't really understand it."

"Liking it is enough." He took a seat across from her and opened a folder on the table, his eyes briefly scanning her resume before lifting to hers. "Are you aware you're interviewing for a position in our Marketing Department?"

Lia felt her face heat up. "Yes, that resume was tailored to the finance position I applied for a couple of weeks ago. I didn't see any entry-level openings in the Marketing Department."

"You're blushing again," he said, a hint of a smile on his lips.

"Sorry," she breathed, shaking her head.

"I'm teasing you," he said. "And we don't advertise for positions in our Business to Business Division. We either hire from within or human resources will identify promising candidates—like in your case."

"I'm definitely interested in marketing."

"Good." He didn't speak for several seconds, his intense gaze meeting hers. "Cecile's right," he finally said. "You're a natural fit for this division." He closed the folder. "Why don't I tell you about the position and then you can tell me what you think?"

"Yes, please," Lia said, barely able to contain her enthusiasm. She was going to leave his office with a job. She could feel it.

Zurtech's Business to Business Division, or B2B, functioned as the Marketing Department's VIP service, responsible for nurturing Zurtech's most important customers.

"The B2Bs sell goodwill," he told her. "And that goodwill fosters loyalty, which ultimately results in increased company revenues. I personally created this division four years ago.

Within the first year, revenue from our select group of clients increased over fifteen percent. The number of clients we now consider elite has quadrupled in the past three years. The personnel in this division are the crème de la crème of my marketing staff, and they are compensated accordingly." He leaned back in his chair, his hands clasped on the table. "I'm not going to lie. This is a competitive division and there is nowhere to hide. I have fifty percent attrition in the first year with my new hires. Some quit, but most are fired or transferred to other divisions." His intense eyes continued to meet hers. "This job isn't for everyone, but I personally feel it is not only the most important division within marketing, but the most rewarding. You are basically paid to pamper and spoil some of the richest and most powerful men and women in the world. The value of the contacts you'll make here is immeasurable."

"There is no product selling?"

"No. You sell our brand. This is high-end customer service. Essentially, it is your job to become friends with our top clients. Friends like to buy from friends. It's as simple as that."

"So, on a day-to-day basis, what does that entail, exactly?" She was a bit confused.

"It entails getting to know our VIPs," he said. "Learning about every facet of their lives—whether they are married, their children's names, their favorite foods, favorite vacation spots, their hobbies, even their favorite color—anything and everything you can learn. The B2B staff has spent the last few years compiling extensive files on our elite-level customers." He leaned forward, placing his elbows on the table, his chin resting on his fists. "We create an energetic, friendly, and pleasure oriented environment, which will feel more like a cocktail party than a meeting, but make no mistake—you are there to work."

He watched her in silence for a long moment. "You still look confused."

"No. I'm just— Where do these interactions with the customers take place?"

"We have suites at most of the venues in the Washington area. We host our clients for sporting events, concerts, even the occasional ballet. We also have the Zurtech house: a ten-thousand-square-foot facility in Great Falls we use to entertain."

"So would my hours be predominately in the evening?" She hated asking, but as exciting as the position sounded, she couldn't leave Taylor five nights a week.

"Not quite." He smiled. "I'm trying to sell the position, so I was highlighting the perks. Most of your time will be spent in the office updating client files and identifying potential elite-level customers both from within Zurtech and from our competitors." He glanced at his watch. "How about a tour and lunch? And then we can talk compensation."

It was a few minutes past 5:00 p.m. when Lia parked her car in her mother's driveway in Tyson's Corner, Virginia. Her mother had proved to be a godsend over the past two years, faithfully serving as Taylor's babysitter while Lia completed her bachelor's degree and then later when she began to work for a temp agency. She was literally living paycheck to paycheck, and there was no way she could afford an outside caregiver. Plus, knowing Taylor was with her grandmother removed some of the guilt she felt for being away for nine or more hours a day.

"Hello?" Lia called out as she stepped into her mother's foyer.

"Hi." Her mother approached from the back of the house. At fifty-five, Elaine was still quite attractive, with dark hair and the same high cheekbones as her daughter. "Well?"

"I got it!"

"Oh, Lia, that's wonderful." Her mother gave her a hug. "I had a good feeling about this one. When do you start?"

"Monday." She followed her mother to the kitchen at the back of the house.

"Monday? That soon?"

"Yes. Their employee-orientation programs begin the first Monday of the month, so it was either Monday or I'd have to wait another month." She set her purse on the kitchen table and turned towards the family room, which was separated from the kitchen by two steps and a wooden railing. "Hi, Taylor."

"Mommy!" Taylor scurried up from her position in front of the television and ran across the room. "You're here!" She jumped into Lia's arms.

"I missed you." Lia gave her a hug. "How was school?"

"Good. I got to be the teacher's helper."

"That's nice. What does the school helper do?"

"Teacher's helper. Not school helper." Taylor laughed.

Lia smiled. "Sorry, teacher's helper. What does the teacher's helper do?"

"She helps the teacher." Taylor smiled. "You're funny, Mommy."

"So are you." She kissed her small, upturned nose. "I love you."

"I love you too." Taylor struggled out of her arms. "Can I watch the rest of my show?"

Lia glanced towards the television and was relieved to see a cartoon on the screen. "Sure," she said to Taylor's quickly retreating back.

"Hi, Frank," she said to her stepfather as he came into the room. Frank Law, her mother's husband of just over eight years, was one of the nicest people Lia knew. After a career in the government as a program manager, he'd retired the year prior and spent most of his days in his garden or golfing.

"Hi, Lia." He smiled. "I'm sensing congratulations are in order?"

"Yes, I start Monday."

"Very good." He patted her arm before leaving to join Taylor.

"Would you like something to eat?" Elaine asked.

"No, thanks. I had a late lunch." She lowered herself onto one of three barstools lining a granite island.

"I want to hear all about it," Elaine said before setting a bowl of tortilla chips and guacamole onto the counter. "Tell me everything."

Lia quickly recounted details of her new position to her mother. "And," Lia said after several minutes, pausing with a chip at her mouth, "I get a clothing allowance. Well, not exactly an allowance. I meet with a personal shopper at the Neiman Marcus at Tyson's, and I'll be completely outfitted. Zurtech has an account—it's all paid for."

"Neiman Marcus?" Elaine's eyes widened. "Wow!"

"I know. I feel like pinching myself. It seems too good to be true."

2

"Nice picture in the Washingtonian." Tony Prossi, one of three founding partners of the law firm of Prossi, Stuart and Craig, stepped into Joseph Craig's office.

Joseph lifted his gaze from his computer screen. He'd been profiled in the latest issue of *Washingtonian* as one of the ten most eligible bachelors in Washington. "It's not like they gave me a choice. You wouldn't believe how many women read that magazine."

"You're fighting them off, are you?" Tony lifted his eyebrows.

"Yes, I'm fighting them off." He gripped the arms of his chair as he pushed himself to his feet and then he was crossing to the bar in the corner of his office. At six foot four, with dark, wavy hair and a model-worthy face, Joseph Craig didn't need assistance attracting the opposite sex. He had an almost untamed air about him that women found irresistible.

"I hear the cute weather woman from NBC was all over you last night."

"We were all over each other." He turned from the bar with a glass of water. "And I've been paying for it all day. I'm exhausted. There was no stopping her. She went down on me in the back of the cab on the way to her place."

"I'm sure it was painful for you," Tony said dryly.

"It was." He laughed. "I'm getting too old for this. I got about a minute's sleep last night."

"And here I thought you were about to pop the question to Kathy," Tony said, referring to Joseph's girlfriend, a former model and the owner of a plush art gallery in Alexandria, Virginia.

"I probably should."

"And this is why you were screwing the weather woman?"

"We're not exclusive."

"Does she know that?"

Joseph shrugged. "We haven't discussed it."

"I bet." Tony glanced at his watch. "I'm off. See you Monday."

"Wait—wait." Joseph followed him to the door. "I was going to ask if you wanted to go up to New York for the weekend. There's an opening at a gallery. A new artist I want to see."

"New York City in August? No thanks."

"Come on, when was the last time you were up there?"

"Not even tempted. Have a nice weekend."

"You're getting boring, Prossi," Joseph called after him as he left his office.

Joseph Craig and Tony Prossi started life on the same day in hospitals six hundred miles apart—Tony the first son of a young senator and his wife, both of prominent Virginia families, and

Joseph the son of an eighteen-year-old girl who would later become a maid at the estate of a prominent Massachusetts family. And when they met twenty-one years later, they were law students at one of the most prominent colleges in the country. As their lives started the same day, their paths to becoming attorneys too started the same day.

The illegitimate son of a maid would receive the same education as the senator's son. Joseph spent his entire life with the affluent, not as a servant or as an equal, but as an outsider striving to be like them because they were all he knew. His childhood home was on one of the largest estates in Massachusetts. His neighbors had names like Kennedy, Rockefeller and Vanderbilt. He shared their world, but not their status. He was a no one in a world of someones and he knew it, had known it since almost the beginning.

As a little boy, he often sat on the porch off the small two-bedroom cottage that served as his home, staring at the mansion where his grandmother worked and asking why his house was so much smaller. "Because we come from different places, Joseph," his grandmother would say. "We only live here because I work for the Williamses. This is their home... Most people live in much smaller houses." But Joseph never saw those smaller houses.

His grandmother, Elizabeth Craig, came to the United States from England when she was thirty-one years old. Recently widowed, with a ten-year-old daughter, she was hired by Mr. and Mrs. Theodore Williams as a maid and provided a small house on the estate.

Elizabeth's daughter, Helen, grew into a beautiful young woman with platinum hair and green eyes. She turned the heads of men wherever she went. And the summer before she was to begin her freshman year in college, she turned the head of Richard

Jefferson Eastwood III, the oldest son of Mr. Williams's banker, Richard Jefferson Eastwood II. He came to the estate to attend a Fourth of July party and noticed Helen sitting on the porch of her cottage reading a book. He was charming and handsome, and when he asked her if he could call her she said yes. He never mentioned he was getting married in September.

Helen lost her virginity that summer. She was in love and never doubted the dashing Richard would one day be her husband, until one Sunday morning in August when she was lying next to him in bed and his telephone rang. He spoke to the other person only briefly, but before he hung up he said, "I love you too" into the receiver. When Helen asked who he was speaking to he told her it was his fiancée and was surprised when she seemed shocked by the admission. "It has nothing to do with you," he said. "I want to keep seeing you after I'm married."

Devastated, Helen listened to him as he explained how they came from different "stations in life" and he would never even entertain the notion of marrying someone with her background. A month later she discovered she was pregnant. Richard, his wedding two weeks away, was in his office when Helen called.

"Helen, hello," he said, obviously pleased to hear her voice until he learned the reason for the call. "Are you sure it's mine?"

"Of course I'm sure. You're the only man I've ever been with."

"I'm not going to marry you. I'm marrying Elise next week."

"I'm having your baby!" she cried. "You have to marry me."

"I'm not marrying you, Helen." His voice was cold. "Even if I wasn't marrying Elise, I wouldn't marry you...My family would never accept you."

"But...but I'm pregnant."

"That's not my problem." He hung up the phone and several days later she received a letter and check in the mail.

Helen,

This letter in no way acknowledges responsibility for the predicament you've found yourself in. I am not in love with you, have never been in love with you, and would never want to father a child with you.

If you are in fact pregnant, I recommend you terminate the pregnancy immediately. I've enclosed five hundred dollars to pay for the procedure.

I will be getting married next week. Please stop calling my office.

Richard

Helen never spoke to Richard Eastman III again. Seven months and two weeks after receiving the letter, she gave birth to a ten-pound boy and named him Joseph. Joseph had a full head of curly black hair, a cleft in his little chin and the hint of deep dimples in his cheeks.

Elizabeth never discussed the pregnancy or birth with her employers. The Williamses thought it odd when Helen stopped attending college after only one semester, but didn't realize she was pregnant until the spring when it became impossible to hide. Even then Elizabeth didn't bring up the obvious fact that her single daughter was pregnant. And when she asked for a few days off in late May to take care of her daughter, there was no mention of the baby.

Joseph was three weeks old the first time the Williamses met him. Helen, who was out walking with him in the garden, came around a corner and almost collided with them. "Oh, I'm sorry. I didn't know you were here," Helen said, quickly turning.

"It's okay, Helen," Mrs. Williams assured her. "We came out to meet your baby."

"Oh." Helen turned back, surprised. "His name is Joseph," she said with the hint of a smile. She moved the blanket down from his face so they could see him. "He weighed ten pounds."

"He's beautiful," Mrs. Williams said, her eyes moving from the baby to her husband. "Isn't he, Theodore?"

"Yes." He didn't take his eyes from Joseph.

Later that day, Mr. Williams approached Elizabeth and asked if he could have a few moments of her time. "Of course, Mr. Williams." She followed him down the long marble hallway leading to his study. "I know I should have asked your permission before bringing him home from the hospital, but she had nowhere else to go," she began nervously as soon as he closed the door.

"Elizabeth, your grandson is welcome here." He led her to a leather chair beside a fireplace before taking a seat himself. "Does Richard know? It's obvious, Elizabeth. He's a perfect replica of him."

Elizabeth showed Mr. Williams the letter Richard Eastman had sent to Helen and the two never again discussed Joseph Craig's paternal roots. Joseph grew up not knowing he was the illegitimate son of Richard Eastman III. His mother told him he was the son of a Frenchman she met during a trip to Europe the summer after graduation—a man who died in a car accident before they were to be married.

Almost from the beginning, it was obvious Joseph inherited more than the Eastmans' looks. He inherited his grandfather's keen intellect. Richard Eastman II was a brilliant financier. His son, Richard III, was gifted both academically and athletically.

Joseph inherited it all. He taught himself to read when he was three. He was beating Mr. Williams at tennis and chess by the age of eight. He was witty and shrewd, and Mr. Williams spent hours counseling and teaching the boy. Joseph attended a prestigious private day school through eighth grade and then was accepted to the exclusive Choate Rosemary Hall in Connecticut for high school.

The week before he left for Choate Rosemary, Joseph was in his mother's closet searching for his birth certificate when he found a large manila envelope. Inside were several newspaper clippings about the founder of a new brokerage firm, Richard Eastman III. He read through each article and then he found the letter Richard Eastman had sent his mother almost fifteen years earlier. It took him a moment to comprehend what it meant. His father wasn't a dead Frenchman. He was from Massachusetts and he had three Roman numerals after his name.

Joseph read the letter thirty times, never mentioning the discovery to his mother. She seemed to have almost convinced herself he was the son of a Frenchman, telling him dozens of stories over the years about the handsome man who swept her off her feet. She'd even given him a name: Jean la Montagne.

Instead, his father was an American who wouldn't give up a fiancée to marry the seventeen-year-old he'd impregnated. Joseph was the only student in his high school not sharing his father's name. He was the only student who was the son of a servant. He was still popular with the other students and teachers, but he knew he was different. When he went home on break it wasn't to mansions like his friends. He went home to a small cottage he shared with his mother and grandmother. While his friends were vacationing in the South of France, Aspen and Palm Beach, he was helping his mother polish silver.

He spent his whole life on the edge of his father's world. He became fanatical about proving his worth to his classmates and had inherited the brains and natural athletic ability to do it. He excelled at everything in high school, becoming captain of the rowing team, tennis team and debate team.

Like his father and grandfather before him, he graduated valedictorian of his class. He was one of three students in the country that year to receive a perfect score on his SAT, and he was accepted to Yale University. After graduating magna cum laude with a degree in English, he took the LSAT and received a score high enough to gain admission to Harvard Law School.

During his final semester before graduation, Joseph's grandmother died of a heart attack and Tony offered to drive him home. When they arrived at the estate, they were greeted by Mr. and Mrs. Williams, and within minutes they were offering Tony a room in the main house.

Joseph excused himself and was almost in tears when he reached the cottage. He found his mother curled up on the couch crying, and as he pulled her into his arms he too began to cry. Later, when the Williamses called to invite them to the main house for dinner, Joseph declined.

He was sitting on a porch swing, drinking his fourth Heineken, when Tony strolled up the path from the main house hours later.

"Hey." Tony stopped several yards from the porch. "You okay?"

"I'm fine." He took a long swig from the bottle in his hand.

"This place is unbelievable," Tony said glancing towards the gardens to his right.

"You mean your parents' place in McLean isn't like this?"

"Hardly. We're paupers compared to this."

"I wonder what that makes me." Joseph kicked off the porch with the tip of his loafer, sending the swing back in a wide arch. "What's lower than a pauper?"

"I was kidding," Tony said. "How's your mother?"

"She's sleeping. Cleaning up after other people all day is hard work."

Tony watched him in silence.

"Has your mother ever made a bed, Tony?" Joseph asked, not looking directly at him, but off towards the main house.

Tony brought his eyebrows together, confusion marring his handsome features. "Of course."

"You mean you didn't have a maid?"

"Not that lived in the house."

"So you had one that came during the day, but went home at night." Joseph's gaze moved from the house to Tony.

"No. We had a service come to the house a couple times a week."

"Did you ever think about those women?" He jumped off the swing and closed the distance between them in several long strides. "Where they went when they left your fancy house?"

"No, Joseph, I didn't." Tony met his eyes. "What in the hell is wrong with you?"

"Nothing...nothing at all." He tilted back his head as he finished his beer and then he tossed the empty bottle onto the porch. "Shouldn't you be getting back to the Williamses? I mean, the servants' quarters are somewhat below you, aren't they, Prossi?"

"I only agreed to stay up there because I thought you'd want some time alone with your mother...It's not a big deal, Joe."

"To you maybe." Joseph moved to walk past him, but Tony gripped his arm. "Take your hands off me," Joseph snapped, his eyes moving to the hand on his arm.

"What are you going to do, Joe? Hit me?" Tony moved his head back so he could meet his friend's eyes. "You're going to hit me because Mr. Williams invited me to stay in his house so you could have some time alone with your mother?"

"That's not why he invited you." Joseph roughly shook his arm free and turned to face him. "He invited you because your father's a fucking senator and he thinks you're too good to stay here." He waved his hand towards the cottage.

"That's bullshit." Tony placed his hands on his hips. "He invited me to stay there because of you."

"You're naïve," Joseph said dismissively, before walking off in the direction of the gardens.

"I'm naïve?" Tony jogged to catch up to him and then fell into step beside him. "The man just spent an hour and a half talking nonstop about you."

"Right." Joseph shook his head, continuing forward. "I'm sure he gets a real kick out of the success of the maid's son."

"That guy is proud as shit of you. He has a folder an inch thick with clippings of your accolades. Jesus, Joe, even I was impressed. You had a perfect fucking SAT?"

"What?" Joseph's head turned in Tony's direction.

"He talks like you're his grandson. He thinks you're brilliant."

"He said that?" Joseph stopped at the entrance to the gardens. "He said I was brilliant?"

"Yes." Tony nodded. "You are, Joseph. You're the smartest guy I know. And you're a great friend, but this obsession you have about where you come from is destructive."

"That's easy for you to say. You're the son of a senator."

"You don't see it, but people respect you, Joseph. And they respect you for your accomplishments, not your father's."

"They'd respect me more if my last name was Prossi."

"That's not true."

"What if my last name was Eastman?" he asked, his eyes intense. "Would they respect me more if I was Richard Eastman IV?"

Richard Eastman III was a senior partner at Eastman and Brothers, one of the most successful investment brokerage firms in New York City.

Tony opened his mouth, but then closed it. "If you were Richard Eastman's son, you'd be rich and spoiled and probably never work a day in your life."

"And what if I was his bastard?" he asked, meeting Tony's eyes. "What would I be like then?"

Tony stared at him for several seconds and then his eyes widened. "Fuck—why didn't you ever say anything?"

"What was I supposed to say? 'Hi, I'm Joseph Craig, Richard Eastman's bastard'?"

"I don't know...Do you know him?"

"No." Joseph's eyes dropped to the ground and he kicked at the dirt under his shoe.

"So he never supported you?"

Joseph actually laughed aloud. "Yeah. And that's why I grew up in a fucking shack behind a mansion." He swung his leg back and kicked a small rock into the air.

"You've never tried to contact him?"

"No." Joseph shook his head. "When I meet Richard Eastman, I don't want him to have any illusions that I'm after his money...I'm going to be established on my own first."

Three years out of law school, after serving as a clerk to a US Supreme Court justice and then working at a private law firm for two more years, Joseph partnered with Tony Prossi and Kevin Stuart, a successful trial attorney and friend of Tony's father, and opened the doors of Prossi, Stuart and Craig. Within two years they were the "hottest" law firm in Washington, DC, and their rates were the highest in the city. Separately the men were brilliant litigators, but the chemistry created by the partnership brought them up to the level of genius.

Joseph's mother was killed in an automobile accident the year he turned thirty. Joseph returned to Massachusetts for the first time since graduating from Harvard. When he disembarked from the plane at Logan International Airport expecting to see the Williamses' chauffeur, he instead was greeted by the eighty-two-year-old patriarch of the family. Theodore Williams smiled as Joseph walked towards him.

"Mr. Williams." Joseph held out his hand as he stopped before the elderly man. "This is a surprise."

"Hello, Joseph...I'm so sorry about your mother." Instead of taking the hand Joseph offered, Mr. Williams wrapped his frail arms around him. "We loved her, Joseph," he said when he finally pulled back, tears glistening in his tired blue eyes.

"I know." Joseph smiled sadly. "She loved you too." And she had. Two years earlier he tried to get her to move to Washington.

"This is my home," she'd told him. "I don't want to leave." And there was nothing he could say to convince her otherwise. She was content to be someone else's servant, even preferred it over any other option he presented. "They're my family, Joseph...I love it here," she'd said. He called her once a month and flew her down to Washington the next two Christmases, but their relationship wasn't close and their conversations were superficial.

As the limousine wound its way down the long road leading to the Williamses' home, Joseph's eyes took in the familiar scenery. And then Theodore Williams turned to him and invited him to stay in the main house.

The funeral was small and intimate, and afterwards Joseph shared a scotch with the older man in the study where they used to play chess.

"Joseph, there are some things...things you have a right to know," Mr. Williams said as his shaky hand brought his glass to his lips. He was staring at the fire, sitting in a high-back chair beside Joseph, the same chair he'd sat in when he talked to Elizabeth about her grandson thirty years earlier. "I'm not young, and I want to make sure you know the truth before I die."

Joseph's eyes swung to the profile of the older man. "About Eastman?"

The old eyes turned from the fire and looked directly into his. "You know?"

"That Richard Eastman was the man who got my mother pregnant? Yes, I've known since I was fourteen. I found a letter."

"Your mother never said—"

"She didn't know. I never discussed it with her."

"I learned when you were a month old, and I contacted your grandfather."

Joseph sat up straighter in his chair. "They knew?"

"Yes. Your grandfather and father knew. They never told your grandmother. Your grandfather paid for your education," he said. "He was very proud of you, Joseph."

"What do you mean he paid for my education?" Joseph pulled his eyebrows together in a frown. "I received grants."

"To college. But he paid for Choate Rosemary. He asked them to tell you they were scholarships."

Joseph shook his head from side to side. "He had no right... You had no right." He abruptly stood and walked to the window.

"You were his grandson...his only grandson. He wanted to help you."

"And my father?" Joseph turned from the window. "How did he play into all of this?"

"I don't know. I've never discussed you with him...but he was there. He attended all your graduations."

"My graduations?" Joseph turned from the window.

"Harvard, Yale, Choate Rosemary. He and your grandfather attended them all."

"They had no right!"

"Your grandfather was so proud, Jo—"

"He didn't have a right to be proud! He had nothing to do with who I am. My mother and you...You were the only ones I wanted. You were the ones who were there for me when I was growing up."

"Your grandfather was a good man, Joseph. You remind me of him."

"No!" Joseph glared at him. "I'm a Craig, not an Eastman. I would never not acknowledge my son or grandson. I'm nothing like them."

"Joseph," Mr. Williams began weakly.

"Don't mention them to me again," Joseph said coolly. "Don't mention them again." And he didn't. Theodore Williams died a few months later, and as Joseph stood before three hundred mourners at the private service, delivering a eulogy at the request of the family and honoring the only father figure he'd ever known, Richard Eastman III sat in the audience.

"Mr. Craig?" His secretary's knock preceded her entrance into his office. At sixty-one, Martha Godfrey was without question the top secretary at the law firm. Originally Tony's, she'd come to Joseph a year and a half prior after a small scandal erupted involving him and his very attractive secretary. The brief indiscretion cost the firm a fine secretary and close to one hundred thousand dollars.

Joseph looked up from the stock portfolio displayed on his computer screen. "Yes?"

"Ms. Paige is here to see you."

"Hello, Joseph." Kathy stepped around his secretary. "Goodbye, Martha."

"It's okay, Martha." Joseph pushed back his chair. "Switch the phones to the answering service and start your weekend." His gaze shifted to Kathy as he came to his feet.

Kathy Paige was the epitome of beauty with long, straight blonde hair, large catlike green eyes, full lips and a perfect complexion. Standing a smidgen under six feet without shoes, she had the head-turning appeal of a movie star. "You haven't called me in three days," she scolded as she slid her perfectly manicured hands up his chest. "Where have you been?"

"Working," he said before brushing his lips over hers, his hands lightly gripping her hips.

"You could have at least texted." She trailed her lips along his jaw as she leaned her body into his. "I missed you."

"I've been busy."

"Too busy to answer my texts?"

"Pretty busy. And I'm still busy. I have a few things I have to wrap up."

"Come on." She flicked her tongue over the sensitive skin behind his ear. "Haven't you missed me? I'm sure you have time for a break." One of her hands was at the front of his pants.

Joseph closed his eyes, breathing deeply as she rubbed him through the thin material of his trousers. "Baby—"

"Your body doesn't want to go back to work," she whispered against his ear.

"I have things I've got to get done today," he insisted, but his hands had slid from her hips to her butt, and he was propelling her backwards towards the door.

"I hate it when you don't call before the weekend. I don't know whether or not to make plans."

"I'm sorry." He pushed her back against the wooden door, his lower body pressing in to hers. "I should have called." He slipped one hand beneath the hem of her dress, slowly trailing his fingers up the inside of her thigh. "Jesus," he said deeply, slipping a finger into her. "You're so wet." A second finger joined the first. He sank his fingers in and out of her for several seconds. "Is this for me?"

"Yes," she breathed, pushing against his hand.

His free hand dropped to his belt. "Go lean over my desk," he whispered against her ear, removing his hand from beneath her dress. He turned the lock on his door before following her across the room, his eyes traveling over the back of her legs and butt.

"Joseph—"

"Shh. Bend over." He placed a hand on the center of her back, slowly pushing her upper body forward until she was lying over his desk. "Spread your thighs a little." He moved his knee between her legs. "Good." He pushed his pants and briefs down just enough to free himself and then without warning thrust his hips forward, plunging inside of her. He pulled out slowly before ramming into her again, dropping his mouth to the back of her neck as he increased the rhythm of his thrusts, the sounds of his body slapping against hers magnified in his office.

He freed her breasts from the confines of her dress, kneading them with one hand as he continued to pump in and out of her, her cries of pleasure filling the air. "You're too loud," he warned, but she continued to cry out, her moans growing louder. "Quiet," he whispered, with no real conviction, his body driving into hers. He reached around her, running his fingers over her clit. "Come for me, baby," he said a moment before she screamed out, her body clenching around him. Seconds later, he groaned deeply, his body collapsing over the back of hers.

"You're bad," she said a short time later as she adjusted her dress.

"I'm bad?" He chuckled as he pulled up his zipper. "You're the one who showed up at my office not wearing underwear."

"I didn't hear you complaining a minute ago."

"I'm still not complaining," he said as he buckled his pants. "But know when you show up in my office without underwear I'm going to fuck you."

She slipped her arms up around his neck, her green eyes meeting his brown ones. "Is that a promise?"

He lowered his head, pausing with their lips inches apart. "You're intoxicating," he whispered before settling his lips on hers.

She ran her hands down his back, continuing until they reached his butt, her hands pulling his lower body into hers.

"Give me a minute, babe," he said against her mouth. "I don't recover that quickly."

"Sometimes you do."

"Not today." He intercepted her hand before it reached the front of his trousers. "Not today." He stepped around her and dropped down into one of the two club chairs facing his desk.

"So where have you been?" She lowered herself into his lap.

"What do you mean?"

"I mean," she began, moving a thumb to his lower lip and rubbing at a lipstick stain, "why haven't I heard from you for three days?"

"I told you. I've been busy." He opened his mouth and tried to capture her thumb. "Come to an opening in New York with me for the weekend."

"I can't. I have to work tomorrow." She began to finger the hair falling just above his collar. "Don't go away. I missed you this week."

"Did you?"

"Desperately. Where were you last night? I must have called you ten times. It just kept going straight to voicemail."

"We settled the case against WNTC and they took us out to celebrate. At some point, my phone died."

"When did you get in?" She frowned. "I dropped by your place at two in the morning."

"Why?"

"Why? Why what? Why did I stop by or why do I want to know when you got in? Regardless, the answer is the same—because you're my boyfriend."

"Do we really have to get into this right now?"

"Get into what? Joseph, what time did you get home last night?"

"I didn't." He met her eyes.

"You didn't?" She pulled her eyebrows together. "Did you sleep here?"

"No."

"Oh my God!" She scrambled off his lap. "You were with someone else."

He dragged his hands down his face. "I had a lot to drink and I—"

"Did you have sex with another woman last night?"

Joseph didn't answer as he met her eyes. "I had too much to drink."

"Did you have sex with another woman?" she repeated, her voice more angry now than hurt.

"We never said anything about other people."

He'd barely uttered the words before she slapped him hard across the face. "You bastard!"

"Jesus!" he yelled, pulling his head back. "Fuck!" He lifted his hand to his watering eye. "What in the fuck is wrong with you?"

"I hate you! You climb out of another woman's bed this morning and then have sex with me in your office the same afternoon," she began, her face contorted in hurt and anger. "You have no respect for me."

"That isn't true." He continued to touch his reddening cheek.

"What do you think? I'm your whore?" She was livid.

"No, God no." He reached for her hand.

"Don't touch me," she whispered, jerking her hand out of his reach. "You have absolutely no respect for me."

"That isn't true. Now sit down so we can talk about this."

"Talk." She shook her head, tears now evident in her eyes. "There's nothing to talk about."

"Kathy, I—"

"You what? What?" Her voice caught. "Did you know yesterday was our one year anniversary?" She angrily wiped at the tears falling down her cheeks. "I am such an idiot. I thought things were going well between us." She crossed towards the door.

Joseph was out of his chair and following, reaching the door as she began to pull it open. "Don't." He closed the door, pressing his body against the back of hers, his mouth at her ear. "I'm sorry. I made a mistake."

"Let me go, Joseph," she whispered, crying now. "I want to leave."

"I'm an idiot," he said. "Don't leave."

"This is over. You aren't capable of a committed relationship." She pulled unsuccessfully on the door. "Let me out!"

"Not until you let me talk."

"Open the door!"

"Calm down," he said through clenched teeth, one hand moving to her shoulder. "I want to talk to you."

"Open the fucking door!"

"Hey." There were three loud knocks on the door. "What in the hell is going on in there?" It was Kevin Stuart's voice.

"Nothing," Joseph said.

"Kevin, he won't let me leave," Kathy cried.

"Joe, open the Goddamn door!" Kevin banged again.

Joseph stepped back, his jaw clenching and unclenching as Kathy swung open the door, pushed past Kevin and the half dozen associates gathered outside the office, and fled down the hall.

"What in the hell?" Kevin asked after slamming Joseph's door. Several inches shorter than Joseph with a husky build and thinning blond hair, Kevin had an uncanny resemblance to Bruce Willis. "We could hear the two of you all the way in the lobby."

Joseph crossed to his bar and poured himself a generous amount of scotch.

"Until today there were actually associates on board who had never seen you put on a public display with some female," Kevin fumed.

"I'm not in the mood." Joseph pushed past him and dropped down in the chair he'd been sitting in with Kathy moments earlier.

"Oh, you're not?" Kevin raised his eyebrows, his hands on his hips, standing directly in front of Joseph's chair. "And do you think we were in the mood to listen to your love quarrel as we met with clients?" The muscles in his jaw were shaking as he spoke. "It sounded like you were raping her in here."

"Yeah, well, I wasn't. She was breaking up with me."

"Let me guess." He tapped his lip with his index finger. "She found out you fucked the weather lady last night."

"How did you—"

"Know you fucked her? I was sitting next to you, Joe. Her foot was in your crotch half the night. And we all know how much restraint you have." He dropped down into the empty chair and reached into his jacket for his cigarettes.

"You can't smoke in here."

"Go to hell," Kevin said through the side of his lips as he lit the cigarette. "You drive me to it." He inhaled deeply, leaning back in the chair as he blew out a stream of smoke. "You've got to stop this, Joe. Half the office heard you."

"So I saw."

"I mean having sex with her. Everyone within your general vicinity could hear her. They were standing around gossiping about it when the yelling started."

Joseph briefly closed his eyes. "Nothing's happened in this office since Tanya left," he said, referring to his ex-secretary who cried sexual harassment when he tried to break off a one-month relationship. It was easier to pay her off than deal with a scandal, but Kevin was still pissed about it. The money came right off the top of their profits and he seemed to resent Joseph more as time passed.

"I know. I was starting to believe you actually changed and, until last night, I thought you were serious about Kathy. You're priceless, Craig."

"Why don't you go home to your wife? I've had about all I can stomach of you for a day."

"You're not alone there." He leaned forward and stubbed out his cigarette in a decorative ashtray on his desk.

"That isn't an ashtray," Joseph said.

"I know." Kevin smirked as he stood up. "Have a nice weekend."

3

By the end of her second week in the B2B Division, Lia had digested enough information to feel completely overwhelmed. There were two distinct branches within the division, one tasked with identifying new elite clients, either from within the existing customer pool or from outside the organization, and the other with nurturing and sustaining established relationships. Lia was part of the latter group.

She spent nine hours a day reading files and attempting to memorize as many facts as possible about the several hundred clients identified as "elite". Unfortunately, the task was proving daunting. The names, faces and details all seemed to blend together. She leaned back in her chair in her small cubicle, wondering if she should take a break.

"Tell me you aren't trying to memorize every file."

Lia glanced up to see a petite woman in a smart pants suit who couldn't have been more than five feet tall, with short brown hair, huge brown eyes and a friendly smile.

"Hi," the woman said holding out her hand. "I'm Kay Thompson."

Lia returned her handshake. "I'm Lia Merrick." She knew instantly the other woman wasn't a B2B. The B2B women only wore skirts and dresses. A week after Lia's appointment with the personal shopper at Neiman Marcus she was issued a complete wardrobe consisting of business suits, skirts and both day and evening dresses. Lia considered her clothes a uniform.

"Do you want to go to lunch?" Kay asked. "I was a B2B. I can give you a few pointers that will hopefully keep you from pulling your hair out."

"That would be great," Lia said, instantly liking the other woman who was certainly being more helpful than any of the B2Bs. Most barely acknowledged Lia, and the ones who did weren't offering advice, they were merely sizing her up.

"I just returned from vacation," Kay said as they walked towards the elevators. "Otherwise, I would have saved you from what I'm guessing was an overwhelming week."

"There is just so much to absorb," Lia said, "and everyone is busy. I'm not sure who I'm supposed to talk to when I have a question."

"Didn't Stan assign you a mentor?" Kay pushed the down button for the elevator.

"Yes, Carmen Gonzalez."

"Carmen!" Kay exclaimed before quickly covering her mouth, her eyes looking around. She didn't speak again until they were alone in the elevator. "I'm sorry, but sometimes men are so stupid. Carmen is the last person who should be assigned that role."

"I can't argue with that."

Carmen Gonzalez was one of the original B2Bs and, according to Stan, held a wealth of information on the workings of the division. Unfortunately, she didn't appear interested in sharing this vast store of knowledge with Lia. And it wasn't because she was busy with her own work. Lia figured she spent seventy-five percent of the day arguing on the phone with someone named Marcos, who Lia was ninety-nine percent sure wasn't a client.

"Just forget about Carmen," Kay said. "She's worse than having no mentor."

When they were seated across from each other in the cafeteria, Kay asked, "Have you been to any client functions yet?"

"No. Stan wanted me to orient myself with the client folders a bit more first."

"Reading about all the clients is a waste of time," Kay said. "The majority don't attend the functions." She leaned forward and took a sip of her Diet Coke. "When it's time for you to attend, Stan will send you an email with a list of which clients are attending a particular function. That's when you familiarize yourself with the client files."

"That sounds more manageable." Lia speared a piece of lettuce with her fork. "How long were you a B2B?"

"Not long. Probably less than three months, but Stan liked me, so he transferred me to his Strategic Marketing Division."

"You didn't like B2B?"

"I didn't like it or dislike it," Kay said. "I was still trying to figure everything out and then one day Stan called me into his office and said it wasn't working out."

"Why?"

Kay shrugged. "I have no idea. That's how the B2B works: Stan brings people in and he either likes them or he doesn't."

She lifted her hands. "And if he doesn't, you hope he offers you another position."

Lia felt a knot of apprehension in the pit of her stomach. "He did say the attrition rate in the first year is over fifty percent."

"More like ninety percent. There is a reason the B2B girls who make it are so uppity."

"That's a lot of pressure," Lia said, almost to herself.

"You'll be fine." Kay patted her hand. "I shouldn't have said anything."

"No, I'm glad you did."

"Obviously Stan saw something in you he liked. And he probably gets better and better at identifying that 'it' quality. I was part of the original group." Someone behind Lia caught Kay's eye and she waved. "Claudia! Here's someone who can definitely help you assimilate," she said, returning her gaze to Lia.

"How was your vacation?" Claudia asked, stopping beside the table.

"Incredible! Have you met Lia Merrick?"

"No." Her gaze shifted to Lia. "I've seen you around, but we haven't officially been introduced. I'm Claudia."

"Hi." Lia smiled. She'd seen Claudia getting out of a Porsche that morning and figured she was doing well as a B2B. She was stunning, with silky black hair falling just past her chin, dark brown eyes, flawless skin and a voluptuous body which undoubtedly turned men's heads wherever she went.

"Join us for a minute." Kay scooted over to make room. "Lia's trying to learn her way around and who better to answer her questions than you?" She turned to Lia. "Claudia's been a B2B since the beginning and, unlike her friends, is willing to talk to underlings from other departments."

Claudia rolled her eyes. "You're not an underling."

Kay smiled. "I came upon Lia earlier trying to absorb all the information in all the elite-client folders. I told her she was wasting her time."

"I just don't know what to expect," Lia said. "I don't want to be unprepared when I start attending the client functions."

"Don't worry about any of that." Claudia met her eyes. "Stan wants you to mingle. That's it. The clients will like you or they won't. Just be yourself."

"Told you." Kay said.

"Okay." Lia nodded, still unsure.

"I like meeting new people and partying, but if you don't"— Claudia shrugged—"then it probably isn't for you. Or maybe you'll attend a few functions like Kay here," she said, patting Kay's forearm, "and meet the man of your dreams."

Lia's eyes swung to Kay. "You dated a client?"

"Dated?" Claudia laughed. "She married him."

Lia was surprised. "So Stan doesn't mind—I mean, he doesn't care if we date clients?"

"Nope." Claudia shook her head. "Are you going to finish that?" She eyed the remaining half of Kay's sandwich.

"It's all yours." Kay slid her plate to Claudia. "Maybe if you opened your eyes and looked around a little, you'd meet the man of your dreams at one of the client receptions."

"No way." Claudia shook her head. "That is definitely not going to happen."

"So you don't date the clients?" Lia asked.

She looked down at her perfectly manicured nails. "I didn't say that."

"She doesn't say much," Kay said. "Claudia never shares the details of her private life."

"Maybe because there's nothing to share." She continued to study her nails. "How about you, Lia? Is there anyone special in your life?"

"Just my daughter."

"You have a daughter?" Claudia lifted her eyes. "You're divorced?"

"It was final less than a month ago."

"Hi, everyone." A tall woman with striking green eyes and long blonde hair stopped beside their table. Her tailored dress clearly identified her as a B2B. Like Claudia and every other B2B, she was extremely attractive. Lia had never seen so many attractive women in an office setting and knew being beautiful was one of Stan's B2B prerequisites.

"Kathleen, have you met Lia Merrick?" Kay asked.

"No." Her gaze shifted to Lia. "Hi."

"Hi." Lia smiled politely.

"Kathleen only has three months on you," Kay said. Her eyes swung back to Kathleen. "And guess who Stan assigned to be Lia's mentor? You won't believe it."

"Who?" Kathleen tucked her hair behind her ears.

"Carmen."

"Carmen?" Her mouth dropped open, her eyes swinging from Kay to Lia, then back to Kay. "You're kidding."

Kay shook her head. "No, I'm serious."

"Oh my God. What could she possibly teach someone besides how to talk on the phone? That's it," she said in a low voice. "This proves what I've suspected since the day I arrived. They're sleeping together. There's no other explanation. I have never seen her do a lick of work, so obviously she's doing him."

Claudia rolled her eyes. "I don't think so."

"You don't?" Kathleen shifted her gaze to Claudia.

"No. I don't."

"Then explain to us exactly what she's doing, because when she's here—which isn't very often—she's talking on the phone. And considering she's speaking Spanish, my guess is she isn't talking business."

"I have too much of my own work to do to worry about what Carmen's up to," Claudia said. "In fact, if I don't leave now I'm going to be late for a call." She patted Kay on the back and gave Lia a smile before walking off.

— ~ —

Six dozen red roses and six weeks after the altercation in his office, Joseph, dressed casually in a tan cashmere sweater and black pants, climbed out of his black Mercedes in front of Kathy's art gallery on King Street in Old Town, Alexandria.

Kathy looked up as he entered. "What do you want?" she asked coolly, stepping out from behind a desk in the corner of the gallery. She was alone in the shop and dressed casually in loose camel-colored silk pants and a black turtleneck, her blonde hair pulled back in a clasp at her nape.

"You," he said, walking slowly towards her. "I want you."

"Joseph," she began, shaking her head. "I can't. I—"

"I'm an asshole." He moved his hands to the sides of her face, staring down into her green eyes. "I'm sorry I hurt you." He lowered his head and kissed her softly on the lips. "Give me another chance." He kissed her again. "I need you." He kissed her again and she began responding, her body leaning forward into his. "I need you so much," he said again before opening his mouth over hers, eliciting a moan from her as she wound her arms up around his neck.

"I hate you," she whispered when he finally lifted his head, her tear-filled eyes meeting his.

"I love you," he said. It was the first time he'd said those words to a woman.

Hours later they lay naked in her bed, their bodies entwined, a light sheet pulled over them. "Joseph?"

"Hmm?" His voice was deep with sleep.

"I want to talk." She slipped out from beneath his arm and situated herself on the pillow beside his, their faces just inches apart as they lay facing each other. "Did you have a good time in San Francisco?" She had joined him on a business trip to San Francisco the week before his indiscretion with the weather woman.

"Of course."

"Why didn't you call me that week? We have this incredible five days together and then nothing."

"I was working."

"You couldn't spare five seconds to send me a text? To ask how I am? To let me know you were thinking about me?"

"I don't think you realize how much I work."

"I think I do. You're out of bed by four thirty every morning. Even the nights you have time for me, you don't arrive until after nine. I think I know exactly how much you work."

"Then I don't understand what you're asking."

"I guess I'm asking if I came to your mind at all during those three days."

"I'm sure you did. I have a dozen things on my mind at any given moment. I'm in the office before six and not out until after nine. And I'm working. Any distraction, any interruption just extends the day."

"It takes two seconds to return a text. You have your phone with you all the time. You just ignored my texts."

"No. I didn't ignore them. I get a hundred texts a day. I can't answer them all—I'd never get anything done if I did."

"But I'm supposed to be your girlfriend. I'm not a business text."

He ran his hand down her arm. "I understand and I'm going to do better. I'm not going to lose you again."

"I feel like you only think about me when you want to have sex."

"That's not true."

"You never call me unless you're trying to coordinate a time to come over. We never talk just to talk," she said. "If we talk it's because you want to come over and have sex."

He sighed. "That isn't true."

"Yes, it is." She pushed herself up on her elbow. "Did you even think about me that night? I mean when you were taking off your clothes to be with another woman, did you—"

"Kathy, don't." He gripped her upper arm. "It was a mistake. I apologized. It's not going to happen again. Now lay back down."

"No. I need to talk about this."

He rolled onto his back and flung an arm over his eyes. "It meant nothing to me."

"Well, it meant something to me." She pushed his arm away from his face so she could see his eyes. "Who was she?"

"No one."

"I want to know. Just tell me."

"No one. Look, Kathy," he began as he sat up, "I'm not getting into this with you. I told you I was sorry."

"Oh, and that's enough? You think it's over now because you said you're sorry?"

"Obviously not." He threw his legs over the edge of the bed.

"How many times did you make her come?"

"Oh, for God's sake! I'm not doing this." He crossed to a chair and picked up his pants.

"How do you think it makes me feel to know you were inside another woman? That you came inside another woman? Where are you going?"

"Home," he said, roughly pulling up his pants. "I have apologized to you every way I know how, and you have a right to be pissed off. Hell," he said, throwing up one of his hands, "no one could blame you if you never wanted to see me again, but I refuse to hang around and be punished for something I don't have the power to change." He shrugged into his shirt. "I never lied to you," he continued. "Until today we never said anything about other people." He picked up his socks from the floor and sat down on the chair. "You're going to have to decide whether you can forgive me for this."

"Don't leave," she said. "I don't want you to leave."

His hands stilled in the process of pulling on a sock. "Kathy?"

"It just hurts, knowing you were with someone else. How would you feel if you knew another man was with me?"

"Not good." He crossed the room, lowering himself onto the edge of the bed beside her. "I'm sorry." He touched the side of her face. "I wish it hadn't happened and I promise you it will never happen again." He kissed her lightly on her lips. "I love you."

━ ━

"Hi, sweetie," Lia said after opening her front door. It was a Sunday in mid-October, and Taylor was returning from a weekend with Ned.

"Mommy!" Taylor hugged and kissed her before turning back to her father. "Can you stay and play with me for a little while?" She grabbed one of his hands. "Please?"

"Not today, Taylor. Daddy has to leave," Lia said, having no desire to spend even an extra minute in his company.

"Yes. I have to go. Candice is home waiting for me." He set down her overnight bag and kneeled down to give her a hug. "I love you, sweetie."

Lia watched them, an emotion akin to hate simmering within. She looked forward to the day she could be in his presence without a reaction. As much as he deserved her wrath, she didn't like harboring such negativity towards another person, especially one she once loved.

Unfortunately, he looked good. He seemed to look better every time she saw him. Standing just below six feet with a lean, athletic build, sandy-colored hair and a strong jaw, he'd always been good-looking, but now there was something different about him, which she decided must be his clothes. He dressed like he had money. Even his casual clothes looked expensive.

"When are you coming back?" Taylor continued to hug him.

"Soon." He kissed the top of her head before standing up. His gaze shifted to Lia. "Could I talk to you for a second?"

"Taylor, you can go watch TV. I'm going to walk Daddy out." She followed him out of her apartment and down the stairs, neither talking until he stopped beside his black BMW.

"I'd like to see more of Taylor. Two weekends a month isn't enough."

"Oh." She didn't know why, but she was surprised by the request. "Okay."

"I could pick her up from your mom's for dinner a couple nights a week. Tuesdays and Thursdays work for me."

"Tuesdays and Thursdays are fine except next week. A week from Thursday is Halloween."

"I know. I'd like to take her trick-or-treating."

Lia shook her head. "I'm taking her trick-or-treating."

"Where?" He swung his gaze around the apartment complex. "Here?"

"No. I'll take her in my mom's neighborhood."

"Lia, let me take her. We live in a nice neighborhood and there's a girl next door the same age that's going to go with us. She wants me to take her. She told me."

"Too bad."

"Too bad'?"

"Yeah." She met his eyes. "She's going with me, Ned. If you'd like to come over and join us that's fine, but I'm not missing out on Halloween with Taylor."

"She's my daughter too."

"I know. And that's why I invited you to join us, because God knows I have no desire to spend an evening with you."

"You're not being fair. You have her all the time."

"That was your choice. It's cold. I'm going inside." She turned and walked towards her building.

Several hours later, stretched out on the couch with a glass of Baileys and crème, she was berating herself for the conversation with Ned. She didn't want to play the role of bitter ex-wife. She didn't even want him anymore, yet knowing he'd cast her aside for someone else still burned. Her husband, a man she once loved and adored, left her for another woman. He'd known both women, slept with both women and chosen Candice.

She took a sip of her drink and reminded herself she wasn't supposed to be thinking about Ned. Her thoughts drifted to

Zurtech. The task of processing what appeared those first few days as an insurmountable volume of information was no longer so intimidating. And she knew enough to ask intelligent questions of Kay and Claudia, who turned out to be valuable resources. She'd begun lunching with them regularly.

The receptions were somewhat baffling. Getting paid to drink alcohol and eat seemed an odd concept, but she supposed it was akin to making business deals on the golf course, with one small exception: As far as she could tell, no business was ever discussed at the receptions. The gatherings reminded her of the mixers she attended in college when she was a member of the Alpha Delta Phi. The B2B staff members were the sorority and the clients were the fraternity, only the participants were ten to thirty years older.

At nineteen, they were fun, but at twenty-eight and recently divorced, she found them depressing. Hanging out with what appeared to be mostly married men and stroking their already-inflated egos was neither rewarding nor challenging work, and she found it incomprehensible Claudia could actually enjoy herself at the get-togethers.

She picked up the television remote and began surfing through the channels. Over the past year, television had become her refuge from the loneliness of the late hours after Taylor was in bed, but at 9:45 p.m. on a Sunday, the options appeared slim.

"...now let's move to your personal life," Anderson Cooper was saying to his guest when Lia passed through CNN. She pushed the up-arrow key to return to the program, the man across from Anderson catching her eye. He was gorgeous, with wavy dark brown hair and large light brown eyes surrounded by black lashes so thick she could see them on the television. "The *Washingtonian* named you the most eligible bachelor in Washington. How does that make you feel?"

He smiled, revealing a set of perfectly straight white teeth and deep dimples in his cheeks. "Honored?" Lia put her hand over her heart, knowing if a man like him showed up at one of the receptions, it wouldn't be so boring.

"You're thirty-four years old and have never been married. Is that correct?"

He reached for the coffee mug on the desk and took a sip before responding. "That is correct."

"Any plans to get married?"

"Not at the moment." He leaned forward and set down the mug.

"You're going to make me work for every detail, aren't you?" Anderson asked.

He shrugged and the smile returned. "You're lucky I'm answering any of these questions."

"You've been dating Kathy Paige for quite a while."

"Close to a year."

"She's a beautiful lady."

"Yes, she is."

"Any talk of marriage?"

He smiled again. "Didn't I already answer that question?"

"No. I asked if you had any plans to get married. Now I'm asking if you've discussed marriage with Kathy."

He moved a hand over his mouth and shook his head. "I've already answered that question. Let's change the subject."

Lia rolled onto her side, continuing to watch the interview, not actually listening to the words, but feeling almost mesmerized by his eyes and deep voice. Not one to partake in unattainable fantasies, she was surprised by her reaction to the man and later, when she awoke on the couch after dreaming she'd had sex with him, she knew she was in desperate need of a boyfriend.

4

ia met Eric Nettles the day before Halloween. She arrived a little late to a reception at the Zurtech House, wearing a black strapless dress falling just above her knees. She was looking around to see if she could spot Claudia when she saw him. He was seated at a small round table by himself, watching her as he puffed on a cigar. When she met his eyes, neither of them looked away. Within seconds he was at her side.

"You're new." It was more of a statement than a question, but she nodded. "And you have amazing eyes." He held out his hand. "I'm Eric Nettles."

"Hi." She smiled as she returned his handshake. "You work with Claudia Kelly." She remembered her name from his file.

"For now." He didn't release her hand, his eyes continuing to meet hers. "Are you going to tell me your name?"

"Oh, I'm sorry." She smiled. "I'm Lia Merrick."

"It's nice to meet you, Lia Merrick." He released her hand, but continued to stand a bit closer than socially appropriate, the male appreciation undeniable as his eyes feasted on her face.

She recognized him from the picture in his file. He was the Chief Operating Officer at Buznet, the largest wireless communications company in the country and, at forty-two, still single. He had dark hair, graying at the temples, brown eyes and a pleasant looking face.

"And what do you do for Zurtech?"

"I'm still learning."

"Is this your first reception?"

"No. I believe..." She paused, squinting as she thought back. "This is my fourth."

"I suppose that means I've missed at least four, because I would definitely not forget you." He glanced towards the bar across the room. "What can I get you to drink?"

"A Coke."

"A Coke?" He pulled head back. "You need something stronger than a coke."

"I do?"

"You do."

"I don't think so." She smiled to take any bite off her words. "I'd really just like a Coke."

It was past 4:00 a.m. when Lia arrived at her mother's house, and as she tried to quietly close the front door, her mother's voice startled her from behind. "Where have you been?"

Lia spun around, a hand moving to her chest. "You scared me."

"Where've you been? It's four a.m." Her arms were crossed over her chest as she stood in a white robe.

"I went out to breakfast."

"Until four? I was worried sick. I've sent you numerous texts."

"I'm sorry." Lia slipped off her jacket and turned to the closet. "We lost track of time."

"We?"

"I met someone," Lia said after hanging her jacket. "And we started talking and the next thing I knew it was three forty-five."

"A man?"

"Yes, a man. He was so nice and easy to talk to. I feel like I've known him a lot longer than one day. Can you watch Taylor for me Saturday night?"

"Saturday?"

"Yes. He has tickets to some play opening at the Kennedy Center."

"Yes. Of course I can watch her."

Lia's desk phone was ringing when she arrived at the office at 10:15 the following morning. She quickened her steps, hoping to answer before it switched over to voicemail. "Hello?" She set her purse on her desk.

"Did I tell you how incredible your eyes are?"

"About a dozen times." She smiled as she sat down. "I just got in."

"I figured. This is the third time I've called. You neglected to give me your cell number. Do you have lunch plans?"

"Today?" Her mind was spinning. She'd barely slept.

"Yes, today. It's seventy degrees. I know the perfect spot for a picnic."

Her eyes swung to Stan Hall's office. "I don't know what my boss—"

"Stan won't mind. I'm an important client. Do you want me to call him and tell him we have a meeting?"

"No! Let me think for a second."

"I don't have a second. I'll be at your office at noon."

Eric Nettles looked even better in the light of the day, and as Lia watched him in Stan Hall's office, laughing at something her boss said, she suddenly couldn't wait to be alone with him. And he was right. When Stan led him to her cubicle several minutes later, he didn't seem to mind that she was going off to lunch with Eric. "Don't worry about coming back today, Lia," he said. "Enjoy the nice weather."

"No, that's okay. I can get a few more hours of work in after lunch."

"Don't bother." He turned to Eric, clearly indicating his decision was final. "Nice to see you." The two men shook hands and then Stan walked off.

"You look incredible," Eric said as soon as they were alone.

"I don't know if this is picnic attire." She glanced down at her dress.

"It'll be fine for my picnic." He trailed his fingers down her arm. "You're perfect."

"Eric?" Claudia appeared beside them. "I thought that was you."

"Hello, Claudia." He turned from Lia. "How are you?"

"Fine." Her eyes moved from him to Lia, then back. "What are you doing here?"

"Taking Lia to lunch. How come you didn't mention you had a new coworker?"

"I didn't realize that was part of my job description. May I talk to you alone for a minute?"

"Sure." He touched Lia's arm. "I'll be right back."

Lia watched them walk off, surprised at Claudia's displeasure. She was still pondering her reaction when Eric returned a few minutes later.

"Ready?" He was smiling as he approached.

"Is everything okay?" She picked up her purse.

"Yes." He put a hand to the small of her back as they began walking. "Everything's fine."

The "perfect spot" Eric chose for their picnic was the backyard of his very posh home in Great Falls, Virginia, located on a prime piece of real estate along the Potomac River.

He'd evidently called ahead because after parking his Porsche in front of his six-car garage, he led her off to the right of the house and down a cobblestone path that wound them through a cluster of trees and then on to a stretch of perfectly manicured lawn about half the size of a football field with spectacular views of the river. To their right, laid out on the grass, was a red-and-white checkered blanket weighted down on each corner with a small gray stone, and in the center was a larger wicker picnic basket.

"This is beautiful," Lia said softly as she set her purse on the blanket and looked off towards the river.

"I like it," Eric said from behind her as he placed his hands on her shoulders. "Isn't this better than work?"

She nodded, liking the feel of his hands. It had been so long since she'd felt the touch of a man. "I love the sound of the river. It's so soothing."

"It is. If I open my bedroom windows, I can hear it while I'm going to sleep." He turned her until she was facing his house, lifting one of his hands from her shoulder and pointing towards a balcony on the second floor, his chest pressing into her back. "That's my bedroom."

The house was almost as spectacular as the view with a modern design, comprised of numerous levels with floor-to-ceiling windows throughout. "Wow," she said. It was the first thing that came to her mind. "It's incredible."

"You like it?"

"Of course." She continued to admire his house. "It's beautiful. How long have you been here?"

"I had it built a little over two years ago." He stepped back from her, and Lia instantly missed his warmth. "How about some wine?"

She turned back to the blanket and watched him kick off his loafers, then lower himself down. "Are you planning to join me?" His eyes were alight with amusement.

She smiled. "Yes." She followed his lead and began to remove her shoes. "You live in this huge place by yourself?"

"Not exactly." He reached into the picnic basket and retrieved a bottle of white wine. "I have a housekeeper and, as I'm sure you'll agree after tasting this lunch, an excellent cook." He removed the cork and poured two glasses of the clear liquid.

"It's still awfully big even for three people." She sat down on the blanket beside him.

"I didn't build it with the intention of remaining alone." He held out a wine glass, his eyes meeting hers.

"Oh." She felt her face heat up and prayed silently she wasn't noticeably blushing as she brought the glass to her lips.

Like the night before, the afternoon seemed to disappear as they talked and ate a delectable assortment of foods, including roasted chicken salad, cheese and crackers, fruit, an assortment of pâtés and pastries.

"What time is it?" Lia asked hours later. They were lying on the blanket together and she was curled into his side, her head resting on his chest.

"It's four."

She closed her eyes, wishing he said 3:00 p.m. "I've got to go."

"No. Don't go." He tightened his hold on her. "This is too perfect."

"I know, but I have to take my daughter trick-or-treating." She sat up and pushed her hair back from her face as she stared off towards the river. She couldn't remember the last time she'd had such a relaxing afternoon. "This was so nice. Thank you for inviting me."

He rubbed his hand up and down her back. "Can you come back later?"

"No," she said, part of her wishing she could. "I can go to the Kennedy Center with you Saturday night, though. If you still want me to."

"I still want you to. Come here."

She took his hand and let him pull her down beside him, and then he was kissing her and she was kissing him back, and for a moment she forgot she needed to get home. But Taylor was waiting and that somehow managed to penetrate through the haze. "I have to go," she said breathlessly, pulling away and managing to sit up.

"Are you sure you don't want to come back later and listen to the river with me?" He sat up beside her and ran the back of his fingers down her arm. "I guarantee you won't be disappointed."

"I'm sure you're right, but I can't tonight." She met his lips for a brief kiss, and then as she met his eyes, knew he was going to be the second man to ever make love to her.

"Good morning," Lia said as she walked into her mother's kitchen Sunday morning. She'd attended a play at the Kennedy Center with Eric the previous night and then spent the night at her mother's.

"Good morning." Elaine lifted her eyes from the Sunday paper. "What time did you get in?"

"Late." She poured herself a cup of coffee before joining her mother at the table.

"Did you have a nice time?"

"Incredible." Lia recounted every detail of their date, from their dinner at a Georgetown restaurant to the play, and then to late-night drinks at a jazz club in Adams Morgan. "He's amazing, Mom. I've never met anyone like him. He treats me like I'm the most special woman in the world."

"You are special," Elaine said.

"You're my mother," Lia said before taking a sip of coffee. "You're supposed to think that. He treats me a million times better than Ned ever did."

"That wouldn't be difficult," her mother pointed out dryly.

"That's true." Lia took another swallow of coffee. "I just really like him."

"I know, but you have to be careful."

"What is that supposed to mean?" Lia frowned. "You don't even know him."

"That's true, but you're very vulnerable right now. You've been through a lot and I just—I want you to be careful."

"Careful about what?"

"Honey," Elaine began, reaching out and covering her hand. "Don't get defensive. I'm happy that you're excited about him. I just know how lonely you've been these past couple of years. I don't want you to jump into the first relationship that comes your way."

"Why don't you like him?"

"I don't like him or dislike him," Elaine said. "I don't know him."

"Exactly, so why are you being so negative?"

"I'm not. I just want you to take this slow."

"There's something you're not saying. You've been negative about him since day one." Lia leaned back in her chair. "Why can't you just be honest with me?"

Elaine slowly lifted her gaze to Lia's. "Do you really want to know?"

"Yes." Lia nodded. "I really want to know.'

"I think a man who makes it to forty-two without getting married isn't interested in getting married."

"And you think I am? My divorce was just finalized. And anyway, you're wrong about him. We discussed this last night. He said he was putting in so many hours trying to get his company off the ground he neglected his relationships, and then the next thing he knew he was forty years old."

"You said he's forty-two, Lia."

"I know how old he is, Mother. And I think I'm smart enough to realize when someone is lying to me."

"Okay." She returned her eyes to her paper. "You asked what I was thinking and I told you."

"So if he was divorced he'd be perfect?"

Elaine sighed as she lifted her eyes. "I just don't want to see you get hurt."

Elaine wasn't the only one concerned about Eric's intentions. When Lia arrived at the office Monday morning, Claudia was waiting for her in the cubicle she shared with Carmen. "What's going on with you and Eric?"

"Why?" Lia set down her purse.

"I don't think he's right for you."

"How could you possibly know that? You barely know me."

"I know Eric," she said, her voice barely above a whisper, clearly not wanting their conversation overheard. "He's a player, Lia."

"A player?" She was completely lost.

"Yes. He likes to sleep around." She lowered herself into Carmen's chair and waited for Lia to sit down before continuing. "He likes the chase."

"The chase?"

"Once he gets you into bed he'll lose interest."

"Did you sleep with him?"

"Me?" She seemed taken aback by the question. "No. No, I didn't sleep with him."

Lia knew she was lying. She'd probably dated him and still had feelings for him. "But you know other women who have?"

"He's a predator, Lia," Claudia said, meeting her eyes. "Trust me on this."

When Lia met Kay for lunch, she was still stewing over her earlier conversation with Claudia. "Do you know Eric Nettles?" she asked as soon as they sat down.

"Eric Nettles," Kay repeated, looking up as she thought. "Isn't he a bigwig with Buznet?"

"He's their COO. I met him the other night at a reception and he seems really nice."

Kay smiled as she leaned forward. "Did he ask you out?"

Lia couldn't help smiling as she retold the events of the past several days. "He seems so nice."

"He sounds great."

"And then this morning, the weirdest thing happened." Lia recounted her conversation with Claudia.

"Yeah." Kay scrunched up her face. "I wouldn't take anything she says too seriously."

"You wouldn't?"

"Definitely not." She shook her head. "This is the problem with the B2Bs. You're in constant competition."

"So you think Claudia likes him?"

"As a client," Kay said. "I'm assuming he was one of her clients?"

"He is her client, but —"

"Not anymore," Kay said. "He's your client now."

"What?" Lia pulled her eyebrows together. "Why?"

"That's how it works. The elite clients have one B2B they communicate with—not two. If he has an issue with Zurtech, he'll complain to you."

"I wasn't trying to steal him from Claudia. I just liked him."

"It's the way it works. There's nothing to feel guilty about—it sounds like he went after you, anyway."

"No wonder the B2Bs are so rude to me," Lia said. "They're probably afraid I'm going to steal their clients."

"Probably," Kay agreed, "but if you don't, you'll be fired, so…" She shrugged. "It's not like you have much choice."

"How did I not get this?" Lia felt stupid. "Bonuses are based on client satisfaction, so I clearly need clients."

"I never mentioned this before because I like Claudia," Kay began, her voice low, "but she gets around. She sleeps with a lot of men."

"So you think she slept with Eric?"

"I don't know. I know she tried to sleep with my husband."

"You're kidding."

Kay held up her hands. "Before I ever met him. He was at a reception and he said she was all over him and even asked him if he wanted to go up to one of the bedrooms on the second floor."

"Bedrooms? There are bedrooms on the second floor?"

"You didn't know that?"

"No. Why are there bedrooms?"

"For the out-of-town VIPs," Kay said. "It's just a perk Stan offers."

"It seems strange."

Kay shrugged. "I don't think so. It's also convenient if someone has too much to drink. I know the B2Bs occasionally spend the night."

"Hi." Kathleen placed a tray on the table beside Lia. "You aren't going to believe this." She was looking at Kay as she sat down. "Stan just fired me."

"Fired you or transferred you?" Kay asked. "You were transferred, right?"

"What's the difference?" She picked up a carton of yogurt from her tray. "It's not like I have a choice in it."

"True, but fired means you're out of the entire complex."

"I've worked my ass off! This is unbelievable." She tossed the yogurt back on the tray. "I don't even know why I bothered."

"What did he say?" Lia asked.

"Nothing. Just the standard, 'It's not working out.' Can the two of you keep a secret?" Kathleen asked. "Because if what I'm about to tell you leaks out, Steven could get fired."

"Steven?" Lia frowned in confusion.

"He's Kathleen's boyfriend," Kay said.

"And he works in payroll," Kathleen added, glancing around. "So can you two promise not to repeat what I'm about to say?"

Lia considered leaving, not sure she wanted to partake in office gossip, but she was too curious. "I promise."

"I asked Steven to look at Carmen's pay," she whispered. "Her bonus pay last month was five thousand dollars."

"No!" Kay breathed, clearly surprised. "He has to be wrong."

"Afraid not," Kathleen said, continuing to whisper. "I saw it with my own eyes. She's made over a hundred forty thousand dollars so far this year."

"Wow." Kay set down her fork and leaned back in her chair. "That means she makes twice what I make."

"Now do you believe Stan's sleeping with her?" Kathleen asked.

5

Joseph slipped off his two-thousand-dollar Berluti shoes after entering his two-level Pennsylvania Avenue condo. He set his briefcase inside his study to the left of the foyer and then took a few steps down into the large open space comprising the main level of the modern condo. He crossed to a wet bar beside the kitchen, pouring himself a glass of scotch. The condo's main level hosted a large great room with an unobstructed view of the Capitol Building, and an ultra-modern kitchen done in various gray tones.

Joseph frowned as he removed the latest issue of *Money* magazine from his pile of mail, his eyes on the image of Richard Eastman III displayed across the cover. He glanced at the table of contents and then was opening the magazine to a specific page, his eyebrows pulled together as he read.

"You fucking bastard," he said aloud minutes later, tossing the magazine on his coffee table. "Fucking bastard."

The intercom beside the front door buzzed and he crossed to the foyer before pushing a button and speaking into the intercom. "Yes?"

"Ms. Paige is here to see you. May I send her up?" the door-man asked.

"Yes." He unlocked the door and opened it slightly before retracing his steps back into the family room and dropping down onto his large leather couch. He picked up the stereo remote and within seconds, the Boston Pops' rendition of the *1812 Overture* filled the room.

When Kathy entered the condo a few minutes later carry-ing a bag of Thai food, Joseph was stretched out on the couch, his hands linked behind his head. "Hi," she practically yelled. "Could you turn that up a little louder?"

"What?" He touched his ear.

"I said," Kathy began, pausing as she set the bag on the coffee table and picked up the remote, "could you turn that up a little louder?" She began to push the down arrow on the remote.

"Don't." Joseph grabbed the control and turned the music back up. "I want it like that." He brought the hand holding the remote to rest on his chest and lay back down, closing his eyes.

"Well, I don't! It's hurting my ears." She took the remote from him and again turned down the volume. "Why do you want it so loud?"

"Because," he said, sitting up and glaring at her, "that's the way I like it." He took the remote, turning it off altogether be-fore coming to his feet.

"Where are you going?" Kathy asked.

"To take a shower," Joseph answered.

Moments later, he dropped down on the gray comforter on his bed and lay back against his pillows, throwing his arm over his eyes. "Fuck! Fuck! Fuck!"

"Joseph?" Kathy came into the room. "Are you okay?"

"No. Would you get the prescription bottle from the cabinet in my bathroom?"

Within moments she was back, sitting down beside him on the mattress, a glass of water in one hand and a bottle of pills in the other. "These?"

He lifted his arm from his eyes and squinted at the bottle she held towards him. "Yes."

"How many?"

"Two. Thank you." He took the pills from her hand, placed them on the back of his tongue and swallowed them down with water.

"Are you sick?" She touched his forehead.

"Your perfume is making me nauseous. I have a migraine. I need to be alone." His eyes were closed and he didn't open them as he spoke. "Would you turn everything off before you leave?"

"Do you need anything else?"

"Quiet. I just need quiet."

When he next opened his eyes, it was 9:00 the following morning. After brushing his teeth and using the bathroom, he left his bedroom and walked slowly, gingerly across the hardwood floor leading to the stairs.

Moments later, he was leaned back against the counter in the kitchen, watching the coffee brew.

"How's your headache?" Kathy came into the room dressed in a short silk robe.

"It's gone." His eyes swept the length of her body as she approached. "Where did you sleep?"

"In the guest room." She stopped before him, moving her hands up over his bare chest. "You were mean last night."

"I'm sorry." He kissed her forehead before stepping around her and taking a mug from the cabinet. "Do you want some?"

"Have you ever seen me drink coffee? How long have we been dating?" She watched him pour coffee into his mug. "What happened last night?"

"I had a migraine."

"You were also in a terrible mood." She moved up behind him, running her hands up and down his bare back.

"A migraine will do that to you." He took a swallow of the hot liquid, one hand resting on the counter, the other holding the mug.

"If you had a migraine, why did you have the music so loud? I would think that would make it worse." She began squeezing the muscles of his shoulders.

"I didn't know I had a migraine then. God, that feels good."

"What happened in a forty-five minute period to put you in such a foul mood? When I called to get your order for the Thai food you sounded fine."

"Could we get the oil out and do this right? I need a good massage."

Five minutes later he was stretched out, completely naked and facedown, on his bed as Kathy's oil-soaked hands worked the muscles of his shoulders, neck and back. "Are you going to answer my question?"

"What question?"

"The one about the terrible mood you were in when I arrived yesterday."

"I'd rather just enjoy your hands right now."

"Joseph, I'm not going to let this go," she said, her hands pausing. "You're always shutting me out."

"Please don't stop. It felt so good."

"Then talk to me." Her hands were once again moving. "What happened last night?" When he didn't answer, she stopped the massage. "I'm not going to do this unless you talk to me."

"We'll talk when you're done."

"No. If you want me to do the massage, you're going to talk to me now."

"Please." He turned his head and met her eyes. "I don't want to talk while I'm getting the massage. It'll ruin it."

"Do you promise we can talk when I'm done?"

"Yes." He turned his face back into the pillow as her hands once again began to move. "I promise."

"I have to get up," Joseph said several hours later, his arms tightening around Kathy.

She moaned as she turned her face into his chest. "It's Saturday."

"I know." He kissed the top of her head. "You can stay in bed. I'll be back in a few hours."

"No you won't. Where do you have to go?"

"I have a meeting with the Angels," he said, referring to a small investment group he oversaw. "We have a few business plans we have to evaluate."

"Why can't you ever stop?"

He ran his hand up and down her bare back. "We can have a late dinner. You can wait here or I could come to your place when I'm done."

"Wait a second." Kathy pushed herself up to a sitting position. "You never told me why you were so upset last night."

"I have to go to work."

"You promised." She leaned back against the pillows. "You can't leave until you talk to me."

He rolled onto his side and propped himself up on his elbow. "What do you want me to say?"

"I want you to tell me what upset you yesterday." She touched the side of his face. "I want to feel like I'm part of your life."

"You are part of my life."

"I'm part of your sex life. There's a difference."

"That's not true. Don't say that."

"Why were you so upset last night?"

"I read about someone retiring. Someone I possibly wanted to do business with."

"And that brought on a migraine?"

"Yes."

"Why?"

"It just did. It's complicated and I don't want to talk about it."

"So that's it? That's all you're going to tell me?"

"Yes."

"Why is it so hard for you to let me in? I'm in love with you. I want to share your life."

He turned his head and kissed the inside of her palm. "You are sharing my life," he said deeply, his gaze returning to hers. "As much as I'm capable of. You know more about me than anyone."

"Not Tony."

"I've known Tony my entire adult life. I was referring to women, and you're going to have to be patient with me. I'm doing the best I can."

"I know." She leaned in and kissed him lightly on the lips. "I just love you so much."

"I love you too."

—◦—

"They loved you," Kathy said, looking up from her cell phone. It was the Sunday after Thanksgiving, and she and Joseph were driving south on I-270 towards Washington, returning from her parents' place in Pennsylvania, where they'd spent the past four days.

"Did they?"

"Yes." She held out her cell phone. "You can read the text from my mother if you want."

"If they loved me, why wouldn't they let me share a bedroom with their daughter?"

"They're just conservative."

"Do they really believe we aren't sleeping together?" He picked up her hand and brought it to his mouth, kissing the inside of her wrist.

"I'm sure they know," she said, moving her hand behind his neck. "They just don't feel it's respectful to have sex with their unmarried daughter under their roof."

"If I had known that, I wouldn't have let you sneak into my bed."

"Right." She began to massage the back of his neck and shoulders. "You wouldn't have stayed longer than one night. You should have seen your face when you realized we were in separate rooms."

"I'm thirty-four years old. It took me back a bit. But it was fine."

"Of course it was fine—I was in your bed every night. We may as well have been in the same room."

"True." He leaned his head to the side, giving her hands better access to his neck. "God, that feels good."

"You're so tense."

"That's probably because I have about six hours of work ahead of me tonight."

"Tonight?" Her hand stilled on his neck. "You mean you have to work tonight? I thought we could unwind and watch a movie."

"Seriously?" He glanced sideways at her. "We've been unwinding for four days. Did you really think I wasn't going to have to work tonight?"

"No," she sighed, again massaging his neck. "And you didn't unwind for four days. You were on your computer and cell phone half the weekend."

"Kathy, I'm doing—"

"I know," she interrupted. "You're doing the best you can."

"I am."

"I know." She leaned across the seat and kissed the side of his cheek. "And I appreciate you spending the holiday with my family. It meant a lot to me."

It was past 1:00 a.m. when Joseph took off his reading glasses and set them on his desk. He leaned back in his brown leather swivel chair and moved his hands over his face, rubbing his fingers over his eyes. He hadn't seen Kathy for several hours, since she brought him a large plate of Chinese food and iced tea.

He picked up his empty plate and glass and opened the door to his study, walking out into the darkened foyer and then to the kitchen. After putting the dishes in the sink, he went up to his bedroom and found Kathy asleep in his bed.

He crossed to his bathroom, emerging several minutes later, freshly showered and naked. "Hi," Kathy said huskily, her voice barely intelligible.

"Hi."

"What time is it?"

"Late." He lifted the comforter and stretched out beside her.

"I missed you." She snuggled up beside him, her head on his chest, her hand moving over his muscled stomach.

"Do you want to go away with me between Christmas and the New Year?"

"Go away?"

"I'd like to take you to Switzerland. Do you think you could get off work?"

She lifted her head from his chest, meeting his eyes in the darkened bedroom. "You want to go away with me for Christmas?"

"Yes, I want to go away with you."

6

*L*ia stared at her pay statement for a full minute, wondering what she should do. It had to be a mistake. How could she possibly deserve a thousand-dollar bonus?

"Stan?" She knocked on his doorsill moments later.

"Lia. Hello." He looked up from a file. "What can I do for you?"

"I think there may be a problem with my pay."

"What's the problem?"

"I'm not complaining, but..." She paused, crossing to his desk and holding out the pay stub. "I think there may be a mistake."

He took the paper and waved it towards the chair before his desk. "Have a seat," he said before his eyes scanned her pay stub. "No, this is right."

"Oh." She hesitated, not sure what to say. "Well, thanks." She began to stand.

"I've been meaning to talk to you." He held up his hand and motioned for her to stay seated. "I'm very pleased with your work.

I told you when you were hired there was the potential to make a great deal of money in this job."

She nodded and wanted to ask exactly what she'd done to deserve the bonus, but was afraid it wouldn't sound right.

"And after watching you over several weeks," he continued, "I think you could be one of our top producers."

"I hope so," Lia said, pleased with the compliment.

"I'm getting positive feedback from the clients. You may not realize it while you're socializing, but those receptions make our VIPs feel a loyalty to Zurtech they wouldn't feel otherwise." He leaned forward, his hands flat on the desk. "And gaining that loyalty is what makes the B2Bs so important to Zurtech. People like to do business with friends."

"That makes sense."

"Yes, it—"

"Stan?" Carmen interrupted, coming through the door. "We need to talk." She didn't acknowledge Lia as she stopped in front of his desk.

"We were finishing up." He stood, picking up Lia's pay stub and coming around the desk. "Keep up the good work." He ushered her out of the office, but it was obvious his mind had moved past her to Carmen.

꧂

After three weeks and four dates, including the picnic and the show at the Kennedy Center, Lia accepted Eric's invitation to spend the weekend with him at his beach house in Delaware. She knew he wanted to have sex, had known it since almost the first date, and now she too felt ready to take the relationship to the next level. Taylor was with Ned for the weekend, so she didn't have to share her plans with her mother, who she knew wouldn't approve.

Forty-eight hours after first arriving at her apartment to pick her up, Eric was returning to the same apartment and depositing her bag inside her foyer. "Do you want something to drink, or—" Lia began.

"No. I've got to get home." He gripped her shoulders and kissed her. "I'll call you tomorrow."

"Okay." Lia leaned forward and kissed him again. "I had a great time. Thank you."

"Me too." He gave her a half smile. "Next time maybe we can actually leave the house." He winked before turning and leaving the apartment.

After removing her coat, Lia walked into her family room and lay down on the couch, still overwhelmed with memories of the weekend. He was perfect. The weekend had been perfect. She closed her eyes, replaying the details. His cozy beach house turned out to be a sprawling oceanfront estate in Bethany Beach, Delaware. His bedroom, where they'd spent most of the weekend, was twice the size of her entire apartment and opened on to a large deck with a hot tub offering a spectacular view of the Atlantic Ocean.

As she lay on her couch, she could almost hear the sound of the ocean. It couldn't have been more romantic. They'd spent hours in the hot tub drinking and talking, and then they'd make love, either on the bed or the bedroom floor, even once in the hot tub. She sighed at the memory and wished the weekend hadn't gone by so quickly.

"Good morning." Claudia stopped at the opening to Lia's cubicle the following morning.

"Where've you been?" Lia hadn't seen her since before Thanksgiving.

"I went home for a few days," Claudia answered.

"Home?"

"Up to Boston to see my family."

"I didn't know you had a vacation planned."

"I didn't. I needed to get away." Claudia sat down in Carmen's chair. "This place was getting to me."

"Are you feeling better?"

"Not particularly, but that will change soon enough."

"What do you mean?"

Claudia looked around before responding. "I'm looking for another job, but don't repeat that. I want my next job lined up before I give my notice."

"Of course, I would never mention it. But why? I thought you were happy here."

"I haven't been happy here for three years. It's been more about the money."

"Oh, so is that what you were doing in Boston? Looking for a job?" Lia asked

"Pretty much. I was putting my feelers out."

"I'm sorry you're not happy. You've been great to me."

"Right." Claudia laughed without humor.

"Seriously, I've learned a lot from you."

"God, I hope that's not true." She looked up and met Lia's eyes. "You should transfer to Kay's division. Those jobs are less stressful."

Lia frowned. "What do you—"

"Nothing." Claudia held up her hand. "Don't listen to me. I'm feeling sorry for myself. And there's actually a purpose to my being here right now. Stan said you haven't been sending in your weekly client roster."

"What's a client roster?"

"It's a list of the clients you've spoken to at the receptions. You know the emails we receive regarding the attendees?"

"Yes."

"Well, every Monday you should send a reply to that same address and list who you've met with and for how long."

"No one ever told me," Lia said.

"It's okay. That's why I'm telling you now."

"Okay. So every Monday I send in an email listing the receptions I attended and who I spoke to?"

"You don't have to mention everyone. Just the ones you've really met with."

"Last week there was only the Friday-night reception, and I didn't attend it, so I guess I shouldn't send anything this week?"

"You didn't attend Friday night's reception?" Claudia frowned.

"No. I was away."

"With Eric?"

Lia wondered if she was going to get another lecture. "Yes."

"Well, you need to put that."

"Put that I went away with Eric?"

"Yes." Claudia brought her coffee mug to her lips. "And how long it lasted."

"You've got to be kidding. How is that anyone's business?"

Claudia swallowed the liquid in her mouth before responding. "He's a client. Any interaction with clients is Zurtech's business."

"I spent the entire weekend with him," Lia whispered, leaning forward in her chair. "I'm not telling them that."

"Sure you will. They aren't going to judge you. In fact, Stan will like it."

"I don't understand."

Claudia stood. "He likes it when we date the clients. Friends like buying from friends, remember?"

"It's private," Lia insisted. "And I'm not telling him."

"Suit yourself," Claudia said before walking away.

— —

Lia was so busy with Taylor she barely noticed when Eric didn't call on Monday, but by 10:00 p.m. Tuesday she was starting to wonder if something had happened to him.

She decided to call his cell phone. His voice came over the line after three rings. "Hello?"

"Hi, Eric, it's Lia." She was surprised he answered, having assumed the phone would be off and she'd leave a message.

"Hi, beautiful, how are you?"

"Good. I was calling to see if you'd be at the reception tomorrow night."

"I hadn't really thought about it. Are you inviting me?"

She could hear the teasing in his voice. "Sure." She smiled. "Would you like to meet me at the reception?"

"I'd like to meet you right now. Can I come by?"

"Taylor's asleep in her room."

"I'll be quiet. And I'll leave before she wakes up."

"No," she said without hesitation. "She gets up in the middle of the night sometimes."

"Come on. I miss you. I'll only stay for a little while."

Lia laughed at how pitiful he sounded. "If you miss me you can meet me at the reception tomorrow night."

"How about I do both? I'll come by for an hour tonight and then we'll meet at the reception tomorrow."

"No, seriously. I can't. Just meet me tomorrow."

There was a long pause before he responded. "Maybe, we'll see."

Lia slowly lowered the phone, surprised by the abrupt ending to the call. He was mad, she realized. He'd expected her to let him come over with Taylor in the house.

— —

Lia arrived at the reception just after 8:00 p.m. wearing a simple black sleeveless dress and black suede heels, gold earrings and a watch her only jewelry. She was at the bar ordering a gin and tonic when Eric arrived thirty minutes later.

"Hi, beautiful." Eric smiled, leaning forward to kiss her cheek.

"I was starting to worry you weren't going to come."

"I almost didn't." His eyes swept over her body. "I got caught in a business dinner." He moved his hand up and down the curve of her waist. "I had a hard time getting away."

Lia nodded and looked around, wondering if she should push his hand from her waist. It couldn't look professional.

"Let's go upstairs."

"Upstairs?" Lia frowned. "Why?"

"Bedrooms." He met her eyes.

"You're kidding, right?"

"No." He shook his head, his amused eyes meeting her startled ones. "Let me show you."

"No." She shook her head and took a step back, forcing him to drop his hand.

"Why not?" he whispered and then laughed at her horrified expression.

"I'm not going upstairs with you," she said, crossing her arms over her chest.

"Then let's get out of here." He took her hand and headed towards the door. "I want to be alone with you."

"I missed you," he said minutes later.

"I missed you too." She settled back in the plush leather seat of his Porsche. "Taylor is with her Dad, so if you want to go to your place, I—"

"How much did you miss me?"

"What do you mean?"

"I mean," he began, taking her hand and placing it on the bulge between his legs, "I'd like you to suck that."

"Here?" She let out a nervous laugh, unsure whether he was serious.

"Yes, here." He leaned back in the seat, lifting himself up slightly as he undid his pants and freed himself from his underwear. "Come on. It won't bite you."

She could feel her heart rate accelerating and her hands clamming up. Ned was the only man she ever gave a blowjob, and it wasn't in a car. "I don't know."

"You can do it." He moved one of his hands around the back of her head. "Come on." He applied enough pressure to slowly coax her head down towards his lap. "That's it," he moaned as she took him in her mouth.

"Oh yeah," he groaned, moving his hips up slightly as he held her head down. "That's right, babe," he said, spreading his fingers in her hair. "Suck it."

Lia tried not to gag as she moved her mouth up and down the full length of him. He was so hard and so big she wasn't sure how to do it without choking.

"You can't stop now, baby." He held her head down when she tried to take a break, increasing the tempo of his hips, seemingly unable to get his penis deep enough in her throat.

She managed to breathe through her nose and attempted to keep her lips against her teeth so she wouldn't rub them against him, praying he would come so the ordeal would be over. It seemed to take forever, and she was sure she was about to throw up, when finally with a hard thrust of his hips he was coming, his semen spilling into her mouth. He seemed to come and come as the spasms shook his body, and then finally he loosened his hold on her hair and she was lifting her head.

"That was good," he said as he pushed himself back into his underwear. "Man." He blew out a stream of air.

Lia leaned back in the seat, her tongue running along the torn skin of her inner lip. She glanced sideways at him after a few minutes of silence. "Do you want to go somewhere now?"

"You know, I'm really beat." He squeezed her thigh. "Why don't we call it a night?"

"Oh, okay."

"I'll see you Friday night." He reached over her and opened the passenger door. "You'll be here, right?"

"Sure." She picked up her purse from the floor of the car. "I'll see you Friday then." She turned towards him, expecting a kiss, but he made no move to close the distance between them so she climbed out of the car into the cold December evening. "Bye," she said before closing the door. Before she took two steps, he had shifted his car into drive and was skidding out of the parking lot.

━ ━

Lia didn't bother asking Stan if the thousand-dollar bonus in her paycheck was correct Friday morning, but realized if they continued, she'd be making close to one hundred thousand dollars per year and be debt free by April. Unfortunately, the knowledge did nothing to quell the unease she felt after her date with Eric, if giving a guy a blowjob could even be considered a date.

"What's wrong?" Claudia's voice broke into her brooding.

"Nothing," Lia lied, lifting her head. "I'm tired."

"Me too," Claudia said as she sat down in Carmen's chair. "I had an interview yesterday in Boston."

"You did?" Lia forced thoughts of Eric from her mind.

"I called in sick," she whispered. "They paid to fly me up for the day."

"How did it go?"

She glanced around before responding. "I start the first week in January."

"They offered you a job after only one interview?"

"Shh," Claudia said, looking around. "I don't want anyone to know yet."

"Oh, sorry." Lia grimaced.

"It's okay. No one heard you." Her eyes returned to Lia's. "Actually, it was my second interview. I interviewed the first time when I was there last week." She leaned back in her chair and crossed her legs. "I'm not planning to give my notice here until the last minute. I don't want it to affect my bonus pay."

"So you're not taking any time off between jobs?"

"No. I can't afford to. I'm taking a big pay cut, so I'd like to make as much money as I can over the next couple weeks so I can pay some bills."

"Why are you taking a pay cut?"

"Because I'm making a lot of money here and at my level there's no way I'm going to bring in that kind of money somewhere else."

"Why not? If Zurtech's willing to pay you that much, then—"

"Trust me. No one's going to pay me what Zurtech does."

— ~

It was 10:20 p.m. when Lia parked her Honda next to Eric's Porsche in the small parking lot outside the Zurtech house. She stared at his car, feeling a renewed sense of disgust at her behavior two nights before. She thought about going home, not wanting to have to see him, but knew she had to confront him eventually.

She spotted him as soon as she entered the house. He was across the room at the bar, laughing at something Carmen was whispering in his ear, and then he was following her through a door to their right and they were out of sight. Lia took a step in their direction, intending to let Eric know she'd arrived, when Kay stopped her.

"Surprise!"

"Kay! Hi." Lia smiled. "What are you doing here?"

"My husband wanted to come."

"Oh, he's here?" Lia looked around.

"He's in the back room playing pool and discussing business." Kay leaned forward. "I met Eric Nettles. He's really cute."

Lia nodded, her eyes glancing towards the door he had just exited. "I just arrived, so I haven't spoken to him yet."

"He seemed nice."

It took Lia over five minutes to untangle herself from Kay, and then she was opening the same door she saw Eric walk through minutes earlier and stepping out into a dimly lit hallway leading to a staircase. She made her way upstairs, the sound of the music from the main room fading with every step until she could no longer hear it, and then she was walking down a hallway and looking into one empty bedroom after another.

She was about to turn around when she heard Eric's baritone voice, and then she recognized the sound of Claudia and then Carmen. She approached a closed door, her eyebrows pulled together in confusion. "Hello?" She knocked lightly on the door.

"This room's taken," Eric said.

"It's Lia," she said, putting her hand on the doorknob and slowly opening the door. "I was—" She stopped midsentence, pulled the door closed, and then she was covering her mouth and running towards the bathroom.

7

Joseph, along with the other eight partners in the DC office, was in the midst of a heated discussion over whether to represent two former female employees of an international company headquartered in Northern Virginia who claimed part of their job responsibilities was to have sex with important clients. The women served as account executives in the Marketing Department and mainly functioned as liaisons between the company and new and established clients.

"This doesn't even warrant discussion," Tony said. "We don't do sexual harassment."

"Wait a second," Kevin said. "We are not in agreement over whether this is sexual harassment."

"We have three ingredients here," Joseph said. "Sex, workplace, women." He held up three fingers. "That sounds like sexual harassment to me."

"This is much more complex than you two are portraying," Kevin argued. "Zurtech has 35,000 employees in the US,

20,000 at their facility in Silicon Valley and another 15,000 in Reston. This practice could be widespread throughout the company. They are hiring young women fresh out of college, placing them in marketing departments, and then giving them bonuses based on how much sex they have with corporate clients. With a base salary of $50,000, one of these women took home an additional $100,000 in bonuses last year."

"If what you're saying is true, this is prostitution," Tony said. "These women are freely having sex and being paid generously to do so. This sounds like a case for the DA's office."

"That may be true for these two women, but what about the other women who work in these departments? Do you believe every woman Zurtech hires for marketing willingly becomes a prostitute? This has the potential to be a huge class action suit."

Tony laughed aloud. "Now we are back to a sexual harassment case. We don't do, have never done, and aren't about to start representing these types of clients."

"Tony's right," Joseph said. "This case is too dirty. Tell these women to go to the police."

"Can you imagine what's going to happen to Zurtech stock when this comes out?" one of the junior partners asked. "Their stock is currently up twenty percent for the year."

"Not a stock I want in my portfolio," Tony said. "Let's move on."

"Do you want to grab lunch?" Tony asked Joseph as the partners were filing out of his office an hour later.

"I'll take a rain check," Joseph said. "I have to run. We'll talk later."

Moments later, Joseph was in the office of the associate who had conducted the interviews of the Zurtech women. "I want all your notes," he said.

"Kevin told me to call them. He said we aren't going forward with it," the young associate said.

"We're not, but I'm going to personally make the calls."

"Oh, okay." He held out the file.

"Thanks." Joseph took the file and returned to his office.

"Martha," he called several minutes later.

"Yes?" She stepped into his office.

"I want to meet with these two women separately." He held out a piece of paper. "Try to schedule something for this Saturday or Sunday."

"But we're closed on weekends." She looked down at the piece of paper.

"That's alright. I'll be in."

"Do you need me to come—"

"No," he interrupted, shaking his head.

"Okay. I'll arrange it."

"Thank you. Oh, and one more thing," he said before she was out of his office. "Let's keep this between us and bill any of your time involved to general admin."

"May I ask why?" she asked.

"No."

At 11:00 Saturday morning Joseph, dressed in a dark suit, was sitting behind the receptionist's desk in front of the elevator awaiting the arrival of one of the two women involved in the Zurtech suit.

He slowly came to his feet as the elevator doors opened. "Ms. Kelly?" He met the eyes of the young woman coming off the elevator.

"Yes." She smiled. She looked like a dark-haired Scarlett Johansson. Not even her conservative business suit could detract from the voluptuous body beneath.

"I'm Joseph Craig." He walked out from behind the receptionist's desk and held out his hand.

"Please call me Claudia." She returned his handshake, the female interest in her eyes unmistakable.

"Thanks for coming in on a Saturday. With the holidays approaching, it was the only time I could fit you in. I didn't want to wait until after the New Year to talk." He led her down the hall to his office.

"I was surprised you wanted to see me and Lia separately," she said before preceding him into his large office.

He helped her out of her coat before gesturing with his hand towards one of the leather club chairs in front of his desk. "I didn't call you and Ms. Merrick in together because I want to hear each of your stories without influence from each other." He took a seat behind his desk. "You experienced similar treatment at Zurtech, but at different times, with different people. In all likelihood, I'm going to handle your cases separately. At least at this point I think I am." He opened the file on his desk.

"The gentleman I talked to before indicated this might be a class action suit."

"Maybe." Joseph looked up from the file, meeting her eyes. "But that hasn't been decided, and even if we choose to take that course, I would still meet with each client separately."

"I understand. It's..." She paused as she crossed one leg over the other and sat up straighter in the chair. "We weren't sure about your rates, and we thought if we did it together..." She trailed off.

"I'm sorry. I assumed someone discussed the rates with you at your initial meeting," he said. "Regardless of whether we handle your cases together or separately, our rates would be the same. This will cost you nothing unless we get something from

Zurtech. In other words, we take this on at a risk to ourselves and do all the up-front work at no charge. If we win a settlement, our firm takes forty percent off the top. If, on the other hand, we are unsuccessful, you owe us nothing and we basically have to write off the time and money we spend preparing."

"Is the forty percent normal?"

"For law firms of our caliber it is."

"It seems high."

"It's not negotiable." He leaned back in his chair. "My hourly rate is a thousand dollars. We can't afford to invest our time in speculative cases such as yours without the possibility of a large payoff." He watched her. "Would you like to take some more time to think it over?"

"No. I want you." She met his eyes.

He returned her stare. "Good," he finally said, remaining professional. "Let's get started then." He reached into the top drawer of his desk and removed a small digital recorder. "Do you mind if I record our conversation?"

"No. I don't mind."

"Okay. I know you've been through this once before with my colleagues, but since I'm taking the lead on this case, I'd like you to tell me, from the beginning, exactly what happened."

"Okay." She nodded. "A Zurtech representative came to Boston University my senior year to participate in a job fair. I was graduating that spring with a degree in journalism and public relations, and they made it sound like an exciting place to work."

"This was four years ago?"

"It will be four in May."

"And do you recall the name of the recruiter you met with from Zurtech?"

"Yes, Cecile Mann."

"Okay." He jotted the name on his legal pad. "How did she describe the position? What made it sound exciting?"

"I was being hired to work in this exclusive division in their Marketing Department that was responsible for keeping Zurtech's most elite clients happy. I was going to be paid to party with rich and powerful men."

"So they weren't hiring you to sell?"

"They were hiring me to sell brand loyalty. It was the B2B's job to entertain the elite-level clients. To make them feel loyal to Zurtech."

"B2B stands for business to business?"

"Yes." She nodded. "That's what we're called."

"And you accepted the position?"

"Yes. They offered me forty thousand dollars a year and paid for my relocation from Boston to Northern Virginia."

"And how did that compute with what your classmates were being offered?"

"It was fine. My grades weren't the best, and Zurtech was a respected company. Some of my friends with better grades interviewed for the position also, but didn't get it."

"Were they as attractive as you?"

"No," she said, her lips turning up in a smile.

"How soon after you started did you realize you were being hired to do more than entertain?"

"In retrospect, I probably should have known right away, but I think it took me a year to really understand what was happening," she said.

"A year?" He looked down at the file. "It was my understanding the sex started much earlier." He began flipping through the file.

"It did. It started after my third reception, but I didn't understand at the time that the company was encouraging us to have sex."

He looked up from the file. "You were having sex with the clients, but you didn't know Zurtech wanted you to?"

"I was having a relationship with one client."

"What kind of relationship exactly?"

"I don't know." She shrugged. "I was young. At the time, I thought he loved me."

"So you were in a romantic relationship with this client?"

"I don't know how romantic it actually was. We had a lot of sex."

"And where did this sex take place?"

"The first time was in Zurtech's corporate apartment. That was the night we met."

"How did you end up in the corporate apartment together?"

"I don't remember exactly. There was a reception that night at the Ritz-Carlton in Tyson's Corner. I had too much to drink." She shook her head. "When I woke up the next morning we were in bed together at the apartment."

"And then after that first night, you saw him exclusively?"

"Yes. For the next eleven months, I only slept with Alan West."

Joseph's eyes widened in surprise. "Alan West as in West to East Communications?" Alan West was the CEO of one of the largest telecommunications companies in the country.

"That's the one." She readjusted her position in the chair.

"He's married, isn't he?"

"Yes." She nodded. "He was then and as far as I know he is now."

"Where did the sex take place?"

"In the beginning it took place at the corporate apartment and then later at the Zurtech House."

"The Zurtech House?"

"Zurtech bought a 10,000-square-foot house on several acres of land in Reston about three years ago. That's where most of the receptions occur. And there are about six bedrooms on the second floor of the house."

He wrote the word "brothel" on his notepad. "How often did you see West?"

"It varied, but probably twice a week. It all depended on when the receptions occurred."

"Did all of your meetings take place on Zurtech property?"

"Or at Zurtech-hosted functions."

"Like?" he prompted.

"Football games, concerts, cruises. I knew he was married, so I figured it was a convenient cover. We had a place to meet and have sex." She shook her head. "I was an idiot. I never realized what was going on."

"And what was going on?"

"I was being offered as a perk to an elite client." Her gaze shifted to the window, and she didn't speak for several seconds. "I'm not really sure, but I think I was supposed to understand from the beginning." Her gaze returned to his. "After I started sleeping with Alan, bonuses began showing up in my paychecks."

"And you didn't receive any before then?"

"No."

"Do you remember how much these bonuses were?"

"I know exactly how much they were." She reached for her briefcase. "I kept all my pay stubs." She pulled the case onto her lap and opened it up, extracting a two-inch stack of check-sized papers held together with a rubber band. "They're in order of date." She held them out.

He took the pile from her hand and removed the rubber band, his eyes quickly scanning the first twenty-five or so stubs. "You were paid every Friday?" he asked, not looking up from his perusal.

"Yes."

"Your first bonus was seven hundred and fifty dollars?"

"That sounds right."

"And then you continued to receive between seven hundred fifty and a thousand for...." He continued to flip through receipts.

"Eleven months," she said.

"At the time, why did you think you were receiving these bonuses?" His gaze returned to her.

She shrugged. "I thought they liked my work."

"Maybe they did." He leaned forward, resting his elbows on his desk. "Did anyone ever tell you these bonuses were in exchange for sex?"

"Not in those words exactly. But it was definitely implied."

"How was it implied?"

"One day Alan just stopped attending receptions. He cut off all communications with me. I tried to call him and text him, but it was like he dropped off the face of the earth, only he didn't because he was still CEO of West to East Communications. I could see him on the news, and he was still a Zurtech client." She looked down at her hands. "To this day I don't know what happened. What I did." The eyes that lifted to his were tear-filled.

"Maybe you didn't do anything," Joseph said, pushing a box of tissues across his desk. "Maybe his wife found out."

"Maybe." She plucked a tissue from the box and dabbed her eyes. "This is ridiculous—I don't even care anymore. I don't know why I'm crying."

"Take your time," Joseph said. "I know this isn't easy."

"I'm fine," she assured him, meeting his eyes. "I'm fine. What was your last question?"

"How was it implied that you were receiving bonus money in exchange for sex?"

"After Alan cut off all contact with me, my bonuses stopped. I was very upset at the time because I'd gotten accustomed to making a certain amount of money, and then my pay was practically cut in half."

"So you confronted your boss?" he asked when she didn't immediately continue.

"Yes. I went to my boss to find out why my bonuses had disappeared when my quality of work was exactly the same."

"Who was your boss?"

"Stan Hall, the VP of Marketing. He's everyone's boss."

"And what did he say?" Again he prompted when she paused.

"He told me to get over Alan and start spending time with other elite clients." She gave a forced laugh. "I was shocked. I didn't know what to say. When I got over the initial shock, I reminded him I was still attending receptions and mingling with the VIPs, and I didn't understand why he was bringing up Alan. And then he looked me in the eyes and said bonuses were based on the level of satisfaction we were providing the customers."

"And that was it?"

"No. He said if I wanted to start receiving bonuses again I'd have to start giving other clients the same level of attention I gave Alan."

"Did he say anything else?"

"No." She shook her head.

"And then what happened?"

She met his eyes. "Then I began to receive bonuses again."

"Did you get into another long-term relationship?"

She shook her head as her eyes dropped to her hands. "No. I was with a lot of different men. The bonuses were based on the revenues associated with the client," she continued, her voice light. "I made a lot of money."

Joseph came to his feet and slowly walked around the desk before lowering himself into the chair beside hers. "How much?"

She took a deep breath and seemed to struggle to maintain her composure. "About a hundred fifty thousand dollars over the next eighteen months."

"Does that include your salary?" He held out the box of tissues.

She again took a tissue and began to dab at her eyes. "No. I was making an additional forty-five thousand dollars a year in salary."

"You were making over a hundred thousand a year in bonuses."

"Yes."

"Why did your bonus pay more than double after West? You said everything was tied in to revenue. He had to be one of Zurtech's largest clients."

She dropped her gaze back to her hands. "This is hard."

"I know and I'm sorry, but I have to ask these questions."

"I understand." She sighed. "It's very embarrassing, especially telling a man."

"Don't think of me as a man. Think of me as your attorney."

She laughed in response. "That may be difficult."

He returned to his earlier question. "Why the increases in bonus pay?"

"The bonus system wasn't complicated. It was linked to the revenue generated, but it also tied in to the number of clients and the category of the act you performed."

His eyes narrowed. "Elaborate on 'category of act performed.'"

She shrugged. "Just like professionals, I guess. When I was with Alan I was paid at a rate for a single client. Like you said, he was a large client, so his rate was between three thousand and four thousand a month depending on the quarter. Most paid less than that, but..." She trailed off.

"I've heard everything, Claudia. You're not going to shock me."

"I don't want you to think I'm some type of slut or something."

"I think you're a beautiful young woman who got caught up in something not of her own making. Tell me the rest."

She met his eyes for a long moment before finally speaking. "The percentages were increased if you participated in group sex and stuff like that," she said. "I mean, I didn't do it all the time, but the bonuses were very good."

"What is 'stuff like that'?"

"Sex with two clients, or two clients and another B2B, or two B2Bs and a client." She continued to meet his eyes. "You must think I'm awful."

His face remained expressionless. "No, I think your boss is awful. And this was all taking place at this Zurtech House?"

"Yes." She nodded.

"And how did you know the different rates?"

She shrugged. "It wasn't difficult. You figured it out based on your pay."

"No one ever told you straight out how much you would receive for the different acts?"

"No. But before a party, we would receive an email listing the clients attending and the amount they were worth to the company. This was basically your invitation. Once you realized the percentages, it was easy to figure how much you could make with the different clients."

"Who generated this email?"

"I assume Stan Hall. It came from a generic address. I have copies of the emails with me." She reached for her briefcase. "Would you like to see them?"

"Yes, I would like to see them."

She opened the briefcase and extracted a manila legal-sized envelope. Written in black ink in the middle of the envelope were the words "client rosters." She undid the string binding the packet and removed a stack of paper, separated in groups of two by a single staple in the left-hand corner, and held them out to him.

His eyes quickly scanned the sheets. The first page was an email from *Zurtech — bulletin board* to *B2B Marketing Division* with four columns listing client names, company, last quarter revenue, and expected next-quarter revenue.

The second page was an email from *Claudia Kelly* to *Zurtech — bulletin board*, written in memo form, with a subject line titled *Client Interactions*. The memo clearly outlined the "meetings" she'd attended over what looked to be a one-week period. Sometimes she'd list one client, sometimes two, sometimes several, and there were also numerous occasions where other female names appeared. "Would you explain what this second page means?"

"It's actually quite simple. If I was with one client, their name appears alone. Where you see two names, I was with two, and when you see other girls' names, it was more of a group thing."

"Why did you keep copies of the emails?"

"I wanted to make sure my bonuses were correct."

"And were they?"

"Yes. There was never a mistake."

"Okay." He paused for a moment, staring at the sheets in front of him. "Do you know who you were sending your emails to?"

"I assume Stan Hall."

"You never saw a list of prices or percentages or anything that mentioned sex?"

Again she shook her head. "No."

"What about the other women? You must have talked among yourselves."

"Not really. It was company policy that we weren't allowed to discuss our bonuses. And the whole atmosphere surrounding us created this sense of competition."

"There were no men in this division?"

"Unless you include Stan Hall," she said, "but he's the head of all marketing, so he's technically in every division."

"And how many women? At any given time, how many B2Bs are in the division?"

She bit her lower lip as she looked up. "It varies, but probably twenty."

He covered his mouth and began to rub his hand over his chin. "It's hard to believe every woman they recruit would participate. Some of them must have husbands or boyfriends."

"They never have husbands," Claudia said. "Not when they start anyway. And most women don't participate. They are usually fired or transferred out within the first three months."

"And new women are brought in?"

"Yes." She nodded. "Most people don't know what's going on."

"But what about these parties you attended? Isn't that where you were having sex?"

"Yes, but that would only happen in certain areas. The people involved knew where to go."

"Including the clients?"

"Some. They were kind of like us. Some of them knew exactly what was going on and others had no clue."

"Any particular reason you left?" He smiled when she made an incredulous face. "I mean other than the obvious?"

"I don't know. I guess I got tired of it all. I think hiring Lia Merrick was the beginning of the end for me. I mean, up until that point they'd never hired a single mother—and I felt sorry for her when she started dating one of the clients. I felt like I should warn her and I tried, but I guess not hard enough. She was so hurt. I still feel awful about it. I don't want to be any part of it anymore."

"When you quit, did they offer you a payoff of any type?"

"No."

"Do you have anything else for me in your briefcase?" He stood and placed the pile of emails onto his desk.

"No. I think I've given you everything I have."

"What exactly are you looking for us to do for you?"

"I don't know. Make them pay somehow. I feel like I've lost my innocence. That should be worth something."

He turned off the digital recorder. "I'm not sure what I can do for you, Claudia." He leaned back against his desk, folding his arms across his chest as he faced her. "I think what Zurtech is doing is unethical and illegal, but proving that..." He shrugged.

"That's going to be a challenge, and to be honest with you, I'm not sure how much sympathy a jury will have for you. If you had come forward once you realized what was happening, that would be different. But you were knowingly involved for three years."

"What are you saying?" she asked, her face crestfallen. "That I'm not going to get anything after what they did to me?"

"Probably not."

"But you're going to try? I mean, Lia wants to go to the police, but I don't see what that would accomplish. We wouldn't get anything."

"Don't go to the police. That would be a mistake. There isn't enough here to get an indictment, and the chances of proving anything would evaporate quickly if they knew they were being investigated. And in your case, I think you're in a very vulnerable position. If you went to the police they'd probably offer you immunity from prosecution in exchange for your testimony."

"What? I don't understand."

"Having sex in exchange for money is a crime. In my opinion, it's highly unlikely they'd come after you, but it's possible."

She covered her mouth with her hand. "Oh my God, I never even considered that."

"Well, I'm an attorney. It's my job to consider everything. My advice to you is to put this all behind you and go on with your life."

She shook her head, an incredulous look on her face. "So what you're saying is they're going to get away with this? What they did to countless women?"

He shook his head. "No. They're not going to get away with anything. They'll eventually be exposed. What I'm saying is you should be as far removed from them as possible when that happens or you may be looking for a criminal attorney."

"Oh—God." She leaned back in the chair and stared up at the ceiling. "This isn't at all what I expected."

"I'm sorry."

She brought her head forward and slowly came to her feet. "I guess that's it then." She reached for her briefcase.

He pushed off the desk and crossed the room to the coat rack. "I wish I could have told you what you wanted to hear." She followed him to the front of the office and he helped her into her coat. "Oh, and one more thing," he said, his hands resting on her shoulders. "Don't share this information with anyone—for your own protection, you need to keep quiet."

Joseph's Mercedes skidded to a halt at the curb in front of a parking meter at 10:55 the following morning. He only had five minutes to spare before his meeting with the second woman involved in the Zurtech case.

He sifted through the change in the small area in front of the gearshift, but only came up with one quarter. He cursed aloud as he tossed it back. He opened the door and climbed out of the low-slung sports car, grabbing his briefcase from behind the driver's seat before jogging towards the building.

"Good morning, Mr. Craig," an elderly black man said, looking up from his desk when Joseph came through the glass door.

"Wilmer?" Joseph walked past the bank of elevators and straight to the man's desk. "Has a woman been here looking for me?"

"No, sir." He shook his head.

"Thanks." He turned, but after a brief hesitation he was reaching inside his suit jacket and turning back to Wilmer. "Merry Christmas," he said moments later, handing him a hundred-dollar bill.

The older man looked up at him, his eyes wide. "Mr. Craig, your office already gave me money."

"I know, but I wanted to too."

Lia parked her Honda behind a black Mercedes. She allowed herself a quick glance, and for once didn't fantasize about owning the nicer car. No, this time she dreamt of being able to afford it, because if she could afford it she could pay off her mounting debt.

"Are we here?" Taylor asked from the back seat.

"Yes, we're here." She looked at her reflection in the rearview mirror as she applied a fresh coat of lipstick.

"May I have some?" Taylor crawled up between the seats.

"Not right now, Taylor. I'm late for my meeting."

"But, Mommy, you're putting it on." She cocked her head to the side.

Lia turned to Taylor and quickly ran the applicator over her lips. "Now remember, you have to be very quiet. We're going into a law office, and—"

"I know. I know," Taylor said, staring at her reflection in the mirror.

"Come on. We're late." She got out of the car and waited for Taylor to do the same before picking up her briefcase and locking the door. She glanced at the meter, wondering if Sunday was a holiday. Deciding she couldn't afford the luxury of finding out, she stopped next to the meter, digging in her wallet for quarters.

"Let me put them in." Taylor tried to take the quarters from Lia's hand.

"You can do one." Lia handed her a single quarter before glancing at her watch. It was 11:15 a.m. Since learning her mother wasn't available to watch Taylor, she'd gone back and forth on whether or not to even show up today. By the time she'd decided she should, she barely managed to get the two of them ready and out of the house.

"I'm cold," Taylor said.

Lia slipped the remaining quarters into the meter. "Where's your hat?" She walked back towards the car. "Stay right there." She opened the car door and reached into the back seat and grabbed a colorful knit hat. "Here you go." She pulled it down over Taylor's head.

"What about my gloves?" Taylor asked as they walked towards the office building.

"You don't need them, it's just a short walk." She picked up their pace, feeling cold herself as the wind swirled around them. It was in the midthirties, but the wind chill made it feel at least twenty degrees colder, and by the time they reached the building, she felt half-frozen. "Here we are." She opened a glass door and ushered Taylor inside.

"May I help you, Miss?"

Her gaze swung to two men near a bank of elevators approximately thirty feet away. One she assumed was the owner of the voice, an elderly black man wearing a dark uniform, and the other—her eyes met and locked with the eyes of the other. He was the man she'd seen on Anderson Cooper a couple of months prior. "I—I'm here to see an attorney at Prossi, Stuart and Craig," she said, hesitating just inside the door.

"Ms. Merrick?" The man from Anderson Cooper didn't take his eyes from hers as he closed the short distance between them.

"Yes," she said, unable to drop his gaze.

"I'm Joseph Craig." He held out his hand.

"You are?" Her eyes opened wider as she slipped her hand into his. He was extraordinary. The television didn't capture his full essence. She felt her mouth grow dry as she continued to look into his eyes.

He narrowed his gaze. "Have we met?"

"Yes." Lia shook her head. "I mean no. I saw you on CNN a few months ago."

"You were there?" He was still holding her hand.

"No." She smiled. "On television."

He continued to meet her eyes. "Why don't we go up to my office?" he said, finally releasing her hand.

"Oh, Taylor." She suddenly remembered Taylor, who was silently standing beside them. "I couldn't find a sitter so I had to bring my daughter. I tried to call to reschedule, but there was just a recording and I didn't want to stand you up, so..." She trailed off when she realized he was no longer listening.

Joseph Craig was bent down on one knee in his expensive suit and cashmere coat, smiling at Taylor. "You're beautiful," he said softly. "What's your name?"

"I'm Taylor."

"Hi, Taylor, I'm Joseph." He shook her hand. "How old are you?"

"Five," she said after a short hesitation. "I'm in kindergarten."

"Is that all? I thought you were going to say you were in second grade."

Taylor beamed. "I'm tall for my age."

"I can see that. Are you ready for Santa Claus to come?"

She gave him an exaggerated nod. "I can't wait," she said, and then began to recite her Christmas list.

Lia watched the exchange silently, impressed by his ability to bring out the usually shy Taylor. Taylor appeared outgoing while she talked to Joseph Craig, her little body animated as she described the different presents she knew Santa would bring.

After a minute or two he stood up. "She's the most beautiful little girl I've ever seen," he said.

"Thank you."

"After you." He held out his hand towards the elevators.

Lia took Taylor's hand and slowly walked in the direction he indicated, conscious of his presence behind them.

"Would you push the up arrow for me, Taylor?"

Taylor pressed the button and darted onto the elevator as soon as the doors opened. "Look, Mommy, sixteen floors!"

Joseph followed Lia onto the elevator and then inserted a key into a slot above the floor buttons and turned it to the right.

"What are you doing?" Taylor asked.

"I'm releasing a lock so the elevator will be able to open on our floor." He pulled the key out and looked down at her. "Can you reach sixteen, Taylor?"

"I think so." She stepped up on her tiptoes and managed to reach the button. "I did it. I did it."

"Good job," Lia said, her eyes meeting Joseph's. She breathed in deeply, feeling overwhelmed by him.

"You're tall," Taylor said. "Much taller than my daddy."

Joseph smiled down at Taylor. "Maybe you'll be as tall as me one day."

She laughed. "Girls aren't as tall as boys."

"No? I guess they aren't." His eyes again found Lia's. "Your mommy's very tall."

"Not as tall as you," Taylor said.

"No, she's not," he agreed, his eyes not leaving Lia's.

The elevator door opened. It took him a moment to react and then he was holding the door open with his hand and motioning for them to precede him into the lobby.

"Wow," Taylor said, spinning in a full circle as she looked around. "Look, Mommy, a waterfall!" She ran to investigate a rocky fountain beside a seating area with leather couches and chairs.

"I brought my computer so she can watch a movie," Lia said as she stopped beside Joseph in front of a reception desk.

"We can feed it to the projector in the conference room beside my office. That way she can watch it on a big screen." He was again meeting her eyes.

Lia could feel her hands clamming up. She felt like she was standing beside a movie star instead of an attorney, but there was something so familiar, so appealing about him. And it wasn't only his looks. He was magnetic. And then for the first time since meeting him, she remembered Kathy Paige. He was dating a supermodel. A wave of disappointment rocked through her body. She sighed, disgusted by the line of her thoughts—hadn't she learned anything?

"Are you okay?"

"Yes. I'm fine." She forced herself to smile.

Ten minutes later, Taylor was situated in the conference room, watching a movie on the flat-screen television, a soda and cookies before her on the table, while Lia accompanied Joseph to his office next door.

"Let me take your coat," he said, moving up behind her. As his hands touched her shoulders, she felt an urge to lean back against him. She closed her eyes, willing herself to get under control.

"Thank you," she said softly before taking a seat in one of the two chairs facing his large cherrywood desk.

He hung up his own coat before taking the seat behind his desk and opening his briefcase. "I'll be right with you," he said as he began removing some files.

She felt a degree better with the distance between them. She looked around his posh office, admiring the exposed-brick walls and abstract paintings. The room was warm and masculine, like the man sitting behind the desk. And then the reality of why she was sitting across from him hit her and she had a desire to flee, not knowing if she could discuss such a personal matter with him. It had been hard enough with his colleagues.

"Thank you for coming in on a Sunday," he said.

Lia looked down at her hands, willing herself to start thinking of him as her lawyer instead of a man. After her recent experience with Eric Nettles, it was disconcerting to feel such an attraction to a complete stranger.

"Are you okay?" The soothing timbre of his voice had her lifting her eyes.

"Yes." She nodded. "This is—it's awkward discussing this. It's something I'd like to forget ever happened."

"I imagine you would, and hopefully this will be the last time you have to discuss it." His eyes were warm, and Lia felt herself relaxing.

"You don't see this making it to a courtroom?"

"No." His eyes remained locked with hers. "Not based on what I heard from your friend, Claudia."

"She isn't my friend."

"Your coworker," he corrected. "Based on what I've heard, this case will never see the inside of a courtroom."

Lia narrowed her eyes. "Then why did you agree to take it?"

"Why?" He hesitated, seemingly choosing his words carefully. "I like a challenge. This is going to be difficult to prove."

"But if it's never going to make it to a courtroom, I'm confused as to why you're interested. I mean, what's in it for you?"

"If I can find proof to back up your allegations, I'm sure Zurtech would be willing to pay a nice settlement for your pain and suffering."

"I'm more interested in exposing them, so they'll stop recruiting and humiliating innocent women," she said. "It was Claudia's idea to retain your firm. I thought we should go to the police."

"You didn't, though?"

"No." She shook her head. "Claudia talked me into coming here first."

"Good. Don't go to the police." He opened a drawer and took out the small recorder. "Do you mind if I record our conversation?"

"I'd prefer you didn't."

"I like to record so I don't have to take notes during my meetings."

"This whole incident repulses me, and the thought of it being recorded...I can't." She dropped her eyes.

"I understand." He slipped the recorder back into the drawer. "I'll just take notes then." He watched her for a long moment. "Are we okay?"

"Yes, I'm sorry."

"There's no need to apologize. I know this is hard for you." He waited for her to lift her gaze before continuing. "Would you like something to drink— something to settle your nerves?"

"Scotch," she said. She'd never had scotch, but she saw the bottle when they first entered the office.

He raised his eyebrows, hesitating only a moment before standing up and crossing to the bar on the other side of the office. "Ice or water?"

"Uh, how do you normally drink it?"

"I drink it neat, but—"

"Neat is fine," she said, not knowing what it even meant.

"Here you go," he said moments later, handing her a highball glass a quarter full of scotch.

"Thank you." She watched him resume his seat as she brought the drink to her lips. She took a swallow, grimacing as it burned her throat.

"Take smaller sips," he said, watching her. "It's made to be sipped."

"Sorry." She breathed in deeply, avoiding his eyes. She took another sip of the strong liquid, this time forcing herself not to react. Within a few minutes, she could feel a calm beginning to settle in, and then she was looking across the desk and meeting his eyes.

"Can you tell me what happened?" His deep voice sounded almost soothing to her ears.

"Yes." She nodded and began to talk.

One hour, one and a half glasses of scotch and two interruptions by Taylor later, Lia was describing the final reception she attended. "And I followed him back. And there he was, having sex with Claudia and Carmen at the same time." Her voice was light, but devoid of emotion.

"And then what did you do?"

"I went to the bathroom and threw up. And then I went home."

She watched him from across the desk. His head was bent as he wrote something on the legal pad. Her eyes dropped to his hands. His fingers were long and his nails were perfectly manicured. Her eyes traced the veins running up the back of his hands. She imagined those hands touching her. She lifted the glass of scotch to her mouth and finished it in two gulps.

"Do you want more?"

Her eyes met his. "I don't think so," she said. "Not unless you're offering to drive me home."

"I don't mind."

As she met his eyes, she had no doubt he meant it. "No, thank you." She dropped her eyes to her hands. She'd already had more than was prudent and was feeling a warm buzz as a result. "Should I continue?"

"If you're ready."

"The next day when I arrived at work, I confronted Claudia. We weren't exactly close, but we had lunch together sometimes and she knew I was dating Eric. I couldn't understand why she would do that."

"And what did she say?"

"She told me the truth," she said. "She told me everything: the bonus system, the clients, the parties. Everything finally made sense."

"What do you mean? 'Finally made sense'?"

"Why Carmen was making so much money when she appeared completely incompetent. Why all the B2Bs seemed to be in competition with each other. Why there were so many beautiful women. Why Stan transferred out perfectly good employees. I wasn't really even interviewed for the position. He didn't ask me any questions about my skills. He just looked at me and then told me about the position. It was all so obvious once I knew the truth."

"So you quit?"

"Yes, I quit. I gave him a week's notice. I would have left that day, but I wanted to see if I could find proof."

He narrowed his eyes. "And did you?"

"No. There's no proof. That's why I was surprised you wanted to see us." She stood, restless, and could definitely feel the alcohol in her system. "Tell me what I'm missing, Mr. Craig."

"Call me Joseph," he said, his gaze following her as she crossed the office and stopped at the window.

"What am I missing, Joseph?" She stared at the US Capitol, visible in the distance. "I'm here because I'm angry and I want Zurtech to stop what they're doing, but I don't see how you're going to be able to make that happen."

"What they're doing is illegal."

"But doesn't that mean it's a criminal and not a civil matter? Shouldn't we be going to the police?"

"The two aren't exclusive of each other. And I don't believe you have enough information for the police to obtain a warrant."

"Well, how can we get enough?"

"That's my job to figure out."

She turned, her eyes meeting his. He was leaned back in his chair, one ankle resting on the other leg, a pen twirling between his fingers.

"There isn't a jury in this country that's going to give us money," she said.

"What makes you so sure?"

"Claudia knowingly slept with clients for money. That makes her a prostitute."

"True, and that's illegal."

"Of course it's illegal, but she knew what she was doing."

"You didn't," he said. "And I'm handling your cases separately."

She turned back to the window. "I'll come across as a woman scorned. There's no proof I was being used as a perk for clients." Just saying the words left a bitter taste in her mouth.

Joseph came to his feet and crossed the office. "You were an uninformed participant."

Lia turned, surprised to hear his voice so close. He was at the bar, pouring himself a glass of water. "But the only thing that makes me different than any other woman who sleeps with a man is I received a hefty bonus as a direct result."

"This Eric. He knew the system?"

"Oh, yes. According to Claudia, he targeted all the new women." She turned back to the window. "He was a regular."

"Have you heard from him since that night?" He was beside her, his eyes moving over her profile as she looked out the window.

"No, he got what he wanted and moved on."

"And you're sure Zurtech doesn't know why you quit?"

She nodded. "And that's one of my regrets."

"What's that?" Barely a foot separated them. "What do you regret?"

"That I didn't confront him." She could smell his scented aftershave, and realized how close they were standing. "I should have confronted Stan Hall, and told him what a despicable excuse for a person he is."

"It's better that you didn't."

"I guess, but it would have made me feel better." She turned to walk back to the chair and felt unsteady.

"Easy," he said, gripping both sides of her hips with his hands.

"Sorry." She clasped his arms to steady herself and lifted her eyes to his. She felt like a deer with its eyes caught in the headlights, a now familiar feeling of awareness coursing through her body. She couldn't remember ever having such a physical reaction to a man. She shouldn't have had the second glass of scotch. She was no longer thinking clearly. "I—I need to sit down," she whispered. "I just felt a little dizzy." And then she was stepping around him and fleeing back to her chair.

Joseph slowly followed and took the chair beside hers instead of behind his desk. He watched her in silence for several seconds before speaking again. "Do you think higher-ups at Zurtech were involved?"

"I don't know." She shook her head. "I assume Stan was acting alone."

"Why do you assume that?"

"I don't know. I just can't imagine something like this being corporate-wide. He was almost obsessed with knowing everything about these elite clients. And the files we compiled were available only to our division. He would want us to record every detail about their lives."

"Such as?"

"Everything." She reached for her briefcase and pulled out a manila folder. "I meant to show you these earlier." She held out the file.

Joseph took the folder and opened it, his eyes scanning the first sheet, a spreadsheet with dozens of rows and columns. "What am I looking at?" he asked, his eyes narrowing as he continued to study the sheet.

"That's an elite-client profile." She pulled the sheet back from him and turned it towards her, reading the name on top. "This is Alan West's, from West to East Communications." She leaned forward and spread it out on Joseph's lap. "The client's name is here." She began running her finger along the top of the sheet, inadvertently touching his thigh through the paper. "And these columns"—she trailed her finger across the various columns and down several inches on his thigh—"list everything from their children's names"—she paused as she poked the column heading—"to their country clubs"—again she poked the column heading—"to—"

"I get it," Joseph said, abruptly coming to his feet, the sheets on his lap scattering to the floor. "Sorry, my fault." He kneeled down and quickly gathered them up, dropping them on the chair and crossing to the bar, his back to her as he poured himself a glass of water. He quickly drank it down and then poured himself a second glass.

Lia watched him, wondering what had caused his sudden mood shift.

A couple of minutes passed, and then he was returning from the bar and sitting down behind his desk. "Okay. Where were we?"

"I was telling you about the elite-client files." She picked up the papers from the now vacant chair and set them on his desk.

"Right." He took a long swallow of water. "Why did you bring Alan West's file?"

"I brought a few. They're just samples so you could get a gist of the information we gather."

"But why specifically is his part of the group?" He lifted up the spreadsheet.

"His was the first client file I was shown. Stan wanted all files to look like that one. Basically it was the template all elite files should be modeled after."

Joseph studied the spreadsheet in silence for over a minute. "What do these names in the lower right corner represent?" He held the sheet out to her and she leaned forward, her eyes scanning the area he indicated.

"Those are the B2Bs who put information in that particular file."

"So, would I assume he had sex with the three women listed here?" He lifted his eyes to hers.

"Maybe, but not necessarily. I added information to several of the files besides Eric's, and I never had sex with those men."

"Why did he need all this information?" He continued to study the sheet. "What purpose did it serve?"

"He wanted us to know them, so when we interacted with them it was more like they were our friends."

"This is more information than I know about any of my friends. His siblings' names and addresses? His children's school?" He lifted his eyes. "It doesn't make sense."

"That's why I said he seemed almost obsessed with them."

"Are these for me to keep?"

"Yes." She leaned back in her chair, watching him as he slipped the spreadsheet back into the folder and then jotted a few things down on his legal pad.

"The woman from human resources who interviewed you," he began, pausing as he flipped back a few pages in his notes, "this Cecile Mann. She's obviously in on it." He looked up from the page.

Lia frowned. "Why would you say that? I don't—"

"As soon as she discovered how beautiful you are, she contacted Hall."

Lia knew the alcohol in her system was the only reason she didn't blush at his unexpected and matter-of-fact compliment. "I don't think so."

"Why not?"

"Because she was so nice," she said and then instantly felt foolish, realizing how naïve she sounded. "I'm an idiot," she sighed. "You'd think I would have learned by now."

"Learned what?"

"Not to trust people."

He narrowed his eyes. "Why would you say that?"

"You'd have to know my history to understand." The smile she gave him didn't reach her eyes. "I seem to be missing the BS detector."

"I don't think you should fault yourself here," he said, his voice low, almost gentle. "No one would have expected this at a corporation as large as Zurtech." He tossed the legal pad back onto his desk.

"Most of the new hires were transferred out. They were smart enough not to date the clients."

He leaned back in his chair, his eyes continuing to meet hers. "You're very critical of yourself."

"Yeah, well." She shrugged. "At some point I have to stop being the victim."

"So what are you doing now?"

"Hmm?" She frowned, not following him.

"Are you working again? Or are you going to take some time off?"

"I'm looking for a job. I can't afford to take time off."

"What would you like to do?"

"Not marketing." Again she smiled without humor. "I'm good with numbers, so ideally a financial analyst position. I don't have any experience though, so I'll probably just try to find an entry-level position somewhere."

"What geographic area? Northern Virginia?"

She nodded. "But at this point I don't know how picky I can be. I just need a job."

He leaned forward and opened his top desk drawer. "Send me your resume." He slid his business card across the desk. "I have contacts."

"You don't have to—"

"I want to. I'll be in touch after the holidays."

"Thank you."

"As far as the case is concerned, I'm going to do some research on my own, and then I'll let you know how I think we should proceed."

"Mommy, are you done yet?" Taylor's voice preceded her entrance into the room. "My show's over."

"Yes, we were just finishing up."

"I'm hungry," Taylor said as she climbed into Lia's lap.

"Do you have big plans for the holidays?" Joseph asked as he began to gather up his notes.

"Not really. We're going to spend the night at my mother's place. She lives a few minutes away."

"And Santa Claus knows I'm going to be there," Taylor said. "Mommy sent him a letter and told him."

Joseph smiled at Taylor as he closed his briefcase. "Your mom's a smart lady."

"How about you?" Lia asked, deciding if it was okay for him to ask personal questions, she could as well.

"I'll be in Gstaad, Switzerland over the holidays." His eyes again met hers.

They lived in different worlds. "I'm sure it'll be beautiful." She wondered if he'd be with Kathy Paige. "We should go. I'm sure we've taken up enough of your Sunday." She gently pushed Taylor off her lap and stood.

He walked around the desk and retrieved Lia's coat from the rack beside his door before moving up behind her. "Thanks again for coming in," he said as he helped her on with her coat.

"Are you a lawyer?" Taylor asked.

"Yes, I am a lawyer."

"My daddy's a lawyer," Taylor said.

"Really?" Joseph glanced down at Taylor.

"Right, Mommy?"

Lia was facing him again. "That's right."

"Where does he work?" He took Taylor's jacket from the rack and knelt down beside her.

"Blackman and Associates," Lia said.

"Ned Merrick," Joseph said. "I thought he worked for the DA's office." He finished fastening her coat and stood up.

"He changed sides a couple of years ago."

"So your husband's a lawyer." His lips turned up in amusement.

"Ex," Lia corrected. "I gather you know him?"

"I've met him."

"Did you try a case against him?"

"Not personally, but my partners have."

"I'm sure you don't run in the same circles, but..." She hesitated. "I don't want him to know about this."

"Of course." He watched her for a long moment. "Everything, including the fact you're my client, is confidential."

"Thank you."

"Mommy, I'm hungry," Taylor said. "When are we going to eat?"

"Right now." Lia glanced down at Taylor and stroked her hand down the back of her head. "You've been great today. And I noticed a restaurant right across from where I parked."

"Let me take you to lunch," Joseph offered.

"Yeah!" Taylor said, jumping up and down. "Let's go to lunch with Joseph."

Lia glanced at Taylor, surprised again at her reaction to this man who was a perfect stranger. "No, thank you." Lia smiled politely as she met Joseph's eyes. "That isn't necessary."

"I know it isn't. I'd like to. It's the least you can let me do after I dragged you in here on a Sunday."

There were a thousand different reasons she should have said no, but at that moment, looking into his eyes, she couldn't think of one. "Okay, if you're sure."

"I'm sure."

Five minutes later, they were walking towards the lobby exit when the glass doors opened. Lia instantly recognized the woman entering the building. It was Kathy Paige, and as she strolled towards them it was painfully obvious pictures didn't do her justice. Even dressed casually in blue jeans and a dark leather jacket, her blonde hair loose around her shoulders, she was the most beautiful woman Lia had ever seen.

Joseph slowed his steps, almost coming to a stop as she approached.

"Surprise!" Seemingly unaware of the woman and child beside Joseph, Kathy wound her arms up around his neck and leaned her body into his, kissing him fully on the mouth. "I came to take you to lunch." She pulled back slightly and moved her thumb over his lip to wipe off the trace of her lipstick.

"Kathy, I—"

"Thank you for everything," Lia said, not looking at the couple as she reached for Taylor's hand. "Come on, Taylor." She hurried off towards the door.

Joseph cursed softly under his breath. "Wait! Lia, wait!" He stepped around Kathy and trotted after her. "Lia?" He caught up with her as she reached the glass doors. "I thought I was taking you to lunch."

She raised her eyes to his. "It's okay. You didn't know your girlfriend was going to show up."

"I told you I'd take the two of you to lunch."

"It's okay," she said, forcing herself to smile. "We eat on our own all the time. We'll be fine." She pushed open the door. "Say goodbye to Mr. Craig, Taylor."

Taylor held up her small hand and managed a light goodbye before her mother dragged her away.

Joseph dropped his chin to his chest as he sunk his hands into the pockets of his coat.

"Who were they?" Kathy asked as she stopped beside him. "Who was the woman?"

"A client. I told you I had a meeting today, remember?"

"Yes." She stepped in front of him and gripped the lapels of his coat. "But I missed you." She leaned forward and kissed his lips. "And it looks like my timing was perfect."

Hours later, Joseph sat behind the desk in his study, looking over his notes from his meeting with Lia Merrick. He took off his reading glasses and tossed them on his desk, leaning back in his chair as he stared, unfocused, at the ceiling. Moments later he was glancing at his watch and then reaching for his cell phone.

"Sam. It's Joseph Craig...Great...Good...No, just tying up some loose ends before the holidays. I need you to check something out for me...No, it can wait until after the holidays... Right...I have some information and I need your help finding the proof. If you need to hire additional help, don't share anything that isn't absolutely necessary." He went on to explain what he knew about Zurtech. "Oh, one more thing, Sam," he said as they were ending the call. "I want you to do a complete background on someone for me...Lia Merrick."

Twenty miles away in Tyson's Corner, Lia was sipping red wine while she flipped through images of Joseph Craig on her laptop. There were pictures of him on the rowing and debate teams at Yale, pictures of him with Supreme Court justices and dozens of pictures of him with beautiful women. It would have been so much easier if he'd been full of himself. Then she wouldn't have thought about him incessantly all day and typed him into her search engine as soon as Taylor was in bed. But there was something about him. She sighed as she trailed her index finger over the image of him on her computer screen. He had the nicest eyes. What if his girlfriend hadn't shown up? She would have had lunch with him. She closed her computer. He was dating a supermodel, and she'd sworn off men. Why was she even fantasizing about him?

8

Lia was at her small kitchen table going through her bills when a knock sounded on the door the Sunday after Christmas. "Hi, sweetie." She smiled as Taylor came into the foyer.

"Mommy!" Taylor hugged Lia's waist. "I missed you."

"I missed you too. Did you have a good time?"

"Yeah, wait till you see all the things Santa left me at Daddy's. I think Santa was confused and thought I was going to be there on Christmas." She glanced back at her father. "Candice thought so too. Right, Daddy?"

"That's right." He was dressed casually in jeans, a black sweater and a wool coat. All clothes Lia didn't recognize.

"You're going to get the stuff from the car, right Daddy?"

"Right." He smiled down at Taylor. "Let me just get rid of these." He was laden with bags of gifts. "Should I put them in her bedroom?" he asked Lia.

"That's fine," she replied coolly, thinking how much shorter he was than Joseph Craig as he walked away.

"I have lots of new toys," Taylor said. "We left a lot at Daddy's house because there's so much more room there." She slipped off her coat and handed it to Lia.

"Would you go watch TV for a little while?" Lia asked as she turned to the closet. "I need to talk to Daddy alone for a minute."

"Okay."

"Where's Taylor?" Ned asked a few minutes later when he returned from his car with more gifts.

"She's watching TV. I need to talk to you." She felt a stirring of anxiety in her stomach.

"About what? Candice is waiting in the car."

"I need to borrow some money," she said, not quite meeting his eyes. "I'm broke."

"How are you broke? I thought you had some great job with Zurtech."

"I stopped working there a week ago."

"You mean you were fired?"

"I quit," she corrected. "And I don't want to talk about it," she added when he looked like he was going to say more. "I just need enough to help me cover the rent and some groceries. Fifteen hundred or so."

"You quit? Jesus, Lia."

"I don't want to discuss this with you."

"Oh, but you want to borrow money from me?" He opened his eyes wider. "Maybe you should have looked at how low your bank account was before you quit your fucking job. You're unbelievable." He turned and reached for the doorknob. "Borrow the money from your mother."

"Ned, no." She grabbed his arm. "I can't. I owe her too much already. She paid for my school." She hated the desperation she could hear in her voice. She should have just taken another advance on her credit card.

He looked pointedly at the hand gripping his arm. "You aren't my responsibility anymore."

Lia dropped her hand to her side. "Well Taylor is, and based on the cars you drive and the clothes you wear, you aren't hurting for money."

"My clothes and cars are none of your business."

She stared at him, wondering why he hated her so much. He was the one who had left her, and yet he treated her as if she had done something to him. "I'll pay you back."

"I won't hold my breath." He turned and reached for the doorknob.

"Where are you going?"

"To get my checkbook from the car."

He was back several minutes later, a check in hand. "You can thank Candice for this. And we do expect to be paid back."

The check was from Candice Merrick's account. She wanted to rip it up and throw it at him, but she couldn't. She needed the money. She'd overspent in October and November, not realizing her job would suddenly come to an end. And now she was in trouble. She only had one hundred and twenty-five dollars in her checking account, and her rent was due on the first of the month.

"You will tell me when you get a raise, right?" She looked up from the check.

"What do you mean?"

"The child support is based on your income."

"So?"

"So, are you still making the same amount of money you were when we came up with the agreement?"

He turned to the door. "I hand you a check for fifteen hundred and you accuse me of not paying you enough?" He shook his head. "Yeah. I'm still making the same money."

"Aren't you going to say goodbye to Taylor?"

"Say goodbye for me." He opened the door and hesitated. "This is the last time I'm bailing you out, Lia."

——— ～

"Happy New Year, Martha." Joseph stopped in front of his secretary's desk the day after his return from Switzerland. "How was your holiday?"

"Wonderful," she said, looking up from a stack of mail she was sorting. "I see you made it back in one piece."

He smiled. "No tree jumped out in front of me this year." The year prior, he'd returned from his winter holiday with a cast on his arm.

"And how about Ms. Paige? Did she fare as well?"

"Yes, I brought her back in one piece too."

"Good. I hope it was relaxing."

"It was." He set a ring box on her desk. "Please return that to Cartier. You can find the receipt in my email. And would you get Nick Prossi on the line for me?"

——— ～

Lia was reading an online job posting when her cell phone began to ring just after 10:00 a.m. She glanced at the display and, after identifying a Washington DC exchange, brought he phone to her ear.

"Happy New Year, Lia," said an achingly familiar voice.

"Hi, Joseph." She was surprised and pleased at how normal her voice sounded. She'd been consumed with thoughts about him since their meeting.

"How are you? How was your holiday?"

"It was fine," she lied. She'd actually had a terrible week, worrying about money and trying to find a job. "I'm sure it wasn't as nice as yours." She closed the computer and stood up from the kitchen table, the room suddenly not feeling big enough.

"Gstaad is beautiful at Christmastime. Do you ski?"

"When I was younger, but I haven't been since I was married. Ned didn't ski and I…" She trailed off, realizing she was rambling. "No, I don't ski anymore."

"You should take it up again. Taylor's at the perfect age."

"I should," she said, knowing she was a long way from being able to afford to take Taylor skiing. "When did you get back?"

"Yesterday."

"You must be tired." She dropped down onto her bed.

"Not particularly. I slept on the plane."

"Ah, first class," she guessed. "You couldn't say that if you flew in economy."

He chuckled softly. "No and, uh, I wouldn't go to Europe if I had to fly economy. I'm too big for those seats."

"That's true," Lia agreed, imagining him. He was at least six foot four, maybe taller.

"How's your job search going?"

"Slow," she sighed. "Everyone's been away for the holidays."

"I just got off the phone with Nick Prossi."

"Of Prossi Designs?" Prossi Designs was a high-end athletic clothing line.

"That's the one. He's my law partner's brother and a personal friend of mine. He's expecting your call."

"Really?" She couldn't hide her excitement.

"Really. Do you have a pen?"

"Yes." She jotted down the number he recited. "What kind of job? I mean, I'm not being picky. I just want to be prepared when I call."

"I told him you were interested in finance, but your degree is general business so there are other options as well. Nick's a good guy—you'll enjoy working with him."

She gripped the phone. It sounded like he was saying she already had a job. "Thank you, Joseph. You have no idea how much I appreciate this." She closed her eyes, afraid she might cry.

"I'm happy to help. Are you going to call him now?"

"Well, I thought I would do a little research first and then call him in an hour or two."

"Or you could call him now," he said, and she knew he was telling her the job was already hers. "He's expecting your call."

"Thank you."

"You're welcome, Lia. I'll be in touch."

"Hi." Kathy smiled, stepping back from the doorway as Joseph entered her foyer later that evening. "What are you doing here?"

"I needed to see you." He touched her waist as he met her lips for a brief kiss.

"You needed to see me?" She snaked her hands up around his neck as she leaned into him. "You just spent ten days with me."

"I know." He gripped her hands and slowly pulled them from his neck. "We need to talk."

"We do?" She frowned as she stepped back from him, crossing her arms over her chest. "What do we need to talk about?" Her blonde hair was pulled back in a ponytail and her face was free of makeup. "What's the matter?"

"I just—we need to talk."

"Joseph?" She frowned. "What's going on?"

"Nothing." He began walking back towards her family room. "I just want to talk."

"You're not going to take off your coat?"

He retraced his steps to the foyer as he shrugged out of his cashmere coat. Moments later, he was sitting beside her on the white linen couch in her family room, his arm stretched out along the back of the cushions behind her.

"Are you okay?"

He moved his hand to the side of her face, letting his fingers trail over her cheekbone, his eyes following the movement. "You're so beautiful." He met her eyes. "I never stop thinking that when I look at you." He breathed in deeply and let his hand drop back to the cushion.

"Joseph, you're scaring me. Are you okay?" She touched his hand.

"I don't know." His gaze traveled to the sitcom showing on her flat-screen television.

"What's going on?"

He leaned forward, resting his elbows on his knees as he dropped his face into his hands.

"Did something happen at work?"

"No." He turned his head, his gaze meeting hers. "This isn't working for me."

Her face paled. "What are you talking about? What isn't working for you?"

"Us." He sat up and turned to her, his eyes looking into hers. "I can't do it anymore."

"I don't understand." Tears came to her eyes. "We just spent ten days together. I thought we had a good time."

"We did, but it's never going to be more than that. And you're looking for more."

"I've never said anything about more. I've never pressured you."

"Kathy?" He turned his head to the side. "I know what you want, and I'm not the man who will give it to you."

"Joseph—"

"I'm never going to marry you."

She pulled her head back as if she'd been hit, tears coming to her eyes. "I don't understand. I—I thought you loved me."

"I do," he said, reaching out and taking her hand. "I do love you. It isn't you—it's me."

"What does that mean? Did something happen in Gstaad? Tell me what's changed," she pleaded. "I don't understand."

"It doesn't feel right. Something is missing for me."

"Maybe you need more time. Maybe—"

"No." He shook his head. "I'm sorry. I'm so sorry." He brought her hand to his mouth and kissed the inside of her wrist. "I never wanted to hurt you."

"Are you breaking up with me?" she whispered, pulling her hand from his. "Are you telling me you don't want to see me anymore?"

"Yes," he said, his eyes meeting hers. "You deserve someone who—"

"Get out!" she cried, coming to her feet. "Leave." She pointed towards the hallway.

"Kathy?" He came to his feet and moved to her, gripping her arm.

"Don't touch me!" she cried, pulling her arm back. "Get out of my fucking house!"

"Kathy, please. Don't act like this."

"Like what? Like what, Joseph? Like you've broken my heart?" She wiped at the tears that were falling from her eyes.

"It doesn't have to end like this," he said. "We've had a lot of good times we—"

"I don't want to ever see you again," she whispered, meeting his eyes. "I don't want you to call me in a few days because you need to have sex."

"Kathy." He shook his head. "Please, don't. I'm sorry," he said again.

"Me too," she managed to say. "Now please leave."

He watched her in silence for several seconds and then he was crossing to the front door, retrieving his coat and walking out into the chilly January evening.

9

Two and a half weeks after Joseph's call to Nick Prossi, Lia received an official offer from Prossi Designs at an annual salary of fifty-five thousand dollars. So elated by the news, she only felt a minor panic when she received a registered letter from Zurtech the following Friday demanding six thousand dollars in restitution.

It was a few minutes past 5:00 p.m. when Joseph returned her call. "Thanks for calling me back," she said as soon as she heard his voice.

"What can I do for you?" His voice was friendly but professional, and she felt a stab of disappointment, which was ridiculous considering she wasn't interested in a personal relationship.

"First, thank you for calling Nick Prossi. I start working on Monday. It wouldn't have happened without you, so I'm very grateful."

"I'm happy I could help."

"The other reason I called is because I received a letter from Zurtech today."

"What kind of letter?"

"Do you remember the personal shopper from Neiman Marcus I mentioned?"

"Yes."

"They say I owe them six thousand dollars. I signed something saying I'd pay them back if I left before six months. I'm not paying them back. I can't believe they have the nerve to even ask me to."

"Would you email me the two documents?"

"They're hard copies, and I don't have a scanner. Wait, I could go to my mother's and—"

"No, that isn't necessary. Can you meet me somewhere? I just left the courthouse in Fairfax, so I'm in your general vicinity."

"Yes, of course." Her heart instantly began to pound in her chest at the thought of seeing him again.

"Or would it be easier if I came to you? With Taylor and—"

"Taylor's with Ned for the weekend. I can meet you." She didn't want him coming to her apartment. It would be too weird. "Where should we meet?"

"Do you know Pearson's?"

"Yes." She'd never been, but she knew of the exclusive club.

"Can you be there at a quarter of six?"

She glanced down at her jeans. "I'll try."

—   —

Twenty minutes later, Joseph entered Pearson's, a members-only restaurant and lounge in Fairfax County, Virginia. The hostess greeted him by name and then, at his request, led him to an obscure booth in a quiet area of the restaurant.

He'd heard from Sam Malone, who was still in the preliminary stages of his investigation, two days earlier. He'd conducted
a thorough background check of Stan Hall. Hall was married
with two kids, living in a $2 million home in Oakton, Virginia.
His mortgage payment was over $5,000 a month, which wasn't
inconceivable with a salary including bonuses of about $300,000
per year. He'd been with Zurtech for eight years, starting as a division lead and rising to Director of Marketing in less than three
years.

He'd studied business at Penn State, where he received above-
average grades and met the woman he would later marry. Fifteen
years later they were still married, but for the past four years
he'd been having an affair with Zurtech's Director of Human
Resources, Cecile Mann.

The Zurtech House turned out not to be a Zurtech property.
It was owned by Mike Hall, Stan Hall's younger brother, who was
also the millionaire owner of Tia Tacos, a successful food-truck
business with a fleet of over thirty trucks, serving areas on both
coasts. The house was purchased three years prior and, as far as
Malone could tell, was used exclusively by Zurtech's B2B division. Malone figured Hall had arranged to have Zurtech pay his
brother for use of the property.

Malone's investigation of Lia didn't hold any surprises. She
grew up in Northern Virginia. Her parents divorced when she
was still young and her father remarried. She had one brother,
who lived in the same town in California as her father, and three
half siblings. She appeared to be estranged from her father.

Her mother remarried when Lia was twenty, and she appeared close to both her mother and stepfather. Lia married
Ned Merrick the summer after her junior year in college and
dropped out of school to work full-time while Merrick attended

law school. The two had their first and only child, Taylor, a year before Merrick completed law school. Merrick began an affair with Candice Blackman, now Candice Merrick, soon after becoming an associate at Blackman and Associates. Candice's father was the founding partner. Merrick left Lia for the other woman less than six months after taking the position. Lia had briefly moved in with her mother while she completed her undergraduate degree, and she was now living in a two-bedroom apartment off Route 7 in Tyson's Corner. She owed a little over $7,000 in credit card debt and $10,000 on a car lien and had less than $800 in the bank. She had never been arrested and there was no evidence of drug or alcohol abuse. Malone included a couple of recent photos of her, which Joseph had studied for more than a few minutes the evening before.

Joseph glanced at his watch. It was 6:00 p.m. He opened his briefcase and took out some files.

Lia parked her Honda between a Lexus and Land Rover and quickly headed through the parking lot to the restaurant. While she liked nice things, she'd never given much thought to how much money other people made, until recently. As she struggled to make rent, she was very conscious of the thirty-year-olds driving around Northern Virginia in fifty-thousand-dollar cars.

She sighed as she turned and retraced her steps to her car, where she'd left the letters. First, she'd forgotten them in her apartment and had to backtrack five minutes, and now she was trying to go into the restaurant without them. She was acting like she was meeting him for a date instead of a business meeting. And now she was thirty minutes late.

"May I help you?" the hostess asked coolly as she approached.

"Yes. I'm here to meet Joseph Craig."

Lia knew she didn't imagine the widening of the other woman's eyes at the mention of his name. "Right this way."

She felt her heart jump as soon as she saw him sitting in a corner booth in the back of the restaurant and was thankful for the extra time she'd spent on her appearance, even if it was one of the reasons she was late. "Thank you," she said absently to the hostess before slowly approaching his table.

He lifted his eyes when she was still about fifteen feet away, and then he was coming to his feet, looking incredibly handsome in a dark gray suit. "Hello." His eyes were even more incredible than she remembered—a light shade of brown with a depth she could lose herself in.

"I'm so sorry I'm late. I left my place without the letter and had to go back, and then traffic was bad, and—" She stopped, realizing she was rambling. "I'm sorry."

"It's perfectly fine. It gave me time to catch up on some work. Please"—he held his hand towards the booth—"have a seat."

She lowered herself into the cushioned seat, letting her eyes move over his face, noticing his full lips and day's growth of beard.

"What would you like to drink? Scotch, perhaps?"

Her eyes flew to his, and she realized he was teasing her. "I think my scotch days are over."

"If you could just learn to sip, you might actually enjoy it."

She scrunched up her face. "I don't actually like the taste of alcohol."

"A girlie drink it is," he said. "What would you like?"

"A Cosmo."

A waitress appeared, and he ordered Lia's drink. Then he began gathering up some papers and files and slipping them into his briefcase. "May I see the letter?"

"Oh." She reached for her purse, surprised at how quickly he turned the conversation to business. "The copy of the contract I signed is attached."

He slipped on a pair of black reading glasses and remained silent as he read the letter and then flipped it over and read the contract she'd signed. "I'll take care of it."

"How?" She leaned back as the waitress placed the Cosmo on the table. "Thank you," she said softly, her eyes remaining on Joseph.

"Don't worry." He refolded the letter and placed it in his briefcase. "You won't have to pay the money back."

"I wouldn't pay it. I'd rather them take me to court."

"I'll take care of it."

Lia paused, unsure of what to say. She'd been upset about the letter all day, and less than five minutes after meeting with Joseph, the problem was gone. "Thank you."

"You're welcome."

"You've done more for me in the past two weeks than anyone in the last..." She trailed off, dropping her eyes. "Thank you," she said again. "I wish there was something I could do to repay you."

"You could stop thanking me," he said, lifting his glass.

"You got me a job," she said.

"No, your skill set got you a job. I made an introduction."

"That's everything," she said as she carefully lifted her glass to her lips. "Plus, he told me you're his silent partner."

"Did he?" He smiled. "Well, I'm not too silent then, am I?"

"I won't tell anyone."

"Thanks." He winked at her and her heart jumped.

"Does 'silent' mean you aren't involved at all?"

"I have a financial stake in the company, nothing more."

"I saw online that you invest in a lot of companies."

"Online?"

She blushed, realizing she'd basically admitted to stalking him. "I researched you before we met," she lied, her embarrassment growing at the knowing look in his eyes.

"I saw your ex-husband today."

"Really? At the courthouse?"

He leaned back, one hand lightly gripping his drink, the other stretched out along the back of the booth cushion. "In the courtroom. I destroyed him."

"You did?" She didn't attempt to suppress her smile.

"Yes. I enjoyed it."

"I would have enjoyed watching."

"So you're not on friendly terms?"

"No, not at all." She dropped her eyes and took another sip from her drink.

"I'm sorry. It's none of my business."

"It's fine." She sighed. "It's fine." She returned her gaze to his and felt momentarily lost in his eyes. There was something so familiar about him.

"He's not very bright," he said, and they both knew he wasn't referring to his skill in the courtroom.

"That's probably true, but I don't think I am either. I married him." She took another sip of the Cosmo and realized it was almost gone. She needed to slow down.

"Tell me about you, Lia," he said.

"Why?" She raised her eyes to his, surprised at his request.

"I'm curious about you."

"I'm sure your story is more interesting," she said. "In fact, I know it is because I read about you in the *Washingtonian* magazine a few months ago."

Joseph smiled, revealing his deep dimples. "What did you think?"

"I think your story is a lot more interesting than mine."

"But I already know my story. I'd like to hear yours."

"It's boring."

"Humor me. Please," he urged.

For the next ten minutes she gave him a synopsis of her life. "I told you it wasn't interesting," she said as she finished. "No one's going to write my biography."

Joseph watched her in silence for a long moment before finally speaking. "I'm about to say something unprofessional."

"You are?" She couldn't imagine what he was going to say.

"Yes." He continued to meet her eyes. "I've been thinking about you since you came into the law firm. I've been thinking about you a lot." His voice was low and steady. "I want to see you. Socially."

Lia was stunned speechless by his bluntness. And when she recovered she was embarrassed. She'd obviously not done a very good job of masking her feelings. And then she was mad. Mad he'd asked her out when he knew that she knew he had a girl-friend. "Are you sure your girlfriend would be okay with this?"

He brought his eyebrows together in a frown. "Kathy and I broke up."

"Oh." She dropped her eyes. "I'm sorry." She shook her head. "Don't be. I'm not."

Lia closed her eyes as a panicked feeling began to grip her chest. He was so handsome, and she was so lonely, but she knew she couldn't handle getting hurt again. Not so soon after Eric, probably not ever and certainly not by him. "I still can't date you," she rushed out. "I can't."

"Are you seeing someone?"

Lia let out a humorless laugh. "No. And to be honest, I don't think I ever will again."

"May I ask why?"

"I'm not good at it. Every relationship I've ever had with a man ended with a great deal of pain," she admitted, her voice barely a whisper. "Pain for me. I don't want anymore."

"Mr. Craig?" the waitress's voice interrupted.

"Give us a minute," he said, holding up his hand, his eyes remaining locked with Lia's. "I'm not interested in causing you pain," he said as soon as the waitress was out of earshot. "Quite the opposite actually."

Lia dropped her eyes and shook her head. "I can't," she whispered. "I just can't."

"Let me buy you dinner." He reached across the table and covered her hand. "Please."

Her whole body began to tingle in response to his touch, and she felt tears coming to her eyes. The thought of getting up and leaving him and going home to her lonely apartment was intolerable, and yet she knew if she had sense it was exactly what she would do.

"Just dinner?" she asked softly, lifting her tear-filled eyes to his.

"Hey." He ran his index finger beneath her eye, catching a tear. "Don't cry. I'm not the bad guy. I just want to buy you dinner."

It was three hours later and she was beside Joseph, walking across the darkened parking lot towards her car. "Thank you for dinner. It was nice."

"It was." They continued in silence, the only sound coming from the gravel kicking up under their feet as they crossed the parking lot, both lost in their own thoughts.

Lia took her keys from her purse as they approached her car. "This is it."

He opened the door, but she made no move to get in, instead turning to face him. "Thank you again for everything. The job, the Zurtech stuff, dinner." She felt like she could cry again. He was being so nice to her, and she felt overwhelmed with gratitude and something she wasn't prepared to label yet.

"You're welcome." He lowered his head in acknowledgement. "Now get in your car. It's too cold for you to stand out here talking to me."

He was right. The wind had kicked up, and it felt like icicles were forming on her bones. She sank down into the bucket seat and put the key in the ignition, bringing the engine to life.

"I want you to do me a favor," he said. He stepped back from the door and set down his briefcase before reaching inside his coat and suit jacket to extract a brown leather wallet from an inner pocket. "I want you to think about the women you know." He was removing a business card from his wallet as he spoke. "Are you doing that?" He placed the wallet back in his pocket.

"Yes." Her hands were resting on the steering wheel as she looked up at him.

"Do you have a pen?"

"Sure." She took a pen from her center console and held it out.

He took the pen and turned over his business card, cupping it in his palm as he quickly scribbled down his cell and home phone numbers, before handing her back the pen. "Now," he began, squatting down in the opening of the door until they were at eye level, "think how different those women are." His eyes were intense as they met hers. "Men are the same way." He held out his card and she took it, their fingers brushing. "All I ask is you judge me based on my behavior and not any other man's. My numbers are on that card." His gaze dropped to the card in her hand before returning to her eyes. "If you ever want me, personally or professionally, call me." He stared into her eyes for several more seconds before slowly standing. "I'll keep you abreast of what's happening with Zurtech, but don't be surprised if it takes a while."

She nodded. "I understand." Her head was spinning as she tried to absorb the message he'd sent. He was leaving it up to her. If she wanted to see him socially she could call him, but he wasn't going to call.

"Good luck Monday." He stepped back from the car. "I hope you call," he added before closing the door.

Lia rolled down her window when he made no move to leave. "Where's your car?"

"I had it valet parked," he admitted with a smile. "I'm lazy."

"I doubt that." He didn't look lazy. She bet he belonged to a gym where everyone knew his face. "Aren't you going to go get your car?" she asked when he still made no move to leave.

"I will." He pushed his hands down into the pockets of his coat. "I'm going to watch you drive away first."

She smiled. He was nice. He was so nice. "Okay. Bye." She closed the window and put her car in reverse.

He stood in the center of the now empty parking lot, watching her drive off and continuing to watch until the car was completely out of sight.

"I almost forgot," Tony began, dropping back into the club chair in front of Joseph's desk. "Are you using Sam Malone for anything?"

"Yes. Why?"

"His invoice for February, which also included a hefty balance from January, was billed to one of my accounts. I have the invoice on my desk."

"I'll take care of it," Joseph said, absently rolling a pencil back and forth on his desk.

"Just tell me the account. I'll transfer it over."

"I was using him on more than one case." His eyes focused on the pencil as his index finger rolled it forward. "I'll take care of it."

"Alright." Tony put his hands on the arms of his chair and pushed himself up.

Joseph leaned back in his chair as he watched his friend leave the room. Sam Malone had provided an update the week prior. In the past two months, the Zurtech house had hosted one to two receptions a week. Malone had taken dozens of pictures of women he identified from the B2B division and male senior executives, both local and out-of-town visitors, arriving and leaving the house at all hours.

As the weeks passed, it became obvious which women participated in the after-party activities. Malone figured seven of the twenty B2B women he documented were working as prostitutes. These women consistently spent the night in the house, while the others were always gone by midnight. There were more clients than B2B women involved—at least that's what Malone thought—but it was hard to determine an exact number without actually being inside the house.

The same local caterer was used for all events, and it appeared Mike Hall was personally financing the receptions. Zurtech was paying for neither the use of the facility nor the food and alcohol consumed. Why the owner of a food-truck business with no financial connection to Zurtech was funding an operation clearly catering to their elite clients was still a mystery.

"Mr. Craig?" Martha's voice over the intercom broke into his reverie. "Sam Malone is on line two."

"I may have something," Sam Malone said as soon as Joseph picked up the phone. "There was someone at the house at about noon yesterday. He was alone and had a key to the house."

"What was he doing there?" Joseph sat up in his chair.

"I'm not sure yet. He went in for about ten minutes, tops, and then he came out. He was driving one of those big Lexuses, with fancy hubcaps and all shined up, blaring this loud music. Definitely didn't fit into that neighborhood. I ran his plates, and his name is Marcos Rodriguez. He's American, born in New York City. He has a record as long as my arm for petty theft, breaking and entering—that type of thing. But he's been clean six years."

"Alright." Joseph scraped his hand over his mouth and chin.

"He's on the payroll of Tia Tacos. Do you want me to put a tail on him?"

"Yes."

"In addition to the house?"

"Whatever it takes to get some evidence. I'm already twenty-five grand in," Joseph said. "Also, I need you to start sending your invoices for this job to my home address."

— —

Lia was halfway through Taylor's bedtime story later the same evening when her cell phone began to ring. "Mommy, your phone's ringing."

"I know." Lia glanced down at her phone, her heart jumping when she saw the Washington, DC, exchange. She wasn't positive, but she thought it was Joseph Craig's number.

"Aren't you going to answer it?" Taylor asked.

"No," she said, silencing the ring. "I'm going to finish reading you this story. If it's important, they'll leave a message."

As soon as she closed Taylor's door, Lia brought her phone to her ear to listen to the voicemail. "Good evening, Lia. This is Joseph Craig. I have a question regarding Zurtech. I'll be up until at least one a.m."

She closed her eyes as she replayed the message, her pulse accelerating at the sound of his deep voice. She hadn't seen or spoken to him since their dinner at Pearson's, but he was never far from her thoughts. She'd almost called him during the initial week after their dinner, her resolve weak after spending an evening with him, but as the days passed, her determination to take a break from men grew stronger. She had been too hurt by both Ned and Eric and, as much as she was attracted to Joseph Craig, she knew she wasn't in the right mental state for another relationship. Of course, this knowledge didn't keep her from fantasizing about him as she lay in bed each night, visions of his dark, wavy hair and brown eyes swirling through her mind.

She poured herself a glass of wine in an effort to calm the nervous flutter in her stomach. He had a question about Zurtech, but all she could think about was the fact she was going to talk to him again. She went about her normal evening routine, cleaning the kitchen and straightening up the house, her thoughts never far from Joseph Craig and the impending call. It was after 11:00 p.m. when she stretched out on her bed with her cell phone in her hand, her nerves muted but not altogether gone after a glass and a half of wine.

The phone rang several times before his voice came over the line, his breathing heavy from exertion. "Craig."

She closed her eyes, an image of him having sex flashing through her mind. She wanted to hang up, but it was too late. He'd know it was her. "I'm sorry. I thought you wanted me to call you back tonight."

"I did. Hold on for a second." There was a long pause. "I was on the treadmill," he said, his voice less labored.

"Oh." She felt her entire body relax. "I didn't mean to interrupt."

"I was just finishing. How are you?"

"Good." She closed her eyes, letting the sound of his voice wash over her. "How are you?"

"How am I?" He chuckled. "I'm fine."

"I can't believe you're working out this late. Doesn't that make it hard to fall asleep?"

"I'm still a couple of hours from sleep, but it doesn't affect me. How is Taylor?"

"Good. She started reading. It's amazing—one day she's learning her alphabet and then suddenly she can read sentences. And she loves it. She wants to read all the time. The other day I caught her trying to read one of my books. I don't think she could comprehend what she was reading, but she's so proud of the fact she could read it."

"She should be. It's a huge accomplishment. How about her mother? Is she enjoying her new job?"

"I love it," she admitted, and spent the next five minutes telling him about her position. "I'm sorry. I know you called for a reason, and I'm just going on and on, not letting you get a word in."

"No, it's nice to hear your enthusiasm. You sound like you're in a better place than when we spoke last."

"I am," she said, knowing she was acknowledging it to herself for the first time. "I'm in a much better place."

"That's good to hear." He paused for a moment. "The reason I called tonight was to find out if you knew or heard of a Marcos Rodriguez while you were at Zurtech."

"I've heard of a Marcos, but I never learned his last name. He was Carmen's boyfriend."

"Carmen?"

"My first mentor, the one I said never worked and talked on the phone. Marcos was the person she talked to."

"The same woman you caught in bed with—"

"Eric," she finished. "Right, that was Carmen."

"Did you ever see him at the house in Reston?"

"No. We weren't allowed to bring dates to those functions."

"Did you ever meet him?"

"No. Why? Why are you asking these questions about Marcos?"

"I'm just following up on some information," he answered, distractedly. "I have nothing definitive, but I'll let you know when I do."

"Oh, okay." She felt a wave of disappointment, realizing he was about to end the call. She wanted to keep talking to him.

"You've been very helpful. I'll be in touch."

She set her cell phone on her bedside stand before lying back on her bed, reminding herself she wasn't interested in having a relationship, but unable to shake the sadness at the quick ending to their call.

10

"That's Nick's brother at the bar," Margo Katz, one of Lia's coworkers at Prossi Designs, announced as she, Lia and Kim Moore, another coworker, sat at a tall circular table at the Blue Iguana enjoying happy hour on the first Friday in April.

"He's hot," Kim said, following her gaze. "He's an attorney at some fancy law firm downtown."

"Nick's brother?" Lia looked towards the bar. "Which—" Her words died in her throat when she saw Joseph Craig. His back was to her, but she recognized his large frame and dark, wavy hair. There was no mistaking him. She'd thought about him too many times in the months since their meeting not to have his image ingrained in her mind.

"Hello? Lia?" Kim touched her hand.

"Oh, sorry." Lia brought her attention back to her table. "I didn't realize you were talking to me."

"He's hot, right?"

"Definitely." She took a long swallow of her Long Island Iced Tea, trying to calm her nerves as her heart beat wildly in her chest.

"Are you okay?"

"Yes, I recognized someone and I just—I wasn't expecting to see him," she admitted.

"Who?"

Heat came to her face. "It doesn't matter."

"Are you blushing? You are!" Margo teased. "Now you have to tell us. It's an old boyfriend, isn't it?"

"No." She shook her head, embarrassed they saw her blush. "It's really not a big deal. He's an attorney. I needed some legal advice a while ago and met with him a couple of times."

"Is he single? Which one is he?"

"The tall one with dark hair. I think he's—"

"Oh my God! That's Joseph Craig!" Margo gasped. "He was on the cover of *Washingtonian* last fall. You know him?"

Lia's blush deepened. "Barely."

"Barely means yes. How come you never told us?"

"There was nothing to tell."

"He's one of the ten most eligible bachelors in the city. He's gorgeous and rich. You have an in."

"She likes him," Kim said.

"I don't even know him." Her gaze swung between the two women.

"You do," Margo said. "You should see your face."

"I don't date. You two know that," Lia said with no real resolve behind her words. After two drinks, she was having a hard time remembering why she continued to fight her feelings for him.

"You can undo that ridiculous rule in about a minute. Let's go say hi to him."

"What?" Lia gripped Kim's forearm when she began to stand. "No, I'm not going to go over there. He's probably working. It's not like he's alone."

"He's in a bar having a beer with his friends—just like us."

"No."

"So you're just going to let him leave without saying a word to him?"

"How are you ladies doing for drinks?" A waiter stopped beside their table.

"We're..." Margo began, but then hesitated, a smile lighting her features. "She'd like to send a drink to the tall gentleman at the bar. The one in the charcoal suit and blue tie."

"Margo, no!"

"A drink isn't interrupting. It's just saying hello."

"Jesus, didn't you see her last night?" Joseph asked. After spending the day at the Fairfax County Courthouse, he and Tony had stopped to have a drink, but after a text from his girlfriend, Tony was ready to go.

"She has theater tickets. And she wants to eat beforehand."

"You really have your priorities messed up. May I at least finish my beer?"

"Mr. Craig?" The bartender set a glass on the bar in front of Joseph. "This is courtesy of the woman in the dark dress at the table beside the fireplace." He filled the glass with scotch.

"She knows your drink," Tony said.

"Apparently. Or it was a lucky guess." He took a sip of the scotch. "Do you recognize her?"

"No," Tony answered after his gaze shifted to the table. "And I'd remember her. She has incredible eyes. A pale blue color I can see from here."

Joseph spun around before Tony finished speaking, the corners of his lips turning up when his eyes met Lia's. "I'll be damned." He lifted his glass in a silent salute. "It's about time, beautiful."

"Who is she?"

"Someone I'm going to try very hard to wake up beside tomorrow morning. I've been after her since January."

"Is she married?"

"What in the hell kind of question is that?" he asked, frowning. "When have you ever known me to go after married women?"

Tony raised his eyebrows. "You want me to name all of—"

"Jesus, you sound like Kevin. No, she's divorced."

"Then what was the problem? She certainly appears interested."

"You think?" He glanced back at her in time to see her look away. "She's been through some messy relationships. She says she's done with men."

Tony chuckled. "Then why is she sending you a drink?"

Joseph inclined his head. "Good point." He smiled as he took another swallow of the golden liquid.

"Why don't you go say hello so we can leave?"

"Leave? I'm not going anywhere. I'll find my way home."

"I think they're leaving," Margo announced as she watched Tony Prossi set some money on the bar.

Lia refused to look, not wanting to appear too eager, but she knew he wasn't going to leave without stopping by her table. Their eyes had met several times, and the chemistry she'd experienced in his law office and then again at Pearson's was there in full force.

"Wait, he's staying," Kim continued. "Tony Prossi left, but he stayed. Oh my God, he is so good-looking. Are you sure you're off men, Lia?"

"Why?" This was the first time Lia had gone out socially with the two women, but she knew they were single, and on many Monday mornings heard Kim bragging about her sexual escapades over the weekend.

Kim smiled at Margo. "That didn't sound like a 'why' from someone who is no longer interested in men."

"She's right, Lia. You have 'interested' written all over you."

"No, I don't."

"So you don't mind if I move in on him?"

"Not at all. Go for it." Her eyes found Joseph's. He was leaning back against the bar, openly watching her as he sipped at the drink she'd sent him. "No, don't go for it," she said, turning back to Kim. "I do mind...I mean." She shook her head. "I don't know what I mean." But she knew she couldn't stomach watching a relationship develop between him and another woman.

"Relax. I was only teasing. As much as it pains me to admit it, the man seems to only have eyes for you. He's looked over here at least half a dozen times, and he hasn't so much as glanced my way."

"Ladies," their waiter began as he stopped beside their table, "courtesy of Mr. Craig." He placed a shot glass filled with layers of brown, cream and orange liquid in front of each of them. "It's a B-52."

"Someone wants to get you drunk," Margo said as she lifted her shot glass. "Come on, let's not disappoint him."

Lia loosened the scarf around her neck, suddenly too warm. She was going to be in trouble tonight. She could feel it. "Cheers," she said before downing the sweet liquid in two swallows.

"Here he comes," Margo whispered.

Lia watched Joseph make his way towards them, his stride unhurried and surprisingly graceful for someone his height as he navigated through the throng of people mingling about, pausing a few times to return handshakes and pat a couple of backs, but then he was beside their table, his eyes looking into hers, and Lia felt overwhelmed, like she was in the presence of a celebrity.

"Is this a girls-only table, or are boys welcome?"

"Yes."

"Yes." Amusement danced in his eyes. "Coming from your lips, I believe that may be my new favorite word."

She smiled, not as embarrassed as she should have been, thanks to the liquid courage coursing through her bloodstream. "I meant yes, you are welcome to join us."

"Oh, I think you were saying yes to more than that, but we can talk about that later." He continued to meet her eyes for a few more seconds before turning to greet Margo and Kim.

Lia's gaze traveled over him, taking in his broad shoulders, his custom-tailored suit and the gold watch on his wrist. She was thankful she'd decided to wear her black dress instead of the pants suit, knowing it made her look more feminine.

Kim was giggling in response to something he said, and she felt a pang of jealousy in her chest, fearing he might be attracted to her friend. It had been months since he'd propositioned her, after all. What if he was no longer interested? Like Kathy Paige, Kim was blonde with Barbie-like good looks.

"Mr. Craig, may I get you a drink or—"

"A chair," Joseph interrupted as the waiter stopped beside him.

"Of course." The waiter hurried off and, to Lia's surprise, returned in less than thirty seconds with a chair he must have snagged from another area of the restaurant, because there was nothing available in the crowded bar.

"Thank you." Joseph intercepted the chair as the waiter attempted to place it between Margo and Kim, effortlessly lifting it into the air before setting it beside Lia. "I can squeeze in here," he said as he turned to Margo. "Do you mind?"

"No, of course not." She moved her chair so there was enough space for him to sit beside Lia.

"Would you like something to drink, Mr. Craig?"

"Yes, another round for the table." He sat down, his thigh brushing against Lia's as he adjusted his chair. "Wait," he said to the waiter, turning to Lia. "Are you hungry?"

"Hungry?" She was having a hard time concentrating with the feel of his hard thigh pressed against hers. The moment their eyes met, a wave of attraction passed between them, and the jealousy over Kim was forgotten as she became lost in his eyes. He was so close she could see the intricate patterns in his irises. They were extraordinary, with gold flecks mixed in with the brown.

"Bring us some appetizers," he said to the waiter, continuing to stare into Lia's eyes.

"Which—"

"An assortment of whatever you think is good," he interrupted. "Thank you."

Lia was the first to break eye contact, taking a breath as she looked down at her drink. Every nerve ending in her body seemed to be tingling in response to his closeness.

"You changed your hair," he said.

"I just didn't straighten it."

"Whatever you did, I like it."

"Taylor asked me if I forgot to comb it this morning." She smiled at the memory. "I think she prefers it straight."

"Taylor's five. Take it from a thirty-four-year-old man. It suits you."

She could feel him staring at her, and her heart rate, which was already elevated, jumped a notch higher. She needed another drink. "Thanks."

"It's good to see you."

"You too." Another wave of attraction pulsed between them as their eyes met.

"Joe Craig!" A burly man with a head of thick black hair stopped beside their table, gripping Joseph's shoulder. "How the hell are you?"

And so the tone was set for the evening, as dozens of people approached their table to greet Joseph, and a simple "hello" rarely sufficed. By 9:00 p.m., Lia's original trio had expanded into a group in excess of twenty people, and at some point Joseph's arm stretched out behind her chair, the gesture clearly demonstrating a familiarity that made the two appear as a couple, and Lia found herself liking the idea of people assuming they were together.

The Joseph of tonight was full of the charisma she'd seen him exhibit on CNN back in October. He was the center of attention, with everyone vying to speak to him, and though he seemed to enjoy the camaraderie, he never neglected Lia, working to include her in the conversation and remaining attentive to her needs. He ensured her glass was never empty and urged her to try the different plates of food that seemed to continually arrive. She couldn't recall the last time a man had made her feel so special.

At some point, his hand drifted from the back of her chair to her neck, his fingers lightly caressing the exposed skin above her collar, and it felt strangely natural, as if they had been a couple for months if not years.

"Have you had enough?" Joseph asked, his hand cupping her shoulder as he leaned in to be heard over the crowd. "I want to be alone with you."

The warmth of his breath tickled her ear, causing goose bumps to run up her arms.

She turned to him, their faces just inches apart, and she knew the entire evening, from the moment she sent him the drink, had been leading to this moment, and there was no way she had the willpower to resist him. "Okay."

Lia pushed her hands into the pockets of her wool coat as soon as they stepped outside, a gust of wind making the forty-degree evening feel chillier. "Cold?" She heard his deep voice before his arm wrapped around her shoulder, pulling her into his side as they began walking towards the parking lot. After several seconds, he stopped. "I completely forgot. My partner drove today. I don't have a car."

"We could take mine, if you don't mind driving. I'm not sure I'd pass a sobriety test. It's parked in the garage under my building."

"He has everything—my keys, briefcase. It's your fault."

"My fault?" She laughed. "How is that possible?"

"You distracted me." He clasped the front of her coat, slowly drawing her towards him.

"Really?" She didn't even attempt to look serious. "I'm sorry."

"Yeah." His eyes searched hers for a long moment before he dropped his gaze to her lips. "You're going to let me kiss you tonight, aren't you?"

The question caught her off guard, and a soft blush covered her cheeks.

His lips turned up in a smile. "Oh, you're definitely going to let me kiss you," he said, almost to himself, as his eyes returned to hers.

He moved his hands to the sides of her face, taking his time as he tilted her head back and lowered his mouth towards hers. "I've waited a long time for this, Lia Merrick."

He didn't attempt to start slow as his lips covered hers, the passion building between them since December unleashed in one kiss. She slipped her hands beneath his jacket, registering the hardness of his body as she ran them up his chest. She leaned into him, moaning softly when she felt the evidence of his desire pressing into her stomach. She resisted the urge to run her hand over the length of him. She wanted him, needed him. Why had she been fighting this? He felt so right.

His hands remained around her face, cupping her jaw with his palms as he continued to kiss her, his tongue tangling with hers.

The sound of laughter from an approaching group had him stiffening and then lifting his head slightly, his breathing uneven as he rested his forehead against hers. "Where's your car?"

Lia took his hand, leading him in the direction of the parking garage, their pace brisk, both seemingly in a hurry to get to their destination. After several seconds, Joseph's arm again found its way around her shoulders, pulling her against his side as they continued walking.

The silence wasn't broken until they reached her car. "This is me." The words were barely uttered before he was on her, his mouth finding hers as he pushed her back against her car, his body pressing into hers. Lia let her purse fall to the ground as she wound her arms around his neck, her body straining to get closer as he deepened the kiss. She was completely lost, her body on fire as he ground his hips forward, leaving her with no doubt that he wanted her as much as she wanted him.

His mouth left hers as he dragged his lips across her cheek and down to her neck, his stubble rough against her skin. "Jesus," he breathed between kisses. One hand began to squeeze her breast, while he inserted one of his knees between her thighs, fitting his upper thigh into the juncture between her legs.

Lia clung to his neck, her mouth searching and then finding his, no longer thinking as her body's need became all-consuming.

"Not here," he said deeply. "This isn't happening here." She was so lost in her desire, it wasn't until she heard his words that she became conscious of the fact she was trying to unbuckle his belt. "Where are your keys?"

"My purse," she managed, not sure if she was more upset that he'd pulled away from her or that she would have let him have sex with her against her car in a parking garage.

"I live off Route Seven, near the mall," she told him when they were both in the car. Her head was back against the seat, her eyes closed as she struggled for some semblance of control. This wasn't her. She wasn't the type of woman who lost her mind during sex. Sex with Ned had been nice, but it was something for the privacy of a bedroom. What she was experiencing, feeling with Joseph was at a completely different level. Even now, with some distance between them, she wanted to climb across the seat and continue where they left off.

The car was out of the garage and merged into the light evening traffic before she allowed herself to look at him, instantly discovering the short reprieve did nothing to curb her desire. The confines of her car weren't big enough. His scent, a subtle woodsy cologne or aftershave mixed with soap and a hint of scotch and something else that she decided was him served as an aphrodisiac to her senses. She crossed her legs, sinking farther back in her seat as her gaze feasted on his profile, tracing the sharp line of his jaw down to his chin. She raised her gaze to his lips, breathing in as she recalled the feel of them against her own. She clenched her hands into fists, resisting the consuming need to touch him. It had to be the alcohol. There was no other explanation.

"Is the temperature okay?" His voice pulled her from her obsessive internal banter.

"Yes." She watched his hand drop to the knob for the stereo, and seconds later music from her favorite pop station drifted from the speakers. He took her hand and brought it to rest on his upper thigh, entwining their fingers. Her eyes drifted to their hands. His were large and masculine, befitting of a man his size, but there was also something refined about them, the nails perfectly manicured, the veins on their backs visible but subtle. When she began to imagine them touching her, she looked away.

After parking in the lot outside her apartment, Joseph switched off the ignition and turned to her, resting his arm along the back of her seat. "Are you sure?" There was warmth in his eyes, the same warmth she'd caught glimpses of that day in his law firm and again when he stood in the parking lot beside her car at Pearson's, a warmth that couldn't be faked.

She felt a stirring deep inside her chest and reached out, trailing her fingers down the side of his cheek. Where had this boldness come from? She didn't know this version of herself. "Yes."

"Okay." He leaned in and kissed her, his lips brushing softly over hers.

It wasn't until she was preceding him into her apartment that she considered whether she had picked up that morning. It wasn't that she was messy, but she usually straightened up in the evening, too rushed before work to pick up after herself or Taylor.

"Do you want something to drink?"

"No." He was behind her, taking her purse strap from her shoulder and then helping her out of her coat. "Take me to your bedroom," he whispered as he gripped her hips and pulled her back into his body.

Her bedroom was a bit of a disaster, a pile of clean clothes on the center of her unmade bed, a few drawers left haphazardly open from her morning haste, a pair of yoga pants on the floor. "Sorry about the mess." She hurried to the bed and scooped the clothes into her arms, placing them on a wicker chair in the corner before crossing to the bureau and quickly closing the drawers. "I'm not usually this bad." She grabbed the yoga pants and tossed them to the chair. "We overslept this morning and I didn't have time—"

"Relax," he said from behind her, his hands sliding down her arms. "I don't care about any of that." He dropped his mouth to her neck, his lips warming her skin.

She closed her eyes as she leaned back into him, tilting her head to the side to give him more access to her neck. This was really happening. Joseph Craig was in her bedroom, about to make love to her. Again, she couldn't fathom why she ever resisted him.

When he began lifting her dress, her whole body tensed, as she remembered the simple white cotton panties she was wearing. They were comfortable and practical, but certainly not date worthy. Her thoughts shot to Kathy Paige. Joseph dated supermodels. She doubted he had ever seen cotton underwear. She wanted to stop him and escape to the bathroom before he saw them, but as she felt the cool air touch her stomach, she knew it was too late. He was going to see them whether she liked it or not. "Turn around. I want to look at you."

"I didn't expect to bring you home. I never would have worn these underwear if I—"

"Why do you keep apologizing to me?" he asked gently. "Do you really think I'm here to see how neat your house is or what your underwear look like?"

"No."

"Turn around, Lia." His voice felt like a caress. "Please."

She slowly turned to face him, a blush heating her cheeks. As she watched his eyes travel over her body, her insecurities began to dissipate. It was obvious from the heat in his stare how much he appreciated her body.

"Beautiful," he said when his eyes finally met hers. "Take off the rest."

She lifted her hands to the straps of her bra, the desire to please him overpowering any reservations. Maybe she should have been put off by the fact he was still clothed, but she wasn't, and as she stood before him, completely naked and seeing the desire in his eyes, she'd never felt sexier.

He took a step towards her, their bodies so close she could feel the heat of his. "You're perfect." He cupped one of her breasts, squeezing it in his hand as he dropped his head, running his tongue over her nipple before closing his lips around it and sucking it into his mouth.

A bolt of desire shot straight to her groin and she gripped his head, a small moan escaping her lips as he sucked one nipple and then the other, his tongue swirling the tip. Lia pulled his head down, her hands moving deeper into his hair as she pushed her breasts up, lost in the feelings.

He propelled her backwards until her legs bumped her mattress, and then he was following her onto the bed, one hand continuing to squeeze her breasts as his mouth rained warm kisses down her stomach. Lia's hips began to rotate, her body seeking more as he ran his chin over her stomach, his razor stubble rough against her soft skin. "Lie back," he ordered when she moved to sit up, his hand pushing gently against her chest. "Just lie there."

The mattress shifted as he came to his feet and she opened her eyes, watching as he began to shed his clothes. Her level of desire seemed to grow with each piece of clothing he stripped, and as he took off his undershirt, her fingers gripped the sheet beneath her, her need for him all consuming. His chest and arms had just the right amount of muscle. He followed some type of exercise routine that included weights and cardio. She wasn't attracted to the bodybuilder type, and he certainly wasn't that, but he clearly spent hours each week in a gym.

When his hands hesitated at his belt, she raised her eyes to find him watching her. He was watching her admire his body, just as she had watched him admire hers. "This isn't a deal-breaker moment, is it?"

"What?" Her heart dropped. Was there something wrong with him?

"If you don't like my"—he hesitated—"briefs."

She sagged with relief. "Only if they're the girl variety."

He laughed aloud and then she was joining him, the sexual tension temporarily broken as their laughter filled the room. He collapsed on the bed beside her, falling onto his back and throwing his arm over his eyes as he continued to laugh, his shoulders shaking. "What would you have done?"

She propped herself on her elbow, smiling down at him. "I don't know." A vision of him in women's underwear had her giggling again. "You scared me."

"Oh, I know. You should have seen your face. What did you think I was going to say?"

"I didn't know—something bad, I guess. Like there was something wrong with it."

He lifted his arm from his eyes. "God, that was funny." He pushed her hair back from her eyes. "Come here." He curved his hand around the back of her neck, pulling her towards him. "I like that smile," he whispered before meeting her lips. Within moments, he reversed their positions, his body over hers.

She trailed her fingers down his back as the kiss deepened, exploring the contours of his body, his skin warm and smooth beneath her fingers. They kissed for minutes before he left her and repositioned himself at the end of the bed, running his hand down the length of one thigh and then the other, his eyes watching the movement.

"Your skin is so soft." He continued to slide his hand over her thigh, slowly getting closer to the juncture between her legs. "Relax," he whispered when she instinctively kept her thighs together, his hand moving between them. "Bend your knees.

Good, now open them." His mouth dropped to the skin of her inner thigh, his lips running along the same path his hands took moments earlier. "So soft," he whispered between kisses. "So soft." His hands slid beneath her, gripping her butt as he tilted her body up, his tongue running over her soft folds.

Lia cried out, her body arching in response. He flicked his tongue over her clit at the same moment he slipped a finger up into her wet channel. She writhed beneath him, her body on fire. "Oh God," she whispered. "I think I'm going to come." She shamelessly gripped his hair, her body stiffening as she was consumed by an orgasm. He continued to flick his tongue against her clit as he rubbed his finger against her G-spot, stretching the length of her orgasm. "Wow," she breathed when she finally got her breath. "Wow."

He kissed her inner thigh a final time before coming to his feet, and this time when his hands reached for his belt, there was no hesitation. She watched him step out of his pants and then retrieve a condom from the wallet of his discarded jacket. He was wearing black cotton briefs, but there was no masking the size of his penis. It was large like the rest of him, which was proved beyond a doubt when he pushed his briefs down over his hips. He was much larger than Ned or Eric—the extent of her experience—but not in a scary way, more in an awe-inspiring way. He was beautiful.

Without forethought, she was opening her thighs and lying back on the bed, her eyes rising to his, the invitation clear. He sheathed himself in the condom without breaking eye contact, and then he was moving onto the bed, positioning himself between her legs and placing a hand on either side of her to brace himself over her.

She reached up, running her hands over his shoulders. "Please." She didn't want to wait another second.

"Is this what you want?" He lowered his hips, his penis sliding against her wet opening, his eyes continuing to meet hers.

"Yes." She hooked her legs around him, lifting her hips off the bed.

He kissed her softly as he pushed the tip of his penis into her. She rocked her hips up, needing more than he was giving, and then, without warning, he thrust his hips forward, burying himself in her completely. He stayed that way, giving her body time to adjust to him. "You okay?"

"Amazing," she answered, knowing it was the only word that could adequately convey how she felt. His body had stretched her to her limits, but the fullness she was experiencing, knowing it was his body inside of hers, felt right. It was like he belonged.

He lifted his head, his eyes looking into hers as he pulled completely out and plunged into her again. He may have been a stranger, but an undeniable connection flowed between them. "Kiss me," she whispered.

He lowered his mouth over hers, their tongues moving together as his body picked up its pace, his hips rocking forward and back as his body possessed hers. Lia stroked her hands down his muscled arms and then over his back, loving the feel of him beneath her fingers. If only for tonight, this perfect man was hers. She let her hands drift lower, holding his butt as he moved in and out of her, his muscles contracting.

He lifted his head so he could witness their pairing, watching his body push in and out of hers. There were beads of sweat on his forehead, and the muscles in his neck and shoulders were straining from holding his weight off her.

"I love this," she whispered.

He lifted his gaze. "Good, because I'm not close to being done."

"I need to hear you," he said deeply as he lay on his back, holding her hips while she straddled him. "I need to hear you come." He pushed his hips up and she knew he couldn't get any deeper inside her body.

It was their second session of the night, and she'd already come several times. She'd reach a state of arousal so intense his slightest movement could send her into another wave of orgasms, each more intense than the previous, and he was doing it now. As he stared into her eyes, he began to push himself up into her while he pulled forward on her hips, and within seconds she was crying out as she fell forward onto his chest, the orgasm continuing until she thought she would explode.

"I don't think I can take any more," she whispered as she collapsed beside him on the bed.

"Me neither." He rolled her onto her back and settled between her thighs. "You only have to come one more time," he said before thrusting into her again. "Wrap your legs around me."

Lia obeyed, and an orgasm began immediately. As his tempo increased, the intensity of the orgasm increased, and she cried out, her body enveloped in sheer pleasure. Joseph's movements became quicker and more erratic, and when he was right on the brink, Lia reached out and gripped his butt. He yelled out as he found release, his body collapsing over hers. Several seconds passed before he rolled his weight off of her and laid flat on his back, his breathing still labored. "Jesus."

Lia curled into his side and slipped her leg between his as she rested her cheek on his chest. She could feel the strong beat of his heart vibrating from his chest. "I don't think I'll be able to move tomorrow."

Several minutes passed before he spoke. "I knew it would be like this between us."

"You should have told me," she mumbled, barely awake.

His arms tightened around her. "I may never let you go."

"Promise?" she whispered before nodding off.

11

Lia turned her face into her pillow and groaned. Her body felt like—flashes from the previous evening stormed her mind. She had picked Joseph Craig up at a bar, brought him home and had sex with him four times. Memories of the multiple orgasms she'd experienced had her cheeks heating. He knew her body better than she did, and certainly better than Ned ever had. Muscles she previously wasn't aware she had were sore.

The aroma of coffee floated in from the kitchen and her heart did a funny flutter at the realization he was still in the house. She peeked at her alarm clock, which read 11:05 a.m. What time had they fallen asleep? No, "sleep" was too generous a term for the short stretches they took between bouts of sex. He took the phrase "virile male" to a new level.

She pushed herself up on her elbow and took in her room in the harsh morning light. The carpet, once tan, was more of beige color with places worn completely bare. There were two windows overlooking the parking lot and the miniblinds covering them were bent up and in need of replacement. Her bedroom furniture looked relatively new, but that did little to help the overall ambience of the room. What could he be thinking? She was twenty-eight years old and her apartment was in worse shape than her old college dorm. Waves of embarrassment washed through her at the thought of him in her kitchen with the old appliances and worn linoleum floors.

Her gaze focused on his jacket and trousers lying over the arm of the chair in the corner. His suit probably cost more than six months of her rent. Men like Joseph Craig belonged to sophisticated women like Kathy Paige, not single mothers who survived paycheck to paycheck. He was out of her league, and he was probably coming to the same conclusion as he saw how she lived.

She crossed to her bathroom—more a closet with a shower, toilet and tiny sink—and again found herself looking at it more critically, imagining what he saw. It was clean, but that did little to improve the overall appearance. The handle for the faucet was chipped, there was a rust stain in the bottom of the sink and the towel rack had come out from the wall, leaving patches of chipped paint and plaster in its wake. She sat on the closed toilet and dropped her face into her hands. How could she have let this happen when she knew she'd have to see him again? He was her lawyer, for God's sake. This was going to be ten times worse than Eric Nettles' rejection, because she still wanted Joseph. She'd have to make it clear that all future dealings would be over the phone. And what was he even still doing in her house? She wasn't experienced at one-night stands, but was pretty sure the guy didn't usually bother to spend the night.

When she forced herself back out into the bedroom, Joseph had returned from the kitchen and was sitting on the side of her bed, looking down at his cell phone. He raised his gaze. "Good morning."

"Hi." She pulled her robe closer around her.

"I hope you don't mind that I helped myself to coffee." In only his boxer briefs, his hair tousled and his eyes puffy from sleep, he looked younger and more vulnerable than the suit-clad lawyer usually on display.

"No, not at all." Her heart began to pump a little faster in reaction to him.

"I made you some too." He inclined his head towards a steaming mug of coffee on her dresser.

"Thank you." She turned, grateful for an excuse to look away from him. She needed him to leave so she could lick her wounds.

"There was powdered creamer and sugar on the counter, so I assumed you took both."

"I do." She took a sip of the warm liquid, keeping her back to him "Thank you. It's perfect."

"Is everything okay?"

"Yes, I just have a lot to do today and I didn't intend to sleep in so long."

"Come here."

She forced a smile to her face before turning back around. "This isn't a big deal. I'm surprised you're still here."

"Closer." He snagged her free hand and began tugging her towards him.

"What are you doing?"

He took the mug from her other hand before stretching his arm out and setting it on the nightstand. "Saying good morning." He pulled her between his knees and settled his hands on her hips. "Good morning." He dropped his head forward and began to kiss her stomach through the material of her robe, his hold on her hips tightening.

She closed her eyes and gave in to the urge to touch him, letting her hands slide over his shoulders. "I'm not cut out for this."

He pulled back only enough to be able to lift his eyes to hers. "I have news for you, sweetheart. I have no intention of allowing you to crawl back in the shell you've been occupying."

"I don't want to get hurt."

"I'm not planning to hurt you."

"You may not plan it, but that's how it ends for me. That's how it always ends." She felt tears gathering in her eyes.

"It's never ended with me, Lia. I feel something very real for you—something I want to explore."

She looked into his eyes and was struck again by their warmth. They weren't the eyes of a liar. "We barely know each other."

"That's not true," he said deeply. "I've known you since the moment I met you."

Lia's heart rate accelerated at his words. He felt it too "Why?"

"I don't know."

She looked away from him, not wanting him to see how much she already cared. She was afraid. She was so afraid. "How do you know it's not just an attraction? That you'll want me for a couple of weeks and then it will be over?"

"I know what it feels like to be attracted to a woman. You're not the only one vulnerable here. I have been consumed with thoughts of you for months. You're why I ended it with Kathy."

"What?" Stunned by his words, she felt her eyes widen.

"And then you rejected me," he continued. "I know you want me—your eyes have been talking to me since the first time we met. And I knew your wall would eventually come down. I wasn't in a rush."

"I need to think," she whispered.

"No. You need to feel." He curved his hand around the back of her neck, pulling her towards him.

— ⁓

"I have to go. I have a meeting at two." Joseph's deep voice broke into Lia's semiconscious state as she lay snuggled against his side, her head resting on his chest.

"It's Saturday."

"I met you on a Sunday."

"True." She sighed. She hated the thought of him leaving, knowing as soon as he was out the door her mind would start doubting everything she felt.

"We don't have to have another talk, do we?" he asked as if reading her thoughts.

"No, but I need to take this slow. I don't want to jump into a full-blown relationship."

"We've had sex five times in less than twelve hours. You don't expect me to go back to holding hands, do you?"

"No, I'm not talking about that. I don't want this to take over my life. For the first time as an adult, I'm realizing I'm okay alone. I don't want to lose that. I already feel like I don't spend enough time with Taylor."

"Did you skip out on the normal girl training?" he teased. "Don't you now that you're supposed to be demanding more than I can give?"

"I'm serious."

"I work an insane amount of hours—the recurring complaint I've received from every woman I've ever had a relationship with is I don't have enough time. We can take this as slow as you like."

"Are you going to see other women too?"

"And there's the girl."

"Are you?" The thought of him touching other women made her stomach clench.

"I wasn't planning to. Are you going to let me see you more than a couple times a month?"

"Yes."

"And you'll be my plus one if the need arises?"

"Yes." This was really happening. "I know we haven't even had a real date, but I don't want to have sex with you if you're having it with other women too." She may have sounded like a prude, but she didn't care.

"You are the only woman I want." He kissed her softly. "I won't be with anyone but you."

— —

Hours later, knowing she'd go crazy if she spent another minute alone in her apartment, Lia drove to her mother's and joined her in the kitchen, where Elaine was preparing dinner.

"Did I ever show you a picture of Joseph Craig?"

"Joseph Craig?" Elaine frowned. "Why does that sound familiar?"

"He's my attorney for the Zurtech stuff."

"Ah." Elaine nodded. "Why do you have a picture of him?"

"I don't have a picture, picture. It's a picture online from a magazine he was on the cover of last year." She pulled up the image on her phone.

"'Washington's most eligible bachelors,'" Elaine read. "I can see why. He is my type of handsome. This is the one Taylor was going on and on about on Christmas? The one that helped you get the job?"

Lia nodded, watching her mother study the picture of Joseph. "He's even better looking in person."

"Really?" Elaine handed her back the phone "Have you heard from him lately?"

"I ran into him last night."

"And?"

"And he's—he's very charming." She dropped her eyes to his picture.

"Well that's nice, but I was actually asking about your case."

"Oh, we didn't discuss it." She continued to study the picture of Joseph in a custom-tailored suit, standing in the lobby of his law office, his arms crossed over his chest, a look of amusement on his handsome face. A vivid image of what he looked like under the suit flashed through her mind and a sigh escaped her lips.

"Are we developing a bit of a crush on him?"

Lia covered her eyes. "I'm so confused."

"Lia?" Elaine walked around the counter, stopping beside her chair. "Is something going on between you and your attorney?"

"Yes."

"Something romantic?" Her eyes narrowed. "Isn't there an ethical rule against that?"

"I don't know. There's this attraction that won't go away." She finally met her mother's eyes. "I'm so scared." She bit her lower lip and to her horror tears welled up in her eyes. "I don't want to be hurt again and I don't know what to do," she whispered.

"Is he putting pressure on you?"

"No. God, no." She shook her head. "He isn't putting any pressure on me. He's leaving everything up to me." She ran the back of her hand over her cheek, wiping at the tears. "I'm sorry. I'm such a baby."

"Have you been dating him or—"

"No. But I want to, Mom. I really do. I've never felt this way before, but I don't know if I trust my own judgment. I mean, I thought Eric was a great guy and look what he turned out to be." Tears continued to fall from her eyes.

"Honey, are you sure you're telling me everything?"

"I ran into him at happy hour last night. I was with some girls from work and he joined our table." She took a deep breath, trying to calm herself. "You should have seen him. People are attracted to him. They want to hear what he has to say, and he's so smart, Mom. I mean, I've never met someone so smart."

"I don't understand why you're so upset."

"Because I like him, and I don't want to! Can't you understand that after everything I've been through?"

"You don't have to yell, honey. I'm trying to understand."

"I'm sorry. I'm just so confused. I thought after Eric I wouldn't even want to date another man. And now I can't stop thinking about one. I don't know what to do."

"I don't know what to say about Joseph Craig, Lia, because I don't know him. When you told me after Eric you would never date again, I didn't say anything because you were devastated and I didn't want to upset you further. But I knew, or at least hoped, you were being rash. You're too young to never remarry. It's not natural. We're made to be part of a couple."

"I don't want to be hurt again."

"There are no guarantees in relationships. There's always the chance you'll be hurt. You could fall in love with the nicest man in the world, but if he doesn't love you back you're going to be hurt."

"But with Eric and Ned I was deceived. They betrayed me."

"So you're going to let them continue to hurt you by keeping you from a more healthy relationship?"

"But that's just it. I don't know if I have the ability to recognize a healthy relationship."

"I don't think you're giving yourself enough credit. You're a smart girl. I think the signs were there in both relationships and you chose to overlook them."

Her mother was right. She'd chosen to ignore the fact that Ned seemed to lose interest in sex overnight, and with Eric, well, Eric never seemed interested in anything but getting her into bed. "Why would I do that?"

"With Ned, you were young and had these idealistic beliefs about what a marriage should be. And then with Eric..." She shook her head. "Your self-esteem was so low after the breakup with Ned. I don't think you were thinking clearly. But I think you've grown up a lot in the past four months, honey. You have a good job, and I think you're starting to realize you can take care of yourself."

"I am. And I don't want anyone to mess me up."

"No one can mess you up unless you let them. You need to keep your eyes open and trust yourself. Take it one day at a time and judge this man for who he is—not who you want him to be."

⌒ ⌒

Taylor arrived home Sunday evening and promptly announced she was going to be a big sister. "Because Daddy and Candice are having a baby," Taylor said before looking back at her father. "Right, Daddy?"

"That's right," Ned said.

"Daddy isn't actually going to have it," Taylor said. "Candice is, but its Daddy's baby too because they're married to each other."

"That's nice." Lia smiled at Taylor. "Say goodbye to your daddy."

Lia hated the thought of Ned and Candice having a baby, but even that news couldn't damper the warmth that enveloped her whenever she thought of Joseph.

~ ~

When Lia hadn't heard from Joseph by Thursday, she literally felt sick. He'd made love to her five times, basically agreed to a monogamous relationship and then hadn't so much as sent her a text since Saturday. The insecure part of her worried he was a liar, but another part, a deeper part, couldn't believe that was true, so after putting Taylor to bed and having a glass of wine, she picked up her cell phone and called him.

After five rings it went to his voicemail, and she hung up without leaving a message. It was 9:45 p.m. She tried again an hour later and this time left a message when he again didn't answer. And then she lay down on her bed and wondered where he was at 10:45 on a Thursday night.

Joseph opened the door to his apartment a few minutes past 11:00 p.m. After pouring himself a glass of scotch, he dropped down onto the couch in his family room. He'd had a late meeting with Sam Malone, and the latest updates on the Zurtech investigation brought more questions than answers. Marcos Rodriguez was a regular visitor to the Zurtech house, but it was unclear why. He would show up the day after a reception and enter the house alone, then leave ten minutes later. Malone was convinced he was picking something up, but needed more time to figure out exactly what. As far as the connection to Carmen was concerned, Malone had learned they shared a rented home together in Centreville, Virginia, several miles outside of Reston.

Joseph took a long swallow of scotch before laying his head back on the couch cushions. Malone had checked out the other Zurtech facilities throughout the country and, as far as he could tell, Stan Hall was running a lone wolf operation. And the B2Bs' promiscuous behavior wasn't a secret among the business elite of Northern Virginia. According to Malone, the extra perks were a real incentive to many executives. But there was no proof. And why Mike Hall bankrolled the operation remained a mystery. To date, Joseph had shelled out over fifty thousand dollars to Malone and another six thousand to pay restitution for Lia's wardrobe.

He reached into the inner pocket of his suit jacket and took out his cell phone. There were ten texts, five missed calls and four voicemails. He scanned the texts, listened to and deleted three voicemails, and then he was pushing the speaker button and listening to the fourth as he leaned back on the couch and loosened his tie.

"Hi, it's Lia. I thought I'd call and say hello. I hope you've had a nice week. You can call me back, um, whenever—I'm usually up late. Okay, bye, Joseph."

"It's about time, Lia," he said aloud, before tapping the display and bringing the phone to his ear.

"I've been thinking about you," he said as soon as she picked up.

"You have?"

"Obsessively." He unfastened the top two buttons of his oxford shirt.

"Why didn't you call me?"

"Is that a serious question?"

"Yes."

"I didn't think I was supposed to. I thought you were dictating the speed of our relationship."

"I didn't mean you couldn't call me."

"Well, I wish you had told me. I would have called you a dozen times. I've missed the hell out of you."

"You have?"

"I have." He laid his head back and closed his eyes. "Are you going to let me see you this weekend?"

"Yes."

— ⁓

"Is this okay?" Lia asked two days later as she glanced down at her white sleeveless top and black cropped pants. She was standing in the middle of her mother's kitchen, awaiting Joseph's imminent arrival. He was taking her to a 7:00 p.m. Nationals' baseball game in Washington.

Her mother looked up from a magazine. "You look very nice."

"Not too dressy?"

"No, you look perfect."

She felt nervous, very nervous. Once she'd decided to let Joseph in, she felt like she actually lost a bit of control. It suddenly mattered very much what he thought of her.

"I think your date has arrived."

"What? Where?" She turned towards the front of the house. "I didn't hear the door."

"Look outside," Elaine said. "I'm assuming he's the one out there with Taylor."

Lia followed her mother's gaze to the bay window behind the kitchen table, where she was watching an animated Taylor interacting with Joseph, who was standing beside the swing set in the backyard. "That's him." She felt a flutter in her stomach.

"She really likes him."

"I know." Lia continued to watch. "He's handsome, isn't he?"

"Very." Elaine nodded.

Lia gave them about ten minutes before opening the door and stepping out onto the deck and telling Taylor it was time to come in.

"Mommy, did you know Joseph didn't have a swing in his backyard when he was a little boy?" Taylor scraped her shoes across the dirt in an attempt to slow the swing.

"No, I didn't know that." She watched as Joseph reached out and slowed Taylor's swing. "Why don't you bring him up to the house so he can meet Grandma?"

"Isn't that sad about him not having a swing set?" Taylor called out. "I told him I have two."

"Two?"

"Yes, one here and one at Daddy's." She bounded up the stairs and stopped in front of Lia. "Remember?"

"Now I do." She met Joseph's eyes as he came up behind Taylor, and a wave of attraction passed between them. Dressed in charcoal-gray pants with dark shoes and a combed white cotton oxford shirt, the sleeves rolled up to reveal his muscled forearms, he looked casually elegant and very handsome. "I've never seen you in anything but a suit."

"That's not true. You've seen me without it," he said, bringing a blush to Lia's cheeks.

"Mommy, I'm going to go get the picture I made today and show Joseph, so don't leave yet." Taylor opened the French doors and disappeared inside the house.

"God, you're beautiful. If we weren't being watched, I would push you back against that wall and show you how much I've missed you this week."

Lia breathed in deeply, her heart beating wildly in her chest at his words. "That would be my mother." She glanced back and saw her standing in the kitchen, openly watching them through the window. "Do you want to come in and meet her?"

"You're moving a little fast for me," he teased.

"You're funny."

After Lia made the introductions, Taylor shouted from the next room that she couldn't find the picture and Lia went off to help her.

"My granddaughter seems to be very smitten with you," Elaine said as she watched Joseph watch Lia leave the room. "She doesn't usually warm up to people so quickly."

"I'm smitten with her too." He waited until Lia was out of sight before turning to Elaine. "She's beautiful. They both are. It's beyond me how he could have ever let them get away."

"Me too," Elaine said softly, her eyes meeting his. "Me too."

It was the perfect evening for a baseball game. At least, it would have been perfect if Lia had remembered to take a jacket. But the temperature reached seventy-five degrees during the day, and she never considered how cool it might get in the evening. By the time they reached the ballpark, the temperature had dropped at least ten degrees, and Lia was cold just making the short trek from the parking lot to their seats behind home plate. She was contemplating how she was going to survive a nine-inning game when Joseph shrugged out of his suede jacket.

"Here, slip this on."

"No. I'm the one who was too stupid to remember my jacket. You shouldn't have to suffer."

"I'm not cold." He laid the jacket across her shoulders. "Really, come on. Put it on."

Lia thankfully slipped her arms into the sleeves and leaned back in her seat, breathing in the smell of leather mixed with what she now recognized as his scent, a clean soap smell with the undertones of woodsy-scented cologne.

"Do you like barbeque and beer?"

She nodded. "Yes."

Ten minutes later, he returned wearing a Nationals' jacket and carrying a box of food and two beers from Blue Smoke balanced precariously on a cardboard tray.

"I knew you were cold! And you had to buy an expensive jacket because of me."

"I've always wanted a Nationals' jacket."

"You're lying. You probably don't own one item of Nationals' clothing."

"Now I do." He lowered his head and kissed her for the first time that evening.

Three beers and seven innings later, with the Nationals up 9 to 1 over the Dodgers, they left the ballpark and drove to the Lincoln Memorial a few miles away.

"This is one of my favorite places in Washington," Joseph said as they walked hand in hand along the reflecting pool towards the Lincoln Memorial. "I like to run here at night."

"Last time I saw my father, we came here. It was on my sixteenth birthday."

"Really?" Joseph's gaze swung to her profile. "Why so long ago?"

"He lives in California with his wife of..." She paused. "Gosh, it must be close to fourteen years, and they have three children."

"Have you met them—his other children?"

"No." She brought her gaze to his momentarily as they continued to walk. "He left us when I was twelve, and then he slowly weaned himself out of our life. We were standing somewhere right around here when he told me he was married and had been for a couple years and that he had a son." She shook her head, remembering. "It was so strange. I remember looking at him and thinking, 'Who are you?' He had this whole life going on that I was no part of, and in my mind he was still this huge part of my world because he was my father. And then something clicked in my head and I realized he didn't want to be my father, so...I stopped talking to him."

"Just like that?" Joseph slowed as they approached the steps to the memorial. "And he accepted this?"

"Pretty much." She turned to face him. "I mean, I think we represented this huge failure in his life. If he didn't have to see us, he could pretend we didn't exist, except once a month when he signed the child-support check."

"He sounds like a great guy."

"Oh, he wasn't so bad. He was weak."

"Weak?" Joseph narrowed his eyes. "Weak is not being able to keep yourself from having another drink. What he did—abandoning his own children—is criminal."

"I guess, but when I wrote him out of my life I stopped caring. My brother, on the other hand, had a much harder time dealing with it. He moved out there after high school and reestablished a relationship. He's still there now."

"And?" Joseph prompted, when she didn't immediately continue. "Did he reestablish the relationship?"

"I guess, but at a great expense. I mean..." She paused as she lifted her gaze back to his. "He moved three thousand miles away from me and my mother so he could bond with a man who rejected him. I always thought that wasn't really fair to my mom."

"So you haven't spoken to your father since you were sixteen?"

"No, I have. He called when he heard I was getting married, and then again after Taylor was born. I think now that he's older he'd like to have a relationship with me, but I have no desire for one. He hurt me so much during those first four years after he left. I had to push all thoughts of him from my mind, and when I did that, he lost the power to hurt me. Now he's a stranger to me."

"Jesus, I would never put my child through that." Joseph shook his head, the side of his jaw clenching. "Men like him should be jailed."

"I'm sorry." She laid her hands on his chest. "I didn't mean to upset you. I don't know what made me tell you that. I'm a real downer, aren't I?"

"No." He moved his hands to the sides of her face, his eyes looking into hers. "I think you're the most amazing woman I've ever met."

"You do?" Her heart jumped.

"I do."

"Why?"

"Because you're beautiful, and strong, and when I'm with you my mind isn't consumed by the hundred unfinished jobs I have waiting in the office. I'm only thinking of you. You overwhelm me."

As she looked into his eyes, she too felt overwhelmed. "I don't know what to say."

"Say you'll come home with me." He kissed her softly before resting his forehead on hers. "I want you."

"What about Taylor? I—"

"I'll take you home before morning. I need to be inside you."

There was no way she could say no to him. "Yes."

— —

Joseph was alone in the law office when he met with Sam Malone a couple weeks later.

"Thanks for coming in so late," Joseph said, meeting him as he came off the elevator. "This is my only free night this week and I didn't want to wait to see what you found."

Sam Malone was a small, wiry man with a thick head of gray hair and skin that had seen so much of the sun it looked almost like leather. "I prefer evenings," Malone said in his raspy voice as he pulled a thumb drive out of his pocket.

"Where'd that come from?" Joseph's eyes were on the thumb drive.

"A digital video recorder in the house." He followed Joseph back to his office. "And if you have anything against pornography, you may have a problem with it."

Five minutes later, Joseph pushed the stop button on his computer. "Jesus!" He leaned back in his chair. "I suppose this means Hall doesn't leave it to his employees to tell him which clients they've been with." The thumb drive showed the activities in one of the bedrooms from the night before as two women, apparently employees of Stan Hall, were having sex with a male.

Malone dropped down into one of the club chairs. "Every bedroom in that house is equipped with a camera."

"Why?"

Malone shrugged. "Maybe this is how he and his brother get their jollies? Wouldn't be the first pervert I've come across."

"And you think Marcos maintains these video recorders?"

"I know he does. He installed a new one three days ago. I caught him on surveillance video."

"Surveillance video?" Joseph frowned. "You set up surveillance video in the house?"

"Outside. They left the shades open in one of the bedrooms. I had it set up in a tree in the back."

"How did you get this?" Joseph held up the thumb drive.

"The house doesn't have a security system," he said, not directly answering the question.

Joseph leaned back in his chair. "The more I learn, the less I think Zurtech is involved. This sounds like some peep show for the benefit of Mike and Stan Hall. These B2B women get nice bonuses for participating, and the Zurtech clients have easy access to sex with beautiful women."

"Could be."

"There's still no proof this is prostitution." Joseph tapped his fist against his mouth. "All we know for sure is this Marcos Rodriguez is video recording them. How do we even know the Hall brothers are aware this is happening?"

"Rodriguez is being paid by Tia Tacos. They're compensating him for something."

"Maybe they're charging the clients."

Sam shook his head. "Hall wouldn't go through the expense of setting up these cameras just to see who to charge for sex and which girls should receive bonuses, no way."

"But you think he would go through the trouble of setting it up to feed his own personal fetish?"

"I'm not saying it's reasonable, but I think it's more possible."

"What does Rodriguez do with the videos? Have you seen him with either of the Hall brothers?"

"No, never. I'm guessing his girlfriend passes them to Stan Hall when she goes into Zurtech."

Joseph blew out a stream of air. "We've got to be missing something. There is no way the only purpose of this house is to feed some perverted fetish."

"Maybe they're blackmailing the clients."

"I don't know. According to the women I talked to, there were a lot of repeat customers. If you were getting blackmailed based on video, it wouldn't make sense for you to continue to give evidence to your blackmailer."

Malone shrugged. "Maybe they figure they're already paying, so—"

"No. These are intelligent men with high-powered jobs. They're not going to be that stupid. Once they realized they were being recorded, they'd stop coming back."

"Maybe they aren't blackmailing everyone," Malone threw out. "Maybe they only blackmail the wealthiest clients."

"Eric Nettles is worth over ten million, and he's a regular."

"I'm out of ideas," Malone said. "If it's not to bring in money, it's not making a lot of sense."

"It is making Stan Hall more successful at Zurtech. You said yourself, many of the clients like the service being provided. Maybe Mike Hall is funding this to help his brother's career and then they have the added bonus of feeding their perverted appetite."

"Could be."

"I think it's probably time to shelve this investigation, at least temporarily. It's not panning out the way I thought it might," Joseph said.

12

The first Tuesday in September, Lia was standing before the mirror in her bathroom, putting on the final touches of her makeup when Taylor stopped outside the door. "Mommy, I have a tummy ache."

"You do?" She hadn't mentioned her stomach bothering her when Lia set a waffle and milk in front of her ten minutes earlier.

Taylor nodded, her lips turning down as she put her small hand over her belly. "It hurts."

Lia laid her hand over Taylor's forehead. It felt normal. "Why don't you go lie down while I finish getting ready? Maybe it will stop hurting before it's time to go to the bus stop."

Twenty minutes later, Lia found Taylor curled up on the couch under a comforter watching television, her uneaten food on the coffee table. "Your belly still hurts?"

"Uh huh." Taylor didn't look away from the cartoon on the television. "You better call Grandma."

"You're not pretending to be sick so you can stay home, are you?" It certainly wouldn't be the first time.

"No, it hurts."

"That'll be Grandma," Lia said when there was a knock on the door forty-five minutes later. She carefully lifted Taylor's head from her lap and slipped off the couch. "I'll be right back."

"That was fast," she began as she opened the door, stopping midsentence when she saw an unfamiliar man standing in the hall.

"Lia Merrick?"

"Yes." She considered closing the door, but in khakis and a plaid shirt, he looked harmless.

He handed her a legal-sized envelope. "Have a nice day." He turned and was down the stairs before she had time to react.

She stepped back into the apartment and closed and locked the door before her eyes went to the envelope in her hand. *Blackman and Associates*, it read in the left-hand corner: Ned's law firm. She unsealed the top of the envelope and lifted out the document inside, her eyes moving to the top of the first page. *Motion for Modification of Custody*, it read.

"What?" It had to be a mistake, but as her eyes scanned the contents of the document, she realized with horror there was no mistake. Ned was seeking custody of Taylor. "Oh my God." Her free hand, shaking now, moved to cover her mouth. This wasn't happening. This couldn't be happening. He wouldn't try to take Taylor. She ran to the family room and grabbed her phone from the coffee table.

"Where's Grandma?" Taylor asked.

"She isn't here yet." She fled the room. After three failed attempts, she finally dialed Ned's office number correctly and leaned back against the kitchen counter, one hand covering her eyes, the other holding the phone. "I need to speak to Ned Merrick," she told the secretary.

"I'm sorry, he's in a meeting. May I—"

"This is an emergency regarding his daughter," Lia interrupted, not even recognizing the sound of her own voice. "Tell him it's his ex-wife." She could hear her heartbeat in her ears as she waited for him to come on the line. It took over five minutes.

"I guess you got the papers."

"What are you doing? You can't seriously plan on trying to take her from me."

"Yes, I can. And I do."

"Ned! This is ridiculous. I'm her mother!"

"And I'm her father. And I believe Candice and I—"

"Candice! Candice is not Taylor's mother."

"But I'm her father. And I believe we can provide her with a better home." His voice was cool, controlled, and Lia wanted to reach through the phone and squeeze his neck.

"You son of a—"

"Mommy, who are you yelling at?" Taylor was at the doorway, her eyebrows pulled together in a frown.

"No one, sweetheart." Her gaze shifted to an uncharacteristically pale Taylor. "Go back and lie down." She forced herself to smile. "Everything's fine."

As soon as Taylor turned back towards the family room, Lia headed for her bedroom. "Are you still there?"

"Yes. What is she doing home from school?"

"None of your fucking business," she bit out. "No judge in this state will take her from me and give her to the woman who broke up our home."

"Lia, think about what's best for Taylor. We have a house with a yard, and you—"

"Go to hell! I'm her mother, and you're the reason we're living in this apartment. You must really hate me, Ned."

"This isn't about you. This is about what's best for Taylor."

"That is such bullshit!" She could barely stomach another word from him. "How could you possibly believe she would be better off without me?"

"Candice is going to go to part time after the baby is born. Taylor won't have to go to daycare anymore."

"Daycare? She goes to my mother's after school, not daycare."

"Right, she has to go to your mom's house. If we had her, she would come straight home after school and play with her friends."

"Straight home to Candice?" God, she hated him. "She isn't anything to Taylor. She's a whore who had an affair with her father." She'd lost her temper, but she no longer cared. "You'll never get her from me. You're a bastard, Ned." She ended the call and threw the phone across the room, bouncing it off the wall.

"Lia?" Elaine's voice preceded a light knock on the door. "Lia, are you okay in there?"

"No!" She opened the door, her eyes immediately falling to Taylor. "Taylor, you're sick. You should be lying down." She was amazed at how normal she could sound when she felt like her whole world was disintegrating.

"But what was that noise?"

"Nothing. I dropped the phone and it hit the wall. Now please go lie back down." Lia's panic-filled eyes found her mother's. "This came." She held up the legal document, her hand noticeably shaking.

"You have to call Joseph," Elaine said, looking up from the papers moments later, tears in her eyes. "You have to call him right away."

"Mom?" Fear gripped her chest at the worried expression on her mother's face. "They would never give her to them," she whispered. "Would they?"

"Just call Joseph. He'll know what to do."

"Oh my God." Lia covered her mouth. "You think he could get her."

"No, I never said that, but you need to call Joseph."

Lia nodded and picked her cell phone off the carpet, thankful it wasn't damaged. "I'll call him." She was numb. She felt like she was in the middle of a nightmare and any second she'd awaken. She called his cell, but it went right to voicemail. "I need his office number." She never called him at work. He called her during the day occasionally, but usually they spoke in the evening.

"Where is it?" Elaine asked.

"In my purse." Her eyes frantically searched the bedroom, having a hard time concentrating. "It must be in the kitchen."

"I'll get it," Elaine said, holding up her hands. "Just wait here." Within seconds she was back, the purse in hand. Lia was sitting on the edge of her bed with her head between her knees.

"I feel like I'm going to be sick." Lia had broken out into a cold sweat. "I can't believe he would do this to me."

"Where's the number?" Elaine asked as she dug through her purse.

"In my wallet." Lia took the wallet from her purse, fumbling with it until she had his card in her hand. "Here." She picked up her phone and attempted to push the numbers to his office, but she couldn't seem to concentrate long enough to push the ten numbers into the phone correctly.

After her fourth unsuccessful attempt, Elaine took the card and phone and quickly punched in the number. "Here." She held out the phone to Lia.

"Prossi, Stuart and Craig. Mr. Craig's office," a crisp female voice said.

"This is Lia Merrick. I need to speak to Mr. Craig."

"I'm sorry, Mr. Craig isn't available right now."

"When will he be available? I need to speak to him. This is an emergency."

"I'm sorry, what is your name?"

"Lia Merrick."

"Are you a client?" came the cool reply.

"No. Yes." Lia shook her head. "I was, but now I'm just a friend, but I have a legal matter I need to discuss with him. It's urgent," she rushed out.

"He'll have to call you back. He's in a meeting and he can't be disturbed."

He was there, and she wasn't putting him on the phone. "Please—just tell him it's Lia Merrick. I know he'll take my call."

"Why don't you give me your number, and I'll have him call you back this afternoon?"

This afternoon! She couldn't possibly wait that long. "I need to talk to him now!"

"I'll tell you what. Give me your number and I'll try to get the message to him."

"O-okay. Thank you." Lia quickly recited her number and ended the call. "He's in a meeting," she said to her mother. "She said she'd get him my message. He should call me right back."

She'd been dating him close to five months and, although they started out slow, only seeing each other twice a week, in the past two months she had started spending the entire weekend with him when Taylor was with Ned. Even on the weekends Taylor was home, it was rare for her not to see him both Saturday and Sunday. The Zurtech case seemed to have been permanently shelved because of a lack of evidence, but Lia rarely thought of her time there anymore. The irony that she would never have met Joseph if not for Zurtech hadn't escaped her.

She waited by the phone for fifteen minutes before once again calling his office. "Prossi, Stuart and Craig. Mr. Craig's Office."

"This is Lia Merrick again. Did you give Mr. Craig my message?"

There was a short pause. "I haven't had an opportunity yet, but—"

"This is an urgent matter! I'll stay on the line until you give him my message."

"He is in a meeting with another client. As soon as he comes out for a break, I will give him your message."

"If you don't put him on the phone right now, I'm coming down there!"

"I'm sorry, but," his secretary began, apparently unperturbed by the threat, "I've been instructed not to disturb him. But I will deliver your message as soon as he takes a break."

"Thanks for your help," Lia bit out sarcastically before ending the call.

"I'm going to his office," she announced a moment later from the doorway to the family room, where her mother was sitting on the couch next to a sleeping Taylor.

"He called back? I didn't hear the telephone."

"No. He's in a meeting and she won't disturb him, so I'm just going to go."

"I'm not sure if that's such a good idea." Elaine met Lia at the door and followed her to the foyer. "I think you're too upset to drive."

"Mom, I'm fine." Lia slipped on her raincoat. "I have to talk to him."

An hour later, Lia was stepping off the elevator into the law offices of Prossi, Stuart and Craig, her purse in one hand and the yellow envelope from Ned's office in the other.

"May I help you?" A young, very attractive receptionist looked up from the mail she was sorting.

"No, thank you. I know where I'm going." Lia continued to walk through the lobby and then down the hall she knew led to Joseph's office.

"Excuse me." The girl came up beside her. "You can't come back here. I need to announce you."

"That's okay. I'll announce myself." She didn't bother to look at the girl as she continued to Joseph's office. As she came to a stop in front of his secretary's desk, the receptionist was still on her heels. "I'm Lia Merrick. I need to see Mr. Craig." Her eyes were directed at the heavyset woman sitting behind the desk outside of what she knew to be his office.

"I'm sorry, Martha," the receptionist said. "I tried to stop her."

"It's okay." Martha rose from her chair, her eyes not leaving Lia's. "I'll take care of it." She waited until the receptionist left before continuing. "Ms. Merrick, I explained to you on the phone Mr. Craig is in a meeting and cannot be disturbed."

"And I explained to you it is urgent I speak with him!" Lia could feel herself becoming more agitated. "I received some legal papers today," she began, holding up the yellow envelope, "that I need to discuss with him."

"I understand, but it's going to have to wait because Mr. Craig is discussing another *urgent* matter with another client right now."

"Well it's not as urgent as mine!" Lia's voice broke. "My ex-husband is trying to take my daughter from me."

Tony frowned and met Kevin Stuart's eyes across the conference table. They were in a preliminary meeting with a potentially huge client—one of the country's largest automobile manufacturers—and Joseph was talking, outlining the approach they'd take to defend them against a class action suit brought on by two dozen clients who suffered injury due to faulty brakes on one of their models.

"Why don't we take a short break to stretch our legs?" Kevin suggested when Joseph paused to look down at his notes.

Joseph's eyes moved from his notes to his watch. It was 11:00 a.m. They'd been meeting for an hour and a half and they'd be breaking for lunch in thirty minutes. His eyes shifted to Tony, who was already out of his chair and headed for the door, Kevin on his heels. He frowned, confusion evident on his face, and then he caught a glimpse of her as Kevin shut the door. It was Lia, noticeably upset in his lobby.

"What's going on out here?" Tony's eyes swung from Martha to Lia as he came out of the conference room, followed by Kevin.

"I'm trying to explain that Mr. Craig isn't available right now."

"I need to speak to him," Lia said, her voice breaking as she met Tony's eyes.

"Look, you're going to have to calm down and lower your voice," Tony said through clenched teeth. "This isn't a Goddamn bar. This is a law firm."

The door behind them banged open and Joseph practically flew to Lia's side. "What happened? What's the matter?"

"Joseph! You have to help me," she cried as she gripped the lapels of his suit jacket. "Ne-Ned is...tr-tr-trying to get Taylor."

"What?" He frowned. "Baby, you're going to have to slow down."

"Why don't you take her into your office?" Kevin patted Joseph's back.

Joseph's eyes remained locked with Lia's as he gently gripped her upper arms and propelled her slowly backwards until they were in the privacy of his office, his foot kicking the door closed. "Take a deep breath and tell me what's going on."

"Ned wants custody of Taylor."

"He wants custody?" Joseph brought his eyebrows together. "He wants full custody of Taylor?"

"Yes," she whispered, the tears once again falling from her eyes. "The papers were couriered over today." She lifted the yellow envelope.

"He's not taking her from you." He moved his hands to each side of her face. "Do you hear me? He's not taking her from you."

"I'm so scared," she whispered, tears continuing to fall from her eyes.

"There's nothing to be scared of," he said deeply, his brown eyes intense. "I'm serious, Lia." He moved his thumbs along her cheeks, wiping at the tears. "I would never let that happen."

"But I don't have any money. And he has an entire law firm at—"

"You have me, and I have a lot more at my disposal than he does. Do you understand?" He continued to hold her face, his eyes looking in to hers.

"Yes." She nodded, biting on her lip. "Yes."

"Now, let me see those papers."

"I don't get it." Kevin dragged his hands down his face. "He wasn't part of that meeting. How does he even know her?"

"What are you talking about?" Tony paused with a coffee mug at his mouth. They were standing outside Joseph's office, waiting for him to come out so they could continue the meeting.

"The woman in there with Joseph is Lia Merrick. She was one of the plaintiffs in the sexual harassment case against Zurtech we didn't take last year."

Tony shrugged. "He must have met her while she was here, because we ran into her this spring at a restaurant in Fairfax, and he definitely knows her."

Kevin sighed. "Only Joseph."

"We've got to get back in there," Tony said, glancing at his watch. It was 11:10 a.m.

"You go ahead. I'll get Joseph."

Joseph looked up from the papers when he heard the knock on the door "I'll be right back." He touched Lia's knee before standing and crossing to the door. "You're going to have to go on without me," he said as soon as he pulled open the door and saw Kevin.

"What?" Kevin laughed. "This is your meeting, your case. What do you mean, 'go on without you'?"

Joseph glanced at his watch. "You're going to break for lunch in twenty minutes. The two of you can handle it. I'll rejoin the meeting after lunch."

"They chose this law firm because they want *you*. You can't skip out on lunch."

"I'm not done here. And I'm not going to abandon her."

"Then don't," Kevin said. "I'll get one of the associates to talk to her."

"No. She's upset. I'm not leaving her. Tony was in here all day with me yesterday preparing. He can handle this for two hours."

"This account could be the biggest thing you bring in all year. You couldn't possibly want to jeopardize that for her." His voice was low but intense.

"She needs me right now. Tony can handle this." Joseph continued to meet Kevin's eyes.

"Get your head out of your Goddamn pants for a minute," Kevin snarled. "This account is way too valuable to mess with. You can't do this."

"Watch me." Joseph stepped back from the door and slammed it in Kevin's face.

Kevin stared at the closed door for several seconds. "Fuck!" He turned to Martha. "How long has this been going on?" He threw his thumb towards Joseph's closed door.

"I didn't connect the name to the Zurtech case when she called, but I knew the name sounded familiar, so I looked back through his appointment books and then I remembered that he asked me to set up a meeting with the two plaintiffs from that case last December."

"What?" Kevin walked closer to her desk. "He met with Lia Merrick about the Zurtech case?"

"I don't know. It's all a vague memory now. But I specifically remember setting up the appointments, and that's the last I ever heard of it. As far as I know, he hasn't met with them since." She threw her hands up in the air. "They may have called. I've been searching my brain, but I really don't recall. I'm sorry."

"Well?" Lia asked when Joseph removed his glasses and looked up from the document. "Is it bad?"

"No."

She sunk back into the couch, relief surging through her. "So what happens now?"

"The two of you will go before a judge and argue the case." He stood and crossed to his desk, pushing the intercom on the phone. "Martha, are you out there?"

"Yes."

"Would you see if you can get John Bianchi on the line for me?" Moments later, he was rejoining Lia, running his arm along the couch behind her. "John Bianchi is a good friend of mine and the best family-law attorney in the city. He'll take good care of you."

"But I want you." Lia could feel her anxiety returning. "I want you to be my lawyer."

He took her hand. "I'm a trial attorney. I don't handle divorce and child custody. John is the best. He'll do a much better job than I ever could."

"But I trust you." Her eyes pleaded with him to understand. "I don't want to go through this with someone else."

"I'll be there every step of the way. I won't leave you. I just want to make sure you win. And believe me, Lia. John always wins."

"Mr. Craig?" Martha's voice came over the intercom. "Mr. Bianchi is on line one."

⚊ ⌢

Joseph looked up from his computer when there was a knock on his office door hours later. "Come in."

"We need to talk." Kevin, followed by Tony, entered his office.

"If this is about earlier today, I don't want to talk about it. We got the case, so obviously there was no harm done."

"How do you know Lia Merrick?"

"How do I know Lia Merrick?" Joseph's eyes met Kevin's. "I met her when she was here for the Zurtech case."

"I don't see how. Wasn't that the same day you and Tony were at that conference in Philadelphia?"

"Well, I met her." Joseph's gaze moved to Tony. "What is this?"

"We're just trying to figure out what's going on. Martha said you told her to call them in to meet with you."

"Martha said, huh?" He gnawed on his lower lip. "Why were you discussing me with my secretary?"

"It was Kevin, actually."

"Why don't you just answer the question, Joseph?" Kevin asked.

"Because it's none of your business." He leaned back in his chair. "And I take offense to the fact that you're checking up on me behind my back."

"We wouldn't have to if you didn't do things behind our backs. Why did you meet with them on a weekend when you knew no one would be in the office?"

Joseph stared back at him, no expression on his face. "I was curious about them, so I called them in to tell them we weren't taking their case."

"Just so you could see them?" Kevin asked, his eyes narrowing in suspicion.

"Yeah, just so I could see them. Is there anything else?"

"Joseph, come on." Tony leaned back in his chair and put his hands behind his head. "You have to admit your behavior was a bit out of character today."

"I don't have to admit anything. I had a friend who needed me, and it obviously had no effect on the outcome of today's meeting."

"But it could have," Kevin pointed out, "and you put the needs of your girlfriend before the needs of this firm."

"Fuck you, Kevin. I skipped out on lunch—big deal." He narrowed his eyes. "Why are you making such a huge deal about this? We got the case."

"That's not the point! First you meet with these women on your own, without telling anyone," he began, grabbing one of his fingers, "and then you walk out of a meeting when you're in the middle of a presentation," he finished, grasping a second finger. "That's not how you act in a partnership."

"You know, Kevin," Joseph began, leaning forward in his chair and placing his hands flat on his desk, "maybe if you spent more time cultivating clients of your own and less time worrying about me, you could bring in seventy-five percent of the money I do for this firm."

"Fuck you!"

Joseph's gaze swung to Tony. "Get him the fuck out of here. I have work to do." He turned back to his computer and began pressing keys.

Thirty minutes later, there was a knock on Tony's office door. "Come in."

The door opened and Martha, her face red and lips turned down, walked into the office. "I was just fired. Mr. Craig just fired me."

"What?" Tony came to his feet.

She swallowed before continuing. "He didn't like that I discussed his meeting schedule with Mr. Stuart."

"I'll talk to him."

"No." She shook her head. "He told me as of today, I'm no longer needed. He said he didn't trust me anymore and that he couldn't have a secretary he couldn't trust. I'd forgotten, but when he told me to make those appointments with the Zurtech plaintiffs, he'd specifically told me not to mention them to anyone." Her hands were clasped tightly before her as she twisted them together. "He was very angry."

"You haven't lost your job, Martha." Tony slipped his arm around her and rubbed her back. "You're a valued secretary at this firm and I, for one, do not want to lose you."

"I've been with this firm since the beginning, and I don't fancy looking for another job."

"Well, you don't have to. We'll find another position for you."

◦— ◦—

"I can't believe he would do this to me," Lia said later that evening. She'd carried a sleeping Taylor, who seemed to be a degree better, to her bedroom and was now seated across the table from her mother in her small kitchen, pushing a piece of chicken around on her plate. "I mean, why couldn't he have called? He was planning this for who knows how long, and he never said a word."

She'd been obsessing over it all day, unable to understand how a man who at one time claimed to love her more than anything else in the world could, in the matter of two years, leave her for another woman, marry that other woman and now try to take her little girl. It was inconceivable to her, and she couldn't seem to keep herself from trying to understand.

"I don't think he's doing it to you, Lia," Elaine said. "He isn't giving any thought to you or your feelings."

"I know, and that's what I can't understand. I can't eat." She pushed her plate to the center of the table. "I don't know why I even tried."

"Lia, eat. You're too skinny." Elaine frowned. "You shouldn't let him upset you so much."

"Mother, please! How can I not be upset when he's trying to take Taylor away?" She dropped her face into her hands. "I can't believe this is happening. What is he thinking? He's known me since I was nineteen years old. How can he do this?"

"How can he do this? This is the same man who cheated on you with another woman for six months and then left you for that woman. He isn't someone with a high moral character, and this is more evidence to that fact."

"But I don't understand why he didn't discuss it with me."

"You have to stop expecting him to act like someone who has respect for you. I doubt he respects anyone. He's selfish and self-centered, and what he did today is consistent with those qualities, not the qualities you seem to want to give him."

13

oseph rounded the corner leading to his office at 5:15 the following evening and looked around, confusion etched on his features. "Has Lia Merrick arrived?" He approached the temp sitting behind Martha's old desk.

"No." A woman of about thirty-five with stylishly short brown hair and large brown eyes looked up at him. "Her mother called about an hour ago and said she couldn't make it."

"Did she say why?"

She dropped her eyes to a sheet of paper on the desk. "She said to tell you Taylor is sick and that they were taking her to Fairfax Hospital."

Lia turned from the window in the small waiting room on the fourth floor of Fairfax Hospital at the same moment Ned and a very pregnant Candice came through the door.

"What's going on?" Ned's eyes found Lia.

"Probably her appendix," Elaine answered when, after several seconds of silence, it became obvious Lia wasn't going to. "The school nurse called Lia at two and said Taylor was having stomach cramping and had a low-grade fever, so she picked her up and took her to the doctor."

Taylor had appeared fine in the morning, so Lia mistakenly thought whatever was bothering her the day before had left her system.

"So they're operating on her?" Ned asked as he lowered himself onto a chair beside Candice.

"Yes." Elaine answered.

Lia turned back to the window, not wanting anyone to see the tears in her eyes. This was hard enough without having to deal with Ned too. She knew her mother had called him. She didn't have a choice, considering he was scheduled to pick Taylor up at her house at 6:00 p.m. And she'd expected him to show up, but she never considered the possibility he'd bring Candice.

Elaine touched Lia's arm. "Do you want a cup of coffee or something?"

"No, thank you." She covered her mother's hand with her own. She didn't want to be alone with Ned and Candice. She'd made the mistake of glancing back at them a moment earlier to find them huddled together, with Candice's head resting on his shoulder. She felt sick to her stomach. "What's taking so long?" Her eyes drifted to the doorway just in time to see someone who looked very similar to Joseph walk by. A second later, he was back and her throat constricted when she realized it was him. He'd come.

Dressed in a black suit with a smoky-blue shirt and dark gray tie, Joseph looked like he'd stepped out of an advertisement in *GQ* magazine, and as his six-foot-four frame entered the waiting area, the room instantly felt smaller. Not sparing a glance at Ned or Candice, who were openly watching him, he crossed the room to Lia and her mother, lightly embracing Elaine and kissing her cheek before turning to Lia.

"Joseph," Lia whispered.

"Are you okay?"

She nodded and wanted to tell him she was fine, but she couldn't because suddenly she was crying, and the buildup from the last two days found a release in the arms of this incredible man who seemed to be her appointed guardian angel on Earth.

"I'm sorry," she said when she finally pulled back and looked up at him. "I didn't mean to do that."

"Don't apologize to me." He gently wiped the tears from beneath her eyes with his handkerchief. "I'm sorry I couldn't get here sooner."

"I'm just happy you're here." She gripped his hand.

He brought her hand to his mouth, kissing the inside of her wrist as his eyes met hers. "Me too."

"Hello?" A young woman dressed in surgical scrubs walked through the door and glanced around. "Ms. Merrick?"

"That's me." Lia rushed forward. "I'm Taylor's mom."

"I'm Katie Menser, a medical student. Taylor's going to be fine. Her appendix ruptured, but everything was caught in time. Dr. Lombardi is washing up, and then she'll be out to talk to you."

"Where's Taylor?"

"She's still in recovery. A nurse will let you know as soon as she's assigned a room."

"Thank you." Lia reached out and gripped the woman's hand. "Thank you so much."

"You're welcome." She smiled. "The doctor will be right in."

As the woman left the room, Lia turned to Elaine. "Thank God," she said as she hugged her mother. "Thank God."

After a moment her eyes sought out Joseph, who was still standing beside the window, his hands pushed deeply into his pockets as he watched her. She crossed the room and moved into his arms, dropping her face into his neck as he wrapped his arms around her, his hand moving up and down her back. "It's okay." His mouth was at her ear. "Everything's okay."

"Joseph?" A female voice had him lifting his head.

"Hannah?" He smiled in recognition. "You operated on Taylor?"

Lia turned in Joseph's arms as the surgeon approached.

"Yes." Dr. Hannah Lombardi crossed the room to where Lia and Joseph were standing. She gave him a quick hug and kissed his cheek. "You're not the father, are you?"

"No." Ned and Joseph answered in unison.

"I'm the father," Ned said. He crossed to where they stood.

"I'm a friend." Joseph slipped his arm around Lia as his eyes moved to Ned.

"Sorry." Hannah shrugged. She addressed Lia. "She's going to be fine. Her appendix was in the process of rupturing, so we removed it just in time."

As she went on to describe the operation in more detail, Joseph's eyes moved from Ned Merrick to Candice, who remained sitting.

"So how have you been, Counselor?" Hannah asked Joseph when she was done answering Lia and Ned's questions. "I haven't seen you in forever."

"Too long." He turned to Lia. "Hannah used to date Tony, but it turned out she was too smart for him." He winked at Hannah.

"Something like that." Hannah smiled. "How is he?"

"As arrogant as ever." Joseph left his arm around Lia as he chatted with Hannah about mutual acquaintances, the completion of her residency and the law firm. He managed to pull Lia into the conversation, and at least fifteen minutes passed before a nurse came in to give them the room number where Taylor would be taken after recovery.

Lia felt better than she had in two days as she walked towards Taylor's assigned room with Joseph and her mother. Suddenly, Ned and Candice were the outsiders. They had arrived at the hospital knowing Lia was alone and not giving one thought to how she would feel. And then, in a matter of moments, Joseph had shown up and Ned not only learned she wasn't alone, but was dating one of the most successful attorneys in the area.

As they entered Taylor's assigned hospital room, there was a moment of awkward silence as they encountered Ned and Candice. Ned came to his feet, and Lia knew she had to acknowledge him.

"Joseph, this is Taylor's father, Ned."

Ned crossed to Joseph, holding out his hand. "This is a bit of a surprise. I had no idea you knew Lia. Taylor mentions a Joseph, but I certainly didn't connect it with you."

Joseph returned the handshake. "Merrick." He met his eyes.

"And this is my wife, Candice." He turned as Candice approached.

"Hi." She held out her hand. "Actually, we've met. We were on opposing sides during a libel suit last year."

"Hello." Joseph returned her handshake and then was turning back to Lia, clearly dismissing the two. "How about a cup of coffee?" His eyes moved from Lia to Elaine.

"Okay." Lia nodded.

Joseph turned to Candice and Ned, who were still standing awkwardly beside him. "May I get either of you something?"

"A cup of ice water," Candice said.

"Nothing for me, thanks," Ned said.

"I'll be right back." Joseph kissed Lia lightly on the lips before leaving the room.

Ned turned to Lia as soon as Joseph was out of earshot. "How did you meet him?"

"How could that possibly be any of your business?"

Ned shrugged. "I'm curious."

"I bet." She glanced from him to Candice. "Maybe he's my lawyer. I need one, you know."

"He doesn't practice family law."

"Oh, that's right. He isn't my lawyer. But one of his friends is." When Ned didn't say anything, she continued. "Have you heard of John Bianchi?" There was no mistaking the flash of surprise in his eyes.

Ned was surprised again when Joseph returned to the room twenty minutes later, carrying a big brown teddy bear and *Get Well Soon* balloons. A newly awakened Taylor, who'd been wheeled into the room fifteen minutes earlier, lit up at the sight of him and his gifts. "Joseph!"

"Hi, beautiful. How are you feeling?" He leaned down to kiss her cheeks, and she surprised everyone, including Lia, by wrapping her little arms around his neck.

"I'm in a hospital!"

"I know. You're a brave girl." He held up the bear. "You're not too big for teddy bears, are you?"

"No." She gave an exaggerated shake of her head as she reached for the bear. "I'm six."

"That's right. I keep thinking you're eight or nine."

Taylor smiled. "You're funny, Joseph." She glanced to the other side of the bed, where Candice and Ned were standing. "That's my daddy and Candice."

"Yes. I've met them." Joseph didn't move his gaze from Taylor.

"Isn't Joseph tall, Daddy?" Taylor swung her gaze to Ned. "He's very strong too. Grandpa wanted him to help him move a desk and Joseph did it all by himself." When Ned didn't comment, she brought her eyes back to Joseph. "Candice is having a baby, and it's going to be my little sister."

Joseph nodded. "You'll be a great big sister."

"Daddy says my little sister will want me to be with her all the time, but I said I could only be with her sometimes because I want to be with Mommy. Daddy said that will make her sad. I don't want to make her sad."

"I'm sure she'll understand that you have a different mommy, so you can only see her sometimes." Joseph's eyes met Ned's.

"That's what I thought." Taylor turned to Ned. "See, she'll understand, Daddy."

"I'll be back," Lia said softly before leaving the room.

Elaine moved to follow, but Joseph touched her arm. "I'll go." He quickly left the room, catching Lia outside the elevators. "Hey. Are you okay?"

"I'm fine. He's so awful. I couldn't stand to be in the same room with him another minute."

He followed her into the elevator. "How come you never mentioned the pregnancy?"

"I don't know. It's not something I like to think about."

"Come here." He leaned back against the wall as he pulled her towards him. "Don't let them get to you."

"It's just been an awful couple of days." She slipped her arms up around his neck and laid her head against his chest as he enfolded her in his arms.

"I know." He kissed the top of her head. "But she's going to be fine, and I promise the rest of this mess will go away too."

"How come you never mentioned you knew Candice?"

"I didn't know I did until I saw her."

"Did you beat her?"

He smiled against her head. "Of course."

They walked through the hospital lobby and then out into the cool October evening and over to a small courtyard across from the hospital entrance. "I should have brought our drinks," Joseph said. He lowered himself down beside her on a wooden bench.

"It's nice out here." Lia closed her eyes and took a deep breath, taking comfort in the cool fall air.

"And a little cool." Joseph shrugged out of his suit jacket. "Here, put this on."

"No." Lia shook her head, not bothering to open her eyes as she leaned back against the bench. "I'm not going to take your jacket."

"Take it," he insisted, pushing her gently forward so he could slip the jacket around her shoulders. "You don't have any body fat to keep you warm."

"Oh, and you do?" She glanced sideways at him. "You don't have an ounce of fat on your entire body."

"I'm sure I have at least an ounce." He leaned sideways and playfully bumped his shoulder into hers. "And that's probably an ounce more than you have."

"Are you trying to tell me I'm too skinny?"

"No. I'm telling you, you need my jacket more than I do."

"Fine, I'll wear your jacket."

"Thank you."

Lia covered the hand he had resting on his thigh. "Thank you for coming out tonight. It would have been so much harder without you."

"I wanted to be here. You're important to me."

"I like you too." She leaned towards him and met his lips for a brief kiss. "A lot."

Their eyes continued to meet, and Lia could feel her heart rate quicken at the unspoken words being so clearly communicated from his eyes. He loved her. He may not have said it, but she could feel it.

"What?" He smiled. "Why are you looking at me like that?"

"Because I—" She suddenly wanted to tell him she loved him, but she couldn't. She was too afraid. Everything was so perfect between them, and she didn't want to jinx it. "I want you."

"You want me?"

She nodded, smiling at his surprise. "Yes."

He opened his mouth and then closed it. "What about Taylor? Isn't she expecting you to come back?"

Lia laughed at the obvious misunderstanding. "I didn't mean right now. I meant in general."

"Oh."

"Well, don't look so disappointed." Lia laughed. "What kind of person would I be if I deserted my six-year-old daughter an hour after an operation to go have sex with you?"

"I wouldn't judge you," he teased.

"I bet. Did you reschedule our appointment with your lawyer friend?" She suddenly remembered the missed appointment.

"I cancelled and told him I'd call back to reschedule."

"Next week will be better. Oh, I did remember my divorce papers." She patted her purse.

"I'll take them now. I'll have them sent over tomorrow so he can get started."

"Okay." Lia removed a white envelope from her bag and held it out, pulling it back slightly when he attempted to take it. "One thing for the record. I know you're paying for this, and I want you to know I'm going to pay you back every cent. It may take me a while, but I'm going to." She continued to hold the envelope out of his reach. "And you have to agree to let me, okay?"

"No." He shook his head. "I want to do this for you. It's important to me."

"It's not your responsibility. I'm paying you back."

"No." He met her eyes. "You're letting me do this for you."

"Joseph?"

"Don't be difficult." He reached out and took the envelope.

"This isn't over."

"Yes, it is."

She was overwhelmed with gratitude. "You're amazing," she whispered. "No one has ever done so much for me."

"It's nothing you wouldn't do for me."

"I could never repay you for everything you've done for me. You're like my personal guardian angel."

"I'd settle for boyfriend. Okay?"

She nodded and, for the first time in years, felt very lucky. "Thank you."

"You're welcome."

"We better go back up. She's going to wonder what happened to me." She glanced towards the hospital. "Are you ready for another dose of Ned and Candice?"

"I'd like to read these papers." He tapped the envelope on his knee. "I'll be up in about fifteen minutes or so."

"You know, you don't have to hang around." She was probably keeping him from a dozen other things he needed to do. "I've pulled you away from your work enough this week."

"I'm staying. I'll be up after I finish reading this."

Joseph set the agreement on the bench beside him and breathed in deeply, the side of his jaw clenching and unclenching. His eyes narrowed several minutes later as Ned and Candice approached. "Did you write your divorce agreement yourself?"

"Excuse me?" Ned frowned as they slowed their steps.

"There is no way Lia had representation." He held up the document. "No lawyer in their right mind would agree to these terms."

"Lia agreed to them." They came to a stop in front of him. "You'll notice it's signed."

"You're not even providing your daughter with health insurance?"

Ned shrugged. "So?"

"I'm guessing the child support is half of what it should be." He brought his eyebrows together. "Was the judge a relative? Who came up with the child support amount?"

Ned met Joseph's eyes. "It's based on my salary."

"Your annual salary?"

"That's right."

Joseph watched him in silence for a long moment. "I don't believe you."

Ned shrugged. "I don't know what to tell you. It's signed by a judge."

"What kind of man shortchanges the mother of his child to the point she can barely afford rent? Your daughter lives in a fucking dump."

"I'm trying to get her out of that dump. That's the whole point of the motion I filed."

"I suggest you withdraw the motion."

"What?" Ned laughed. "Are you serious?"

"I'm always serious."

"I'm not withdrawing anything. I want Taylor—she'll have a better life with us." He glanced at Candice before returning his gaze to Joseph.

Joseph shifted his gaze to Candice. "I know from experience you are a lot smarter than your husband, so I suggest you talk some sense into him. If you continue down this path it isn't going to turn out well for either of you."

"Obviously you're afraid it will. Otherwise you wouldn't be trying to stop us," Ned said.

"No." Joseph's gaze returned to Ned. "I want you to stop because you're upsetting Lia. And I don't like to see her upset."

"Sorry." Ned held up his hands. "I'm not changing my mind about raising *my* daughter because you don't want Lia upset. That's ridiculous."

"Well, you better hope you're squeaky clean, Counselor, because if you're not, I'm going to prove it."

"There's nothing to prove."

"My billable rate is probably five times yours. And when I uncover the fraud in this document." He slapped the envelope against his leg. "You're going to pay me for my time."

"Is there anything else? It's late and I want to get my wife home."

"No." Joseph continued to meet his eyes.

"Have a nice evening." Ned slipped his arm around Candice and they began to walk away.

"You've become my new project, Merrick," Joseph called after him. "Welcome to the major leagues."

At 8:00 p.m. two days later, Joseph sat across from John Bianchi at the Prime Rib on K Street in DC going over the documents Joseph had couriered to John the day before. "It looks legitimate to me, Joe." John Bianchi looked up from the pay stubs and tax forms. "I agree his pay is low for an associate, but then again, I've never even heard of this law firm."

"I have," Joseph said. "And I don't believe for a second he'd leave the DA's office for eighty thousand dollars a year." He leaned back in his chair. "He's falsified documents at a minimum."

"Assistant DAs don't make a hell of a lot," John pointed out. "There's also the possibility he was only working part time so she wouldn't get much money. I see it all the time. But, just to be thorough, we'll file a motion to increase child support and I'll subpoena his time records—past and present."

"And the custody motion?"

"It's standard. I'm going to need to hire a detective to do some investigating, but given the fact she's got a steady paycheck and he left her for another woman, I don't think it'll be much of a challenge. I'd like to meet with her and make sure she doesn't have any skeletons."

"Her daughter was released from the hospital today, so sometime next week would probably be okay."

John nodded. "It'll have to be in the evening. I'll be in court all week."

"I'll check with her." Joseph picked up his menu and opened it up. "Do you want to eat?"

"Sure. I read something about you in the business section of the *Post* last month. Some kids you invested in at the University of Maryland?"

"Yes, we have our IPO next month."

"You're serious." John looked up from his menu. "You're part of an IPO? An initial public offering? What percent of the company do you own?"

"Forty."

"Forty percent? Jesus."

"You know this is the third IPO I've been part of in the past three years."

"I never heard about the first two."

"I don't know what to tell you." Joseph closed his menu and set it on the table. "I offered the opportunity to you and Prossi early on. You should have taken me up on it."

"Jesus, Joe." He shook his head. "How much money are we talking? Do you have forty percent share in these companies?"

"Not quite. I have partners." He looked up as the waiter approached. "I'd like another scotch and a filet medium rare, a Caesar salad and some asparagus if you have it."

"Do you want—"

"No, nothing else," Joseph interrupted, holding out his menu. "Oh, and a glass of merlot with the filet. Your best sold by the glass."

The waiter nodded, took John Bianchi's order and then disappeared.

"So, are we talking hundreds of thousands or millions?"

"Do you mean how much I'm investing?"

"No." John shook his head. "How much are you making?"

Joseph met his friend's eyes. "I'll put it to you this way: I made more in one IPO last year than I'll make in my entire career as a partner in the firm."

John's eyes widened. "You're fucking serious."

"I'm always serious when it comes to money."

"Then why are you still working as an attorney?"

"Because it's what I like to do."

"Are you still dabbling in the stock market?"

"Of course."

"Did you take a bath last quarter?"

"No." Joseph brought his drink to his mouth. "I take it you did."

"Nasdaq has dropped five hundred points since the first of the year. Everyone's taken a bath."

"Just sit tight. It'll come back." Joseph took a swallow of the amber liquid in his glass before setting it back on the table. "You've only lost money if you sell the stock."

"So you did take a bath.'

"No. I made more in the last quarter than all of last year."

John frowned. "How?"

"I've been selling short. When the market's on a downturn, it's the only way you can really make money."

"Isn't that risky? I mean, my understanding of the process is you're selling stocks you don't own in the hopes the price will go down, but if the price goes up you have to pay up."

"If? Hopefully I'm smart enough to pick a stock that's going to go down."

"So you sell a stock you don't even own, and when it goes down, the brokerage house has to pay you the difference between what it's going for and what you sold it for?"

Joseph nodded. "Say a stock's price is ten dollars a share, and I know it's going to take a dive. If I have enough equity in the market or liquid money in my account, I can tell my broker to sell, say, a hundred shares of the stock."

"Right." John nodded. "You sell a hundred shares of stock you don't even own."

"Correct." Joseph took a sip of his drink before continuing. "Now if the stock goes up to, say, fifty dollars a share, I'm in trouble, because my broker can tell me I owe him forty dollars a share for each of those stocks. So I'd be out a hundred times forty, or four thousand dollars."

"But that would never happen to you." John leaned back in his chair.

"That's right. Not often anyway." Joseph paused while the waitress set a salad before him. "What happens to me is this: I sell a hundred shares at ten dollars a share, hoping the price will fall. And say it does. Say later that day, the price falls to two dollars a share. Eight dollars less than I sold it for. That's my money now. I pick up the phone and call my broker and I make eight dollars times a hundred, or eight hundred dollars, and I never have to spend a dime."

"I must have a block in my head," John said, picking up his salad fork, "because that sounds counterintuitive to me. Is someone actually buying the stock you're selling?"

"Of course."

"How can you sell stock you don't own?"

"They're borrowing someone else's stock. But they're covered because, if it goes up and the original owner wants to sell, I owe the difference. If it goes down, the original owner is losing money, so either way, everyone gets their money."

"Sorry I asked. I'll leave my investing to my broker."

Joseph laughed. "It's really not that complicated. Think of it this way. If you know a bad earnings report is going to come out or some scandal is about to break, like this huge recall of cellphones in the news, you sell short. Takita had to recall six million cellphones because they were catching fire. Does it surprise you their stock price dropped fifty percent over the past week?"

"I never really thought about it, but it doesn't surprise me."

"I thought about it," Joseph said. "And I sold the stock short the first time I heard any mention of it. I didn't know how much further it would go down, but I didn't have any fear it would go back up."

"When was this?"

"I heard about it over the weekend, so I sold it first thing Monday morning."

"How much did you make?"

"I cashed in as the market closed. It had gone down thirty-five percent since Monday morning." He picked up his fork and speared a crouton.

"So how much did you make?" John repeated.

"Thirty-five percent," Joseph answered.

"In dollars," John continued, pointing at him with his fork. "How much did you make in US currency?"

"A lot." Joseph put the crouton in his mouth and began to crunch down on it. "A whole lot."

———

"That'll be your daddy," Lia said in response to the knock on her apartment door Friday evening just after 7:00. Taylor was recovering quickly and didn't seem to be in any pain, but the doctor said she needed to take it easy for at least two weeks.

"Come in." Lia stepped back from the door. She was dressed in a form-fitting black sleeveless dress, a single diamond pendant hanging from her neck.

Ned, wearing a suit and tie, stepped into the foyer. "How is she?" His eyes swept over her outfit and, for the first time in two years, she could see the male appreciation in his eyes.

"She's better. But you're going to have to carry her, because she's not supposed to go up and down stairs."

"Okay." He continued to stare at her, making no move to get Taylor. "Do you have a date with him tonight?"

"A date with who?"

"You know who I'm talking about." He took a couple of steps towards her. "Washington's most eligible bachelor."

"You mean Joseph." She smiled. "As a matter of fact, I do."

"Did he give you that necklace?" His eyes were on the two-carat diamond lying just above her breasts.

"That's actually none of your business."

"You better be careful, Lia," Ned said as he leaned towards her, their faces just inches apart. "He's apparently quite the stud."

"You don't have to tell me." She made no move to step back from him as she met his eyes. "I'm the one dating him, remember?"

Ned's smile didn't reach his eyes. "You and a dozen other women, probably. He can have any woman he wants. He dated Kathy Paige. Have you looked at her lately?" He blew out a stream of air. "I'd give my left nut to spend a night with her."

Lia could feel her heart begin to pump faster. "How nice for Candice."

"You're out of your league. There is no way you're going to be able to keep Joseph Craig's interest."

"And you care because?"

"Because I don't want to see you hurt again."

"That's a joke. You're jealous because I'm dating someone who's a thousand times more successful than you'll ever be."

"Why would I be jealous of you?" His eyes slowly traveled over her. "You're my leftovers, remember?"

She wanted to hit him, to smack him right across the mouth, but she wasn't going to give him the satisfaction of knowing how affected she was by his words. "And now you know what a mistake that was."

His eyes traveled over her for the third time that evening. "The truth is, you couldn't satisfy me anymore."

A knock at the door startled them both and before Lia had time to react, there was a second knock. She opened the door and forced herself to smile at Joseph, who was dressed in a black tuxedo, holding a single red rose in one hand and a porcelain doll in the other.

"You look stunning." He met her lips for a lingering kiss, and then he was stepping back and holding out the rose. "This is for you."

"Thank you. It's beautiful."

"And this is for Taylor." He held up the doll.

"She's in the family room."

"And this is for you." He rounded on Ned, his eyes intense and the side of his jaw clenching and unclenching. "A piece of advice." He pointed his finger in Ned's face. "Never. Ever. Speak to her like that again."

"Whoa." Ned stepped back and held up his hands. "We were having a conversation."

"Don't mess with me." Joseph continued his forward movement until Ned was backed up against the metal closet door and their faces were only inches apart. "I will destroy you."

"Are you threatening me?" Ned swallowed, clearly intimidated by Joseph, who was several inches taller and at least fifty pounds heavier.

"Oh, yes." Joseph placed his hand flat against the door beside Ned's head. "I'm threatening you. I'm definitely threatening you."

"You don't scare me." Ned met his eyes.

Joseph's lips turned up slightly. "I should." He continued to meet Ned's eyes. "The only reason you're not on the floor right now is because there's a lady present."

"Fuck you."

"You're done," Joseph whispered. "Done." He stepped back, his eyes remaining on Ned for several more seconds, and then he was turning to Lia, who was watching from a position next to the door. "I'm going to give this to Taylor." He again held up the doll.

"Okay." She nodded.

He lowered his head and met her lips for another lingering kiss. "I'll be right back."

"He's crazy," Ned said as soon as Joseph was out of earshot. "He's a fuckin' nut."

"And you're done." Lia smiled, taking a sick sort of pleasure in the fear she saw in his eyes.

Joseph apologized to Lia as soon as she closed the door on a departing Ned and Taylor. "I don't usually lose my cool like that."

"That's alright." She ran her hands up his chest and around his neck. "He deserved it."

He gripped her hips, pulling her against him. "I'm not playing around with you."

"I know." She met his eyes and could see the sincerity in the brown ones looking back at her. "I trust you." And she did. It had taken months, and she was still afraid she'd end up hurt, but she trusted him. He was nothing like Ned or Eric. And she'd fallen for him, hard. "How long were you outside the door?"

"Long enough. I was about to knock when I heard him start talking about me."

She dropped her forehead into his chest. "You heard everything? Even the stud comment?"

"Even that. I thought you handled him well, but when he started getting crude I couldn't listen anymore."

"He was awful."

"I'm not one to condone physical violence, but I really wanted to hit him today."

"I'm glad you didn't." She touched the side of his face. "He would have sued you."

"It might be worth it."

"No. He isn't worth it."

"The jury's still out on that one." He kissed her lightly on the lips.

They were in his Mercedes, on I-66 east, headed downtown to a reception, when Lia decided to broach a subject she'd been wondering about from the first day of their relationship. "Why did you stop dating Kathy Paige?"

It took Joseph a moment to respond. "I told you before—I met you."

"And that was the only reason?"

"Yes. I planned to ask her to marry me over the holidays. I had bought the ring. And then you came into my office."

Lia was stunned. "Really?"

He glanced away from the road momentarily, his eyes meeting hers. "Yes."

"But there must have been more. I mean—"

"I met you," he interrupted. "I asked you to lunch—do you think that's how I normally talk to a client?"

"I don't know." She tried to get her head around what he was saying.

"Well, it's not. And after our meeting I realized I wasn't in love with her, not enough to make her my wife, anyway. She wasn't the one."

"But you thought she was for a while."

"Because I had no clue what it was going to actually feel like when I met *the one*."

Her heart jumped at his words, and she turned her gaze to the side of the road, watching the blur of trees. "Joseph—"

"I'm in love with you, Lia. You have to know that."

She swung her gaze back to his.

"I've loved you," he said, "from the moment I saw you standing with Taylor in the lobby."

She could feel tears coming to her eyes. This beautiful, warm, incredible sexy man was telling her he loved her.

"Hey." He took her hand, linking his fingers with hers as he brought them to rest on his upper thigh. "That's not supposed to make you cry."

Lia smiled and wiped at a stray tear rolling down her cheek. "I love you too," she whispered. "I've wanted to tell you for a while, but I was afraid to say anything that would change the relationship. You make me so happy."

Joseph maneuvered the car to the shoulder of the busy road and put it into park. "This is dangerous as hell, but I have to kiss you." He cupped her face in his hands and lowered his mouth over hers, kissing her until she felt almost faint with desire.

14

Lia turned off the light in the family room as a light knock sounded on the front door just after 11:00 p.m. the following Thursday. "What are you doing here?" she asked moments later as Joseph stepped into the foyer.

"I was in the neighborhood."

"You were in the neighborhood?" She laid her hands on his chest as he pushed her back against the wall.

"I had dinner with a client." He slipped his hand under her nightshirt and cupped her breast as his mouth dropped to her neck. "I've missed the hell out of you this week."

"I'm coming out tomorrow." It was Ned's weekend with Taylor, and Lia was in the habit of spending those weekends at Joseph's condo.

"I know, but I wanted to see you tonight." His mouth moved over her neck, his body pressing hers back against the wall. "You're not going to send me away, are you?"

"What about Taylor? She could wake up and come in."

"We'll lock the door. And I'll leave before she has to get up for school."

"Are you sure?" Her voice was breathless. She couldn't think clearly while he rolled her nipple between his thumb and index finger.

"Yes." And then he surprised her by lifting her effortlessly into his arms.

"You're crazy." She laughed as she wrapped her arms around his neck.

"For you." He covered her mouth with his as he walked back towards her bedroom.

"Mommy...Mommy?" Taylor whispered, tugging on Lia's arm the next morning.

"Hmm? Yes? What time is it?" She opened her eyes, squinting at her bedside alarm clock. "Taylor, it's not even five. Go back to bed."

"You're naked. How come you're naked?"

Lia pulled the sheet up to her neck as her gaze swung to Joseph's sleeping body. "Taylor, go turn on the television. I'll be out in a minute."

"But—."

"Taylor, *Arthur's* on," she lied, knowing the mention of her daughter's favorite television show would get her out of the room. "And close the door behind you."

As soon as the door was closed, she reached over and pushed Joseph's bare shoulder. "Wake up. You overslept," she whispered. "Joseph, wake up."

"What?" He sat up and glanced around, the blanket falling down around his waist.

"You overslept, and you forgot to lock the door last night." She slipped out of bed and locked the bedroom door. "Taylor was in here."

"Did she see me?" He fell back against the pillows.

"I don't think so." She shook her head. "I'm not sure." She lifted her nightshirt from the floor and slipped it over her head. "You've got to get out of here."

"Hey." He reached for her hand. "Come here for a second."

"Joseph, there's no time. You've got to get dressed and out of here."

"Come on, just say good morning to me."

"Lower you voice," Lia whispered, her eyes moving to the door. "She'll hear you."

"She knows I'm your boyfriend."

"Mommy?" Taylor banged on the door. "Mommy, why is the door locked? *Arthur* isn't on."

Lia glared at Joseph and motioned with her hand for him to lie down before opening the door and going out into the hall. "Taylor, it's still early. I'm going to take you back to bed."

"What are you doing?" Lia sputtered a few minutes later after pulling back the shower curtain.

"I think it's called showering." Joseph raised his eyebrows.

"But you're supposed to be gone."

"You need to relax." He put his hand up in the stream of the water, causing it to spray out and get her wet.

"Joseph!" She jumped back.

"Lia!" He mimicked the sound of her voice. "You're acting like you're married and your husband's in the next room."

"Have you forgotten I'm in the middle of a custody suit?" She moved her hands to her hips. "If Ned knew you spent the night, he could—"

"Did you lock the bedroom door?"

"Yes. Why?" Lia's eyes swung towards the bedroom.

"Because you need me to make love to you again." He reached out of the shower and clasped her hand.

"Joseph, don't you dare pull me in there." She was under the spray of the shower before she completed the sentence. "Have you completely lost your mind?"

"Yes." He began to remove her wet T-shirt while she attempted unsuccessfully to flee. "I've completely lost my mind over you." He tossed the wet T-shirt in the back of the stall.

"This isn't funny." She pushed against his wet chest. "I don't want to lose her."

"You're not going to lose her." He moved his hands to the sides of her face. "I would never do something to jeopardize your case."

"But it's not setting a good example for her. I don't want her to think it's okay for men I'm not married to, to spend the night."

"Is that a proposal?"

"What?" She blinked her eyes as the water splashed against her face.

"Are you asking me to marry you?" He moved his hands to her hips.

"No." She shook her head, her heart suddenly pounding.

"Because I think I'd say yes." He covered her mouth with his and kissed her until she was clinging to his shoulders. And then he was pushing her back into the tiled wall, and moving his hand to the juncture between her legs. "Your body wants me to stay."

Lia was lost, unable to think past the "because I think I'd say yes" comment, as her body responded to his.

Thirty minutes later, she was still reeling from his words as she lay curled against him in her bed. "So, were you asking me to marry you?" Joseph asked, as if hearing her thoughts.

"You know I wasn't." She kissed him lightly on his chest.

"Because my answer is yes."

She closed her eyes, her heart rate again accelerating. "Don't tease me."

"Lia?"

"Yes?"

"Look at me. Look at me," he repeated, when she didn't respond.

She pushed herself up so she could see his face. "Joseph—"

"Do you really think I would tease you about something so serious?" He covered her lips with his fingers before she could say anything. "I'll be right back." He was off the bed and crossing to his suit jacket.

Moments later, he was on one knee beside the bed. "Give me your hand."

"Joseph?" She let him take her hand.

"You're shaking," he said.

"Are you being serious?"

"I've never been more serious. Lia, will you do me the great honor of being my wife? Will you marry me?"

Lia stared into his eyes. He was serious. And then she felt the ring. "Oh my God." She looked down at her hand. There on her finger was the most beautiful diamond she had ever seen. It was spectacular—a cushioned cut diamond of at least five carats set in a platinum setting, and it was on her finger. "Joseph?" she raised her eyes to his.

"You haven't answered me, Lia."

"Of course I'll marry you." She came off the bed and launched herself into his arms, raining kisses over his face as he fell back onto the carpet. "There is no one on this earth more perfect than you," she said, framing his face between her hands as she met his eyes. "I'm the luckiest woman alive." She lowered her mouth onto his, trying to show him with one kiss how much he meant to her.

"Mommy?" There was a click of the knob, followed by a knock on the door. "Mommy, why's the door locked?"

"I'll be right out, sweetie." Lia didn't take her eyes from Joseph's. "I love you," she whispered. "And now you really do have to leave."

"Is Joseph awake yet?" Taylor's voice came through the door. "Cause I poured him a bowl of cereal."

Lia dropped her forehead onto his chest. "Yes, he's awake." She lifted her eyes to Joseph's, attempting to frown at him, but she couldn't. Instead she was smiling. She and Joseph were getting married. She was going to be his wife.

"We'll be some role models when we tell our grandchildren you proposed to me while we were both naked," she finally whispered, happy tears in her eyes.

— ∾ —

"I think you were right about her ex-husband," John Bianchi told Joseph several hours later as they shared lunch at Kinkead's Restaurant on Pennsylvania Avenue.

"The pay stubs were bogus, weren't they?" Joseph sat up straighter in his chair.

"No. He's actually a clever guy. In fact, if the accountants hadn't screwed up what they sent us, I don't think we could have figured it out."

"Figured what out? What did you figure out?" Joseph leaned back in his chair as the waiter delivered his scotch.

"Are you ready to order?"

"Fish. Broiled. Whatever looks good." Joseph didn't take his eyes from John as he ordered.

"You get a salad and two sides with—"

"Any vinaigrette on the side, and two vegetables."

He tapped his hand impatiently on the table as he waited for John, who took considerably more time, to place his order. "What? What did you figure out?" he asked as soon as the waiter was gone.

"Up until the time he left his ex-wife, he was billing approximately sixty-five hours a week. Once he's out of the house, his billable hours go down to twenty and this continues until a month before the divorce is final, at which time it goes back to sixty-five."

Joseph frowned. "Then the time records are bogus, because there's no way—"

"Let me finish."

"Sorry." He reached for his drink.

"Like I was saying, for a sixteen-month period, he bills approximately eighty hours a month. Except"—he paused as he picked up the top sheet from the documents set out in front of him—"in June of last year, his monthly total is five hundred and twenty-five hours." He held out the sheet to Joseph.

"Five hundred and twenty-five?" Joseph frowned as his eyes scanned the sheet, which listed consolidated totals for each month. "Is this what they sent you?"

"No. One of my associates put that together. What they sent me was daily breakdowns of his time."

"So what is this? He actually billed out five hundred twenty-five hours?" Joseph shook his head. "It's impossible to log so many hours. What did he do, double bill to make up for previous months?" He brought his hand up to cover his mouth as he stared at the total for June. "But that wouldn't make sense. The divorce wasn't final. She could have gotten ahold of this."

"It didn't make any sense to me either, until I noticed the initial in front of 'Merrick.'" He waited until Joseph looked up from the paper to continue. "The time sheets in June were for C. Merrick. All the other months were for N. Merrick."

"I'm not following."

"Look at these." John handed him two more sheets. "See the employee name at the top?"

Joseph glanced at the sheets, noticing one was for the first of June with the employee name listed as "C. Merrick," and the other was the first of May with the employee name listed as "N. Merrick." "So he divided his time between two different names?"

"That's my guess. But something went wrong that month, and all the hours were charged to C. Merrick."

"But it doesn't make sense." Joseph looked from one sheet to the other. "How did he keep the C. Merrick charges from his pay statement? If he were receiving the money, it would be appearing on his biweekly statements, unless they were treated like separate employees." Joseph's eyes met John Bianchi's. "He receives two pay statements, and two W-2s, and Lia only knew about the one."

"That's my theory."

"And when his clients receive the bills, they don't notice which initial is before the 'Merrick,'" Joseph said absently.

"Correct." John paused to take a swallow from his glass. "They're paying for the services of Ned Merrick, and they receive an invoice with 'Merrick' at the top. They aren't going to care what initial precedes the name. All they care about is that they're paying for services they actually receive."

"So you think he has two social security numbers?"

"He must. Which means his law firm knows what he's doing. Which is a bit surprising, but considering his wife's father is the founding partner..." He trailed off. "Maybe one of her relatives works in their Accounting Department. It's an awful lot to risk to save what? Ten, twenty thousand? It's probably more about sticking it to his ex-wife than saving money."

"There aren't any social security numbers on the time sheets?"

"No. I've already checked. They're blacked out."

"So what do we do now?"

"That depends on what Lia Merrick wants. Unless there's a C. Merrick at Blackman and Associates, this guy is in some serious trouble."

"Wait a second." Joseph looked down at the June first time sheet. "Candice Merrick. This is his wife's time sheet."

"Then he's a bigamist, because the date of that time sheet is over three months before the divorce is final."

"Oh, right." Joseph covered his mouth with his hand as he stared at the name. "Just to be safe, I guess we should make sure there are no other Merricks at the firm."

"We already checked." John closed his briefcase and deposited it on the floor beside his chair. "He and his new wife are the only Merricks." He paused as the waiter delivered their salads.

"We've got him by the balls." John picked up his salad fork. "What? What are you looking at?"

"I still don't understand why there were so many billable hours in June."

"He's probably double billing. He screws his ex-wife. He screws his clients. He certainly wouldn't be the first."

—⁓ ⁓

Joseph was freshly showered and dressed casually when Lia arrived at his apartment later that evening. "Are you hungry?" He took her overnight bag from her shoulder and set it by the stairs before following her to the kitchen.

"Kind of." She actually wasn't, but she hadn't eaten all day and figured she needed food.

"I picked up some orange roughy on my way home. I've got it seasoned. I have to put it under the broiler, and I've got rice and asparagus cooking on the stove." He took his cell phone off the counter and looked over the note he'd jotted down after his meeting with John Bianchi.

Doesn't add up:

- Two names
- Two social security numbers
- 525 billable hours in June? Did he bill that many each month?
- What am I missing?????????

"Can I do anything?" Lia was at the stove, lifting the lid off the asparagus.

"Hmm?" Joseph looked up from his phone.

"I asked if I could help."

"Yes, in a second." He crossed to the oven and placed the fish beneath the broiler. "You can set the table. There's a salad in the refrigerator, and you can grab a bottle of Montrachet White Burgundy from the wine pantry...1986." He frowned as he looked down at his phone. "Would you watch the fish?" He left the kitchen before she responded.

"Five weeks," he said aloud moments later as he stared at the calendar on his computer. He picked up his phone and continued the note:

- 5 weeks in June so feasible that he was billing 100 hours per week
- Why the jump from 60? It's not Merrick's MO

He leaned back in his chair, staring up at the ceiling. "What am I missing?"

He sat forward and again began to type:

- Why C. Merrick when his wife would be C. Merrick? Why not something random M. Merrick or O. Merrick? Why C.??????

"Dinner's ready." Lia leaned against the doorsill of his study.

Joseph lifted his gaze to hers. "Candice did take Ned's name, right?"

"What?" She frowned.

"Did Candice take Ned's name?"

"I heard you the first time. I can't understand why that's important to you."

"I met with John Bianchi this afternoon, and there're some discrepancies in Ned's time records. I'm trying to figure something out." He came to his feet. "I need to know if she took his name."

"We have barely been engaged twelve hours."

"And?"

"And you've been distant since I arrived—I was actually starting to wonder if you changed your mind about getting married."

Joseph tilted his head to the side as he met her eyes. "You're serious. I wasn't paying enough attention to you, so you decided I didn't want to marry you? That's how much depth you think I have?"

"No, of course not. It's my past—every now and then it creeps in and makes me have irrational thoughts."

He placed his hands on her shoulders and slowly propelled her backwards until she was pressed against the wall. "What can I do," he asked deeply, his eyes looking into hers, "to make those feelings disappear forever?" He kissed her hard on the mouth as he pressed his body into hers. "I'm thirty-four years old. I've dated a lot of women—I've *known* a lot of women, and until you walked into that lobby and my life, I had no clue what it meant to love another person."

"Joseph."

"Lia, I'm serious. Tell me what I'm doing wrong. Tell me and I'll fix it."

"You're not doing anything wrong." She kissed him. "You're perfect."

"I'm far from perfect, but my love for you is perfect and it's permanent." He kissed her nose. "Okay?"

"I'm sorry. I was so excited, and then I get here and you're completely distracted."

"I'm a man. I can compartmentalize." He kissed her again. "I love you."

"I love you too." She wrapped her arms around his neck. "You make me so happy."

"Joseph...Joseph, are you awake?" It was past 1:00 a.m., and they'd been in bed over an hour.

"No," his sleep-filled voice responded as his hold on her tightened.

"Remember what you asked me earlier about Candice changing her name to Merrick?"

"Mm-hmm."

"She did. In fact, she did it months before they were even married."

She could feel his entire body stiffen, and then he was sitting up and turning on the light, flooding the room with brightness. He was awake.

— ❦ —

When Ned stepped into Lia's foyer Sunday evening, she made a conscious effort not to blurt out that she knew what a snake he was. He'd cheated her out of thousands of dollars, according to Joseph, but she wasn't able to let on that she knew because Joseph was still in the process of gathering the proof.

"Where's Joseph?" Taylor asked after hugging Lia.

"He's at home. You'll see him next week."

"But you're married," Taylor said, frowning. "I thought married people lived together. I thought he was going to live with us." She placed her hands on her hips as she looked up at Lia.

"Married?" Lia repeated, completely baffled. She couldn't believe Taylor had been listening through the door when he proposed, but why else—

"That's right," Ned said. "Apparently he was in your bed the other morning, and our daughter thinks when two adults sleep in the same bed, they're married."

"Oh." Her eyes moved from Ned to Taylor. "We're not married, Taylor."

Taylor brought her eyebrows together. "But he slept in your bed."

"I know." She rubbed Taylor's back. "He was tired."

"You're a great role model, Mom." Ned leaned back against the door and crossed his arms over his chest. "Just the type of mother judges look highly upon."

"You're one to talk," Lia bit back and then forced herself to calm down, remembering Taylor. "Say goodbye to your daddy."

"Bye, Daddy," Taylor said softly.

"Bye, baby." He bent down and gave her a hug and kiss. "I'll see you Thursday." He stood and his eyes found Lia's. "You're making this easy for me."

Lia smirked, no longer fearing he would get Taylor. "I guess we'll see."

15

ony looked up from his cell phone as Jason Broddick, a fourth-term congressman from Massachusetts and one of the firm's clients, stopped beside his table at 1789 Restaurant in Georgetown a couple of weeks later.

"Good evening, Tony."

"Jason, hello." Tony came to his feet and shook the other man's hand.

Jason Broddick was about forty with a tall, lean build, sharp features and an engaging smile. "I don't think you've met my fiancée, Brooke Eastman." Jason slipped his arm around a tall, dark-haired woman in her late twenties.

"No, I don't believe I've had the pleasure." He briefly greeted her, and then Jason was turning to the other two members of his party.

"And these are her parents, Richard and Elise. Richard, Tony is one of the founding partners at Prossi, Stuart and Craig, and of course, Senator Prossi's son."

Tony smiled politely at Elise Eastman and then was turning to Joseph's biological father. "Mr. Eastman." He held out his hand.

"Richard, please." Mr. Eastman gripped his hand. "It's a pleasure." His intense brown eyes met Tony's. "I read you'll be representing Diner Securities in the SEC investigation."

"That's Joseph Craig's case."

"I didn't realize he was a securities attorney," Richard said, his face giving nothing away.

"Joseph has a number of specialties."

"How is Joseph?" Jason asked. "I haven't seen him in months."

"He's great." Tony turned from Eastman to Jason. "Recently engaged."

"Really? When Kathy Paige couldn't land him, I didn't think any woman would."

"Well, someone by the name of Lia Merrick managed."

"I suppose there's something in the air." Jason smiled. "You're not eating alone, are you?"

"No." Tony glanced at his watch. "I'm just being kept waiting. Enjoy your dinner. It was a pleasure meeting all of you." His eyes moved over the group, which responded in kind.

"Be sure to tell Joseph and Kevin I said hello." Jason touched his arm before they continued following their host.

Tony remained standing until they took their seats at a table about fifteen feet away, and then he was picking up his scotch and moving to the other side of his table. As he sat down, he had a perfect view of Richard Eastman.

Lia felt nervous as she and Joseph followed the host to their table at 1789 Restaurant, where they were meeting Tony Prossi for dinner. He was the one man Joseph respected more than any other, and Lia knew his opinion mattered to him.

"Sorry we're late," Joseph said as they reached Tony's table. "It's my fault."

"I never doubted it," Tony said dryly as he came to his feet. "Lia, I don't believe we've ever been properly introduced. In fact, I think I was actually rude to you at our last meeting."

"It's fine." Lia smiled.

"I apologize. I had no idea what was going on with your ex-husband."

"You don't have to apologize. I shouldn't have interrupted your meeting. It really could have waited." She felt like she was rambling, but Tony Prossi had to be the most intimidating person she'd ever met. He was much warmer tonight than the man she'd encountered outside Joseph's office, but he still had an air of aloofness about him.

"Please have a seat." Tony pulled out her chair and then was resuming his own across the table. "How is your daughter? All recovered?"

"Yes, she's a hundred percent back to normal."

The waiter arrived to take their drink orders, and Lia felt herself relaxing as she watched the natural rapport between Joseph and Tony. As the evening progressed, she found herself laughing more and more as they reminisced about their days at Harvard and the early years at the law firm. Tony was definitely the more serious of the two, but Joseph clearly had the ability to bring out a lighter side of him, and Lia found herself liking him very much.

"Joseph!" Jason Broddick stopped beside Joseph's chair. "I thought that was you."

"Jason!" Joseph came to his feet and shook the other man's hand. "How are you?"

"Good. I saw Tony earlier, but I didn't realize you were joining him."

"It's been a long time. This is my fiancée, Lia Merrick."

Jason greeted Lia and then was glancing back towards his table. "I've got to get back before they bring out the cake. It's my fiancée's father's birthday."

"You're engaged?" Joseph followed Jason's gaze towards the back of the restaurant.

"Yes. Make sure you come by the table and meet her before you leave. In fact," he began as he touched Joseph's arm, "as much as you delve into the world of high finance, you'd really enjoy her father. Maybe he'll even give you some investment advice."

"Who's her father?" Again, Joseph's gaze moved to the back of the restaurant.

"Richard Eastman, so make sure you come by. Lia, it was a pleasure meeting you. Tony." He nodded. "Come by and say hello," he said again to Joseph before walking off.

Joseph remained standing as he watched Jason return to his table, and then he was rounding on Tony. "You knew?" His eyes narrowed. "You fucking knew all this time and you didn't say anything?"

"Just sit down." Tony returned his gaze.

"Fuck you!"

"What's going on?" Lia's eyes moved between the two men.

"Sit. Down," Tony repeated through clenched teeth.

Joseph dropped down into his chair. "Fuck!"

Tony leaned across the table, his eyes intense. "Get it together, Joe."

"It's too soon." He met Tony's eyes. "I'm not ready to meet him." He reached for the knot of his tie and began to loosen it. "It's too fucking hot in here."

Tony continued to watch him. "He isn't worth it."

"Joseph?" Lia touched his hand. "What's going on?"

He didn't respond as he picked up his water glass with a shaky hand and brought it to his mouth.

Tony glanced around, and then his eyes were focusing in on their waiter, who was standing at the next table taking an order. "Excuse me," his deep voice rang out, interrupting the waiter. "Pardon me," he said to the couple in the process of giving their order. "We need our check."

"Yes, sir." The waiter hesitated as if deciding whether to finish taking the order, but was rescued when the couple at the table assured him they didn't mind if he prepared the check before taking their order.

"Joseph," Lia whispered, "is everything okay?"

Joseph stared at the white cloth napkin clutched in his right hand, not responding.

"Joseph?" She touched his arm. "Please talk to me."

"What?" He lifted his eyes to hers. "What!"

She pulled her head back as if she'd been slapped, not prepared for his anger. This wasn't a side of him she had ever seen. "What's the matter?"

"Nothing. I'm fine." But he wasn't, and everyone at the table knew it. He shrugged out of the jacket.

In less than a minute the waiter returned with the check, and Tony held out his credit card, not bothering to look at it. And then he was pushing back his chair. "Come on. Let's go." His eyes were on Joseph.

Joseph's eyes moved to Tony. "No. We're not done." He squinted and gripped his forehead. "I'm not letting him ruin my evening." He picked up his spoon and dropped his eyes to his half-eaten chocolate mousse, beads of sweat evident on his forehead.

Tony leaned forward. "You don't have anything to prove. He's the asshole, remember?"

"I'm finishing my dinner."

"Joseph—"

"Please." He held up his hand, his fingers spread out. "Let's finish."

"Okay." Tony's lips were turned down as he watched his friend.

"Who is he talking about?" Lia looked to Tony when it was clear Joseph wasn't going to answer her questions.

Tony shook his head. "Let's just finish eating."

Joseph set down his spoon and brought his hands up to cover his face.

"Joseph?" Lia touched his arm. "Tell me what's wrong." Her voice was barely above a whisper, her eyebrows pulled together in a frown.

He dropped his hands from his face and gripped the arms of his chair. "I've got to get out of here." He pushed back his chair and came to his feet, his eyes briefly finding Lia's. "I'm sorry."

"I'll come with you." She began to stand.

"No! I need to be alone." And without another word he was gone, leaving her with Tony.

Lia was stunned. "I can't believe this. He left me."

"Just give him some time. He'll be okay."

"I don't understand." Her tear-filled eyes met Tony's. "I've never seen him like that. Who did he see that upset him so much? That congressman?" She could feel her face heating up, embarrassed that he'd left the restaurant without her.

"You really need to discuss this with Joseph. I'm sure he'll call you tomorrow and explain. I'll take you home."

"No." Lia shook her head. "That's okay. I'm going to go to his place to make sure he's okay."

Tony took her hand. "This is complicated, Lia, but it has nothing to do with you. Why don't you give him some space?"

Lia slowly pulled her hand from his grasp. "I don't agree. This has everything to do with me. He left me in a restaurant without an explanation. I'm his fiancée."

Tony watched her in silence for several seconds. "Okay, I'll take you to his place."

Twenty minutes later, she opened the door to Joseph's darkened condo and flicked on the foyer light. She assumed he'd come straight home, but a quick search of the apartment revealed that wasn't the case. Two hours later, there was still no sign of him, and she felt nauseous with worry.

She must have dozed off sometime during the night, because she sat up with a start when she heard the front door opening just after eight the following morning. "Joseph?" She was off the couch and in the foyer before he closed the door. "Oh my God." She covered her mouth. "What happened to you?" His royal-blue shirt was splattered with blood, and he had a white gauze bandage on the right side of his forehead.

"I crashed my car." He held up a hand when she moved closer. "I'm fine. Just a few stitches." He stepped around her and crossed to the stairs.

"Joseph. What—"

"I don't want to talk right now," he interrupted. "I've been up all night. They made me stay for observations, so I didn't get any sleep."

Lia followed him up the stairs and to his bedroom and watched as he stripped down to his briefs, pulled back the comforter and lowered himself onto the bed. He lay back on the pillow and closed his eyes.

"You have to tell me what happened. I was sick with worry. I think I deserve an explanation. You left me there at the restaurant, Joseph."

"Lia, please. Not now."

"But I want to understand. I want to help."

"You can help by letting me sleep. I'm tired. I'll explain everything after I sleep."

She wanted to press her point, but he looked pale and exhausted, so instead she turned towards the door. "Alright."

"Lia?" His voice had her stopping in the doorway and turning back to him. "Don't leave."

"I'm not going to. I was going to—"

"Come lie with me."

She crossed to the bed and slowly removed her clothes before slipping beneath the cool sheets beside him. As she lay back against the pillows, he took her hand. "I love you."

"I love you too." She wanted to say so much more, but instead she curled against him and closed her eyes.

When Joseph awoke, he was alone in the bed. He touched the gauze bandage and grimaced. He began to sit up, but almost instantly lay back down. "Lia," he called out, his voice hoarse.

Within seconds, the bathroom door opened and Lia was at his side. "How are you feeling?"

"Lousy. I think my migraine's coming back. They gave me some pills at the hospital last night. Would you look in my jacket?"

Less than a minute later she was handing him a pill and glass of water. "Do you need anything else? Something to eat?" She gently pushed his hair back, her eyes moving over the bandage on his forehead.

"No, I need the pills to kick in." He groaned. "Please close the blinds. I can't take the light."

It took her a minute, but she figured out which button brought down a darkening shade, which bathed the room in complete darkness. She was slowly making her way towards the door when Joseph's voice came from the bed. "Will you lie with me?"

"Of course. Do you want me to rub your back or something?" She slipped beneath the covers and moved her hand over his chest.

"No, just lie with me."

Lia was completely disoriented when she awoke several hours later. It was so dark, and yet she felt rested. Then she remembered the shades. She felt around for her cell phone and a moment later was squinting at the display. It was after 4:00 p.m. She'd basically slept the day away. Her eyes traveled to Joseph, who was stirring beside her, and quickly darkened her phone, hoping it hadn't disturbed him.

"What time is it?" His voice was deep with sleep.

"A little after four. How are you feeling?"

"Better. I'm sorry. God, I'm sorry." He began to sit up, but fell back with a slight moan.

"Still hurts?"

"Yes, but it's different. It could be my forehead or the lack of coffee. It's pounding."

"I could make you some coffee."

"Yes." He sighed. "But after last night, I don't deserve this."

"Shh." She kissed him lightly on the cheek. "I love you. I'll be right back."

"Oh God, my car," he said. "I need to call my insurance company and I need to call my dealer. I need to order another one."

"Joseph, no." Lia put her hand on his shoulder when he moved to sit up. "Let me get the coffee and then we can deal with the car."

He didn't argue as he lay back on the bed. "Would you bring me some crackers or something?"

"Yes. I'll be right back. Do you mind if I turn on the light? I can't see a thing."

A half hour later, after drinking a cup of coffee and eating two biscotti biscuits, Joseph began to get up.

"What are you doing?"

"I need to get my insurance information from the study so I can let them know about the accident. And I need to order another car."

"No, you stay here. You're still pale. I'll get it for you."

Joseph hesitated, but then lay back down. "There's a hidden wall in my study. When you walk, in it's the wall to the left. There's a floorboard that comes up—it's the one in the far corner of the room, farthest from the door. Lift it and you'll see a place for a key. Put the key in and turn it to the right. The wall will open and you'll see my file cabinets. Then look under I for insurance and then A for auto. Then find the folder for the Mercedes S63."

"Where's the key?"

"In my jacket beside my car key."

"Do you need anything else? More coffee?"

"Coffee would be great." He closed his eyes.

"I'll be right back." She kissed him lightly on the lips before leaving the room.

She quickly located the hidden wall and stood back in amazement as the wall disappeared into the ceiling, revealing a space deep enough to contain Joseph's massive collection of files, which seemed better suited for a company than a home. There were hundreds—no, thousands—of files housed in twelve connected maple cabinets lining the entire wall of his study. Most of the files seemed to be companies, but his personal information also appeared to be confined within the cabinet drawers. She noticed a Harvard file and peeked in to see three years of law school transcripts. The insurance section had files titled *health, life, homeowners, liability, accident* and *automobile.* The car section included only the Mercedes and his Land Rover, which was an indication he didn't hold on to outdated information.

When she opened the file labeled *Mercedes,* her mouth fell open. He'd paid one hundred sixty-four thousand dollars for his car, and there was no lien holder. She knew the car was expensive, but thought "expensive" was more like sixty thousand dollars and included a loan with a hefty monthly payment.

"I have the file," she said as she entered Joseph's bedroom.

"Would you call the number for the dealer and give me the phone?"

"Why the dealer? Do you think it's totaled?"

"I have no idea, but I don't want it anymore."

She laughed. "It's practically brand new. I'm sure your insurance will pay to fix it."

"I'm sure they will, and then it will be sold. I'm not driving a repaired car."

"But it's so expensive."

He was lying on his back with his head on his pillow, watching her. "I know exactly how much I paid for the car, and when you

dial the number for me, I'm going to order a new one. Okay?"
His eyes widened.

"Fine." She quickly dialed the number into her cell phone
before handing it to him. "I really think this is extravagant."

"Noted." He met her eyes as he brought the phone to his ear.
"Do you mind bringing me a cup of coffee?"

"Oh, I'm sorry." She left the room and when she returned a
few minutes later with a hot cup of coffee he was off the phone.

"Thank you." He was almost in a sitting position, lounging
back against a stack of pillows, his chest bare, the comforter falling at his waist. He was still a little pale, but not nearly as much
as earlier.

"Doesn't your car have airbags? I can't understand how you
hit your head."

"I wasn't wearing my seat belt. I hit a light pole. The air bags
probably saved my life."

"Oh my God." Lia covered her mouth, feeling sick inside.
He could have been killed. "What happened? I'm so confused."
She lowered herself onto the edge of the bed beside him. "You
left me at a restaurant."

He closed his eyes as if in pain, and then he was opening
them, his gaze meeting hers. "I'm ashamed of my behavior last
night. There is no excuse for what I did."

"I need to understand what happened."

"This isn't something I ever talk about."

"Tony seemed to know."

"He's the exception. I told him back in law school."

"And now you need to tell me. I'm going to be your wife.
We shouldn't have secrets. Did it have something to do with that
congressman?"

He sighed. "Indirectly. The woman he referred to as his fiancée. She's my biological half-sister."

"Your half-sister," Lia repeated, a little confused because he'd already told her he was an only child. "But not from your mother."

"No, from my father. And that's what caused me to lose control last night. I found out he was there in the restaurant."

"Your father was at the restaurant last night with the congressman?"

"Right."

"But I thought you told me you didn't know your father—that your parents never married."

"I don't know my father. I mean, I know he's Richard Eastman, but I've never met him, and last night when it seemed like I was going to for the first time, I couldn't."

"I don't understand. Does he know you're his son?" His father's name sounded familiar, but she wasn't sure why.

"He knows." He dropped his hand, his eyes once again meeting hers. "He's always known." For the second time in his life, he explained how he came to be. How his father had wanted his mother to abort him. How he'd grown up around money, but never had any of his own.

"That must have been hard," Lia said when he finished.

"It was hell. And he left us there. The son of a bitch was worth hundreds of millions and he let my mother continue to work as a maid." His lips turned up in disgust. "Even if he didn't care about her, even if she'd just been an easy lay, how could he let his blood be raised in a tiny two-bedroom house knowing I was going to school with people worth millions and knowing how different that would make me? Their fathers were presidents of banks and CEOs of Fortune Five Hundred companies, and I was the illegitimate son of a servant!"

"Joseph," Lia began, laying her hand on his chest, "calm down. You're going to give yourself another headache. He's a bad person, I agree. But he should be nothing to you. You're a successful attorney. You're a great person. Who cares about him?"

"I do." The normal warmth was gone from his expression. "I want to look him in the eyes and have him explain to me how a father could abandon his only son. I want to look him in the eyes when he answers that question."

"Why didn't you confront him last night?"

"Because I'm not ready yet. When I'm ready, I'll call him on the phone and make an appointment."

"You were fourteen when you discovered his identity. When will you be ready?"

"Soon," he answered. "As soon as I make the *Forbes* list of wealthiest Americans."

"The *Forbes* list?" She realized why she recognized his father's name. "He runs a brokerage house in New York City. He's always referred to as 'the Genius of Wall Street.'"

"Wizard of Wall Street," Joseph corrected. "But he's never made the list. I'm going to."

Her eyes opened wider, having a hard time comprehending what he was telling her. He intended to be on the *Forbes* list of richest Americans. "Joseph—"

"I'm worth over eight hundred million dollars," he said, stunning her. "I'm going to make it."

Lia stared at him, unable to believe what he was saying. He was worth over eight hundred million. She realized he was successful, even figured he made over a million dollars a year, but this—this was mind-numbing. She didn't know if she could look at him the same again.

"Say something."

"I'm speechless." She looked into his eyes, eyes that were familiar and yet suddenly not. "How did you get so much money? Did that man, Theodore Williams—did he leave you his money?"

"No. I made it myself. I started investing in stocks when I was an undergrad at Yale. I put everything I made into it. I took risks. When I graduated from law school, I had close to three million."

"How did you know what to do?" While other kids were experimenting and living it up, he was amassing a fortune.

"Williams taught me a tremendous amount, and I studied on my own. It wasn't hard, and there was luck involved. It was the right time to be in the market. I was basically a day trader."

"Luck?" She laughed. "Luck doesn't make you three million dollars."

"It helps." He pushed back the sheets and began to get up. "I'm going to put on some clothes."

She watched him walk off towards his closet, her mind still in a haze. He didn't live like he had that kind of money. He didn't have a driver or a chef or a mansion in the suburbs, or vacation homes all over the world. He drove an expensive car and wore three-thousand-dollar suits, but so did many lawyers in DC. She was still on the edge of the bed when he emerged from the closet dressed in dark cotton lounge pants and a long-sleeved black T-shirt.

"How did you go from three million to eight hundred million?"

"Investments. I'm still in the market, but I made the bulk of my money through my Angel investments."

"Angel?"

"Entrepreneurs who need cash come to me with business ideas or existing businesses. I invest in them and, in return, get a significant stake in the company. I'm a silent partner."

"Like with Nick?"

"Kind of." He sat on the edge of the bed beside her. "I own a little less than half his company, but funding him was a favor. My other investments have been in the high-tech industry."

"So, what now?"

"I make more as quickly as possible. My father announced his retirement last year. I read it in a magazine and was afraid he had something terminal, but I was wrong. But I still need to work harder. If he dies before I meet him, it would all be for nothing."

"You're serious? Your whole motivation for accruing this wealth is so you can meet your father?"

"It's a little more complicated than that. When I meet him, I want him to have no misconceptions that I'm after his money. I want him to know, to see I don't need anything from him, that I'm much more than him."

"But you don't know him. Why do you care what he thinks about you?"

"I don't care what he thinks about me. I don't care about him. But when we meet, I want him to know what he lost."

She watched him, trying to understand. "And then what? What happens after you've made the list and met him? Do you stop working, or—"

"I don't know." He shook his head. "I've never thought past that day. I suppose that's a decision we can make together."

"I don't understand how you could let someone you've never even met control your life."

"Control my life? What are you talking about?"

"Don't get mad at me," she said, taking one of his hands. "I'm trying to understand."

"Trying to understand what?"

"You're thirty-four years old and you've accrued a large fortune. And you're telling me your entire motivation for accruing this money was so a man you've never met won't think you're a gold digger."

"You don't understand." He pulled his hand from her and walked off towards the bathroom.

"That's right," Lia agreed, following. "And I'm trying to. Please explain it to me so I understand."

"Did you listen to me when I described my childhood?" he asked, turning back to her before entering the bathroom. "Can you even begin to understand how it felt to live among those people, knowing I was his bastard? You can't—you can't possibly, or you'd understand everything I'm doing. I despise him with every inch of my being and I think about it every day. Every day I think about how much I despise him, and one day I'm going to look him in the eyes and tell him that to his face. Then I'll be free." He went into the bathroom

"But you're free now," Lia said, following. "You've chosen to let this hate you have for your father control your entire life."

"That's preposterous. He has nothing to do with my life."

"It certainly didn't seem that way last night. You got yourself so upset you got a migraine and left me in that restaurant. And if what you're saying is true—if your sole motivation for making that money was to make some silly list—then you've given him your freedom."

"You have no idea what you're talking about, no idea what it feels like to be me." He walked into the separate toilet area and closed the door.

"I do know," Lia said, raising her voice. "My father rejected me too. Remember? Except my father knew me when I was rejected. Your father was rejecting your mother. He's never even known you."

"You can't compare these situations. Our lives were completely different. Your father wasn't worth millions of dollars." He yanked open the door and stepped around her.

"Joseph?" Lia followed him back into the bedroom. "Money has nothing to do with this. My brother let the rejection rule his life too. His whole mission in life has been to establish a relationship with my father."

"Money has everything to do with this." He picked up his coffee mug and headed towards the door. "Money rules the world."

"Only if we let it."

He turned back to her, meeting her eyes. "So my announcement that I'm worth eight hundred million had no effect on you? It didn't make you think any differently of me?"

"It didn't change how much I love you."

"It certainly wouldn't lessen it."

Heat came to her cheeks. "That isn't fair."

"It changed the way you look at me, didn't it? You have a little more respect for me than you did earlier today."

"That's not true! I've never cared about money."

He smiled slightly. "You're lying. When I told you, I saw your eyes. They were impressed, just like Eastman's will be, and everyone that's ever known me."

"And that's what's going to make you happy? Knowing that everyone is impressed with how much money you have?"

Joseph gave an exaggerated nod. "Yes, that and imagining how Eastman will feel when he realizes that I have more money than he does."

"So, let me get this straight," Lia said. "If your father was only worth fifty million, you would have met him by now?"

"I suppose so."

"Your whole life goal is to have more money than your father, a person you don't even know? You care so much what this stranger thinks about you."

"Forget it." He turned and headed out of the room. "You don't understand."

"You're right. I don't understand," she said moments later as she joined him in the kitchen.

"That's okay." He leaned back against the counter, bringing his coffee mug up to his lips. "It has nothing to do with you anyway, but you're going to be my wife and I wanted you to know the truth."

"It bothers me though, that you're motivated by hate. That can't be healthy."

"I haven't hurt anyone. And our children are never going to have to deal with the prejudices I had to deal with. No one will ever look down their nose at a Craig. They'll have respect from the moment they take their first breath."

"What I hope is that they respect themselves and other people." She was still having a problem wrapping her head around what he was saying.

"Come here." He set down his coffee mug and pulled Lia into his arms. "They will. They'll take after their mother."

She turned her face into his warm neck, taking comfort in his familiar smell. He was still her Joseph. He was different and yet he was exactly the same, and suddenly the conversation they'd shared wasn't nearly as important. This was the man she loved, the one she was going to share her life with. "I love you."

"I love you too, and this Eastman thing...It's something I have to do. It's separate, completely separate from us."

"Okay." She nodded, hating his obsession, but knowing it wasn't something she could undo.

"We need to set a wedding date. I want to marry you." His lips lowered to hers, and the coffee, Richard Eastman, even the money was momentarily forgotten.

16

Three and a half weeks later, a week before the custody hearing was scheduled and twenty-five minutes after his secretary buzzed him to say Ned Merrick had arrived for their 1:00 p.m. meeting, Joseph pushed the intercom button on his phone and told his secretary to send him in.

"I was about to leave," Ned, dressed in a dark suit, said after entering his office.

"You should have." Joseph lifted his eyes from his computer screen. "I'm busy and I have a lot more important things to do than save your ass."

"Excuse me?" Ned lowered himself into one of the chairs in front of Joseph's desk. "How could you possibly save my ass? Lia's the one who needs saving, considering our custody hearing is a week from today and you've been sleeping with her while my impressionable six year old is in the house. I think you should lose the cocky attitude. That's right," Ned continued when Joseph didn't comment, "I've had a detective watching the apartment and taking pictures for the past month. I think Lia needs to start packing Taylor's bags."

Joseph tapped his pen on his desk as he stared at Ned. "Are you done?"

Ned shrugged. "For now."

"I've found some discrepancies in your time records." Joseph opened a file on his desk. "It seems your wife was mistakenly billing some of your hours on her time sheets." He picked up one of Candice's time sheets and tossed it towards him.

Ned scrambled to pick it up off the floor as Joseph continued. "Your Accounting Department was generous enough to share her time sheets from June of last year with us."

"What in the fuck are you talking about?"

"You were billing approximately a third of your hours on your time sheets, and your wife was claiming the other two-thirds of your hours on her time sheets." He tossed him another sheet of paper. "Based on the June total of five hundred and twenty-five hours, I extrapolated your actual hours out over all your time sheets to correct the errors. For that month, I added a hundred and sixty. In this month"—he picked up another sheet of paper and tossed it towards him—"I added a hundred forty, in this one a hundred fifty." He continued to rattle off numbers and toss sheets at Ned until he'd accounted for seventeen months of records and there were sheets all over the floor surrounding him.

"I know it was a mistake because, if it was intentional, I'd have to report you." He looked up from the folder and met Ned's eyes. "You know, Counselor, it's a disbarrable offense to charge a client for work that wasn't performed."

"What in the hell are you talking about?" Ned was out of his chair. "That work was performed."

"Not by C. Merrick, it wasn't. The work was performed by N. Merrick, and before you waste any more of my time or insult my intelligence further," Joseph continued, holding up his hand, "we've been through the court documents. We know she wasn't even involved with most of those clients. We figure your wife owes you about a hundred thousand dollars."

"You don't know what you're talking about," Ned said, his face red. "All your conclusions are wrong."

"Like I said earlier, we believe they are legitimate mistakes, because if you were actually letting your wife receive money for services you performed so your salary would look lower during your divorce settlement, that would be a federal crime as well. You could be disbarred and go to jail. Of course, we know you're not stupid, so we'll assume it was a computer glitch at your firm. A glitch that seems to have corrected itself based on the recent data, so now there is the little matter of straightening out the prior mistake." He extracted a sheet of paper from the open file on his desk. "Based on our calculations, this is how much money you owe in back child support and rehabilitative alimony." He handed the paper to Ned.

"You're out of your mind," Ned said after studying the sheet for a few moments. "Even if your theory was accurate, which it isn't, these figures are ludicrous."

"They're based on a seventy-hour work week, and we added eight percent interest."

"Eight percent!" Ned dropped the sheet on Joseph's desk. "That's obscene."

"I think eight percent is generous on our part, considering the money should have been Lia's all along and you, or rather Candice, was borrowing it."

"I'm not paying her a dime. Go ahead and disbar me. We'll see how much money she collects then. If I'm out of work, she won't even be able to afford the apartment she's living in now, and she'll have you to thank." He leaned back in his chair and crossed his arms over his chest.

"Have you noticed the diamond on Lia's hand?" Joseph slowly came to his feet. "She's going to be my wife. And based on these figures, I make more in a couple days than you make in a year, so financially it won't make a bit of difference whether you're employed or not. In fact," he paused as he walked around the desk and came to stand directly in front of Ned, "Lia's the one who convinced me it was a mistake. I wanted to report you to the bar without this discussion. But for some reason, Lia didn't want to believe Taylor's father could be such a crook, so I told her I'd discuss it with you and give you the benefit of the doubt."

He reached behind himself and picked up the settlement paper. "It's your choice, Merrick. If it was a legitimate mistake, you can go home and, between you and your wife, scrounge together twenty-five thousand dollars and have a certified check delivered to my office within five days. If I don't receive it, I'll assume it wasn't a mistake, and I'll be forced to turn my evidence over to the bar." He held out the sheet of paper. "It's your decision."

"This is extortion."

"I don't think so." Joseph continued to look down at him. "One more thing before you go." Again, he reached back and picked up a sheet of paper from his desk. "This is the invoice for my time."

"You've got to be joking."

"I don't joke about money." He tossed the sheet of paper at Ned before resuming his seat behind his desk. "I told you at the hospital, if I found any mistakes in your divorce settlement, you'd pay me for my time. I spent twenty hours on you."

"Twenty hours," Ned repeated, looking down at the invoice. "You expect me to pay you twenty thousand dollars?"

"And that doesn't include John Bianchi's time. He said he'd send his bill directly to your office." Joseph picked up his reading glasses and slipped them on. "Any questions?"

Ned's face was pale when he lifted his gaze from the invoice. "I don't have this kind of money lying around."

"Then I recommend you take out a loan. I have another meeting in ten minutes I need to prepare for, so..." He nodded towards the door.

Ned didn't say a word as he came to his feet and headed towards the door to Joseph's office.

"Oh, one more thing." Joseph's voice had Ned turning back towards the desk. "I'm assuming when we meet before the judge next week, we'll be discussing an increase in child support, nothing more."

"No." Ned shook his head. "I still want custody."

"If that's your decision, I'll have no choice but to provide the information I've gathered about you during the hearing. If you could make mistakes like these, you really don't appear responsible enough to be a full-time father."

"You son of a bitch!" Ned crossed back to the desk. "You're blackmailing me into giving up custody of my daughter."

"Careful, Merrick." Joseph leaned back in his chair as he met his eyes. "I don't appreciate your tone or your accusation. I suggest you take a few deep breaths and walk out that door. If you don't, I'll be forced to charge you another thousand for my time."

"You—"

"Now!" Joseph interrupted, raising his eyebrows. "This discussion is over." He closed the folder on his desk. "Another word and I'll increase the invoice you're holding by a thousand dollars."

Ned hesitated only a moment before turning on his heels and leaving the office.

17

*L*ater, Lia would wish she'd never attended the private showing of Picasso's early years at the National Gallery of Art in Washington, DC, but not knowing beforehand she was going to meet Kathy Paige or see Stan Hall, she actually looked forward to the evening.

She couldn't remember ever feeling happier. She was finally debt free, thanks to the check she'd received from Ned, and her days in the small run-down apartment that had been her home for almost a year and a half were finally over. She'd gotten a generous raise at work and, by a stroke of luck, a friend of her mother's needed someone to sublet her townhouse for six months while she was out of the country. Lia had moved in a month earlier.

Joseph seemed more pleased than she was with the move. He'd been trying to convince her to leave the apartment since practically their first date and offered, on more than one occasion, to pay off her debt and finance the move. But she wouldn't let him. She wanted to pay off her obligations without his help and, as she wrote out her last check, becoming debt free for the first time since parting with Ned, she felt elated.

Everything seemed to be working out in her life, and more than a little of the credit was due to the man standing in her mother's doorway, looking incredibly handsome in a black tuxedo and holding two small boxes and a bouquet of flowers.

"What's this?" Lia asked before stepping back so he could enter the foyer.

"This," he said, before pausing to kiss her on his way in, "is for you." He handed her a rectangular box wrapped in silver paper. "The flowers are for your mother, and this," he held up a smaller box, "is for Taylor. You look sensational, by the way."

"So do you." She met his lips for another kiss.

"Joseph, Joseph!" Taylor called as she ran into the foyer, stopping and scrunching up her face when she saw them. "Kissing's so gross."

"Does that mean you're not going to give me a kiss?" He effortlessly lifted her into his arms. "Because I'd really like one."

"Well," she began, wrapping her arms around his neck, "maybe just one." She kissed him on the cheek. "You smell good."

"Do I?" He smiled at her. "This is for you, pretty girl."

"For me?" She took the box from his hand and quickly opened it. "Oh, Mommy, look! It's a heart." She scrambled out of Joseph's arms. "Put it on me, Mommy!"

"Joseph?" Lia looked up from the heart-shaped pendant surrounded by diamonds and sapphires. "Please tell me these aren't real."

"I thought of her when I saw it."

"Put it on me, Mommy! Put it on!" Taylor was jumping up and down.

"You can wear it for a little while, but this is for special occasions only." She clasped the necklace around Taylor's neck. "You can never wear this to school."

"I'm going to go show Grandma."

"Give these to her," he said, holding out the flowers.

She took the flowers and began to leave, but then suddenly turned back and threw her arms around Joseph's legs. "I love you." Not giving him a chance to respond, she sprinted off in search of her grandma.

Lia touched Joseph's cheek, a feeling of pure love swelling in her chest. "You're amazing."

"You haven't even opened your box."

"I'm serious." She kissed him softly on the lips. "I love you. Taylor loves you."

"I count on it. Now open your box."

Lia gasped when she saw the diamond necklace lying in blue velvet. Besides her ring, it was the most beautiful piece of jewelry she'd ever seen. There was a large, tear-shaped diamond in the center with dozens of smaller diamonds along the sides.

"Just as I imagined," he said after clasping it around her neck.

"Thank you for the flowers, Joseph, they're—Oh, my!" Elaine brought a hand up to cover her mouth when she saw Lia. "It's beautiful," she breathed. "Let me get my camera. You both look so nice, and I don't have any pictures of you together."

Moments later, they were standing in the family room in front of the fireplace, Joseph's arm around Lia as they posed for the camera. Within a week, a five-by-seven print of the picture would be displayed on the mantle behind them.

"Stop touching it," Joseph whispered in Lia's ear an hour later as they admired a painting at the National Gallery.

"I'm so afraid of losing it."

"It's insured. If you lose it, I'll get you another."

"I don't want to lose *this one*."

"You won't." He kissed her cheek as he pulled her into his side. "You're making your neck red."

"I'll stop," she said for the third time in fifteen minutes. "I promise I won't touch it again."

"You promise, huh?" He turned her in his arms, his hands running over her hips as he pulled her lower body into his. "And what do I get if you renege on this promise?"

"Whatever you want." She linked her hands behind his neck. "I'm yours all night."

"I have news for you, sweetheart." He kissed her softly. "You're mine all the time."

"And are you mine all the time?"

"Definitely."

A movement from directly behind him caught Lia's attention, and a moment later she found herself meeting the eyes of the very beautiful Kathy Paige. She instinctively began to break loose from Joseph.

"What?" Joseph glanced back over his shoulder. "Kathy!" He dropped his hold on Lia as he turned to greet the other woman.

"I thought that was you." Kathy touched his chest as she leaned in and kissed his cheek. "You look as handsome as ever." She ran her hands down the lapels of his tuxedo.

"And you as beautiful."

In the matter of a second, Lia went from feeling like the most beautiful woman in the world to a wallflower. Kathy Paige seemed too beautiful to be mingling with mere mortals at an art show. She looked like she belonged in Hollywood or New York or wherever other impossibly beautiful people hung out.

"Lia?"

She blushed when she realized they were both looking at her. "I'm sorry, I was just—you're beautiful," she said to Kathy before returning her brief handshake.

"Thank you," Kathy said coolly, her eyes quickly sweeping over Lia before returning their full attention to Joseph. "How have you been, Counselor? Still working a hundred hours a week?"

"Something like that. How are you?"

She bobbed her head from side to side. "Better, much better." She smiled then, and Lia wondered how Joseph had ever managed to stay away from the woman. She looked perfect. "I'm engaged."

"Really?" He raised his eyebrows. "I hadn't heard."

"It's been two weeks." She held out her left hand to show off a three-carat diamond solitaire.

"Congratulations. Who's the lucky man?"

She said a name that meant nothing to Lia, but which Joseph obviously recognized. "I hadn't heard the two of you were dating."

"Then you obviously haven't been asking about me, because we've been living together since June."

"I'm happy for you."

"So how long have you and..." She paused, glancing at Lia.

"Lia," Joseph supplied. "We've been together a little over a year."

"Really." Kathy's eyes widened as her gaze returned to Lia. "Joseph's actually the perfect man until you start pushing for a commitment."

Lia didn't think a moment could get more awkward until she saw Stan Hall walking directly towards them. Her entire body tensed up.

"Kathy, hello!" His booming voice rang out as he approached.

"Stan. Is Zurtech one of the sponsors for this exhibit?"

"No, I have a friend who—Lia?" He smiled in recognition. "Wow, you look fabulous! How've you been?"

"Fine." She dropped her eyes, memories of Eric flashing through her mind.

"Lia used to work for me at Zurtech," he told Kathy. "Is this your fiancé?" His gaze shifted to Joseph.

"Hardly. Stan, this is Joseph Craig. I doubt anyone will ever manage to get him down the aisle."

"Someone is apparently about to. I heard he was here with his fiancée, and when I heard about your engagement, I naturally assumed..." He trailed off as he held out a hand to Joseph. "I'm Stan Hall."

Joseph brought his eyebrows together as he returned the other man's handshake. "Have we met? You look familiar to me."

"Not officially, but I've seen you at exhibits in New York and here."

"He outbid you on the Paikouch pieces you wanted to buy when we were at his opening the November before last," Kathy offered absently. Her gaze was moving between Joseph and Lia.

Joseph narrowed his gaze. "You paid four hundred thousand dollars for a Paikouch. Three times what it was worth."

Stan shrugged. "To you maybe, but I was buying for myself. I don't care about market value. I wanted the sculpture."

"Obviously," Joseph said.

Lia could feel her anger growing as she listened to Joseph carrying on a conversation with the man who'd basically prostituted her. "Excuse me." She fled towards the bathroom.

"Are you engaged?" Kathy asked as soon as Lia was gone.

"Yes." He pulled his attention from Lia's departing back. "I was going to call you."

"It's okay." Her smile didn't reach her eyes. "I wish you would have told me before I made a fool of myself in front of your fiancée."

"I'm sorry." He took her hand, seemingly unconcerned with the fact Stan Hall was listening. "I didn't know how to tell you."

"We've been over for a long time. It's okay. I'm engaged too now, remember?"

"Yes." He glanced back in the direction Lia had gone. "I need to go." His eyes returned to Kathy's. "May I call you?"

"Of course."

"I'll talk to you soon." He kissed her lightly on the cheek and walked off without acknowledging Stan Hall.

Lia stared at her reflection in the bathroom mirror, willing herself to gain control of her emotions. She was so angry with Joseph. She didn't even want to see him. She was just going to get an Uber and go home. As soon as she came out of the ladies' room she saw him, leaning back against the wall, apparently waiting for her. "I'm going home."

"Okay." He brought his eyebrows together. "Are you okay?"

"Actually, no." She walked past him towards the exit.

Joseph caught up with her in several strides, gripping her arm. "Are you ill, or—"

"Or." She pulled her arm from his grasp.

"Lia?" Joseph followed her to the glass doors leading outside and again took her arm. "Would you wait for me to get your wrap? It's cool outside."

"Fine. Get my wrap." She continued to stare straight ahead.

"What is wrong with you?" He stepped into her line of vision and tilted his head to the side as he met her eyes. "Are you upset with me?"

"I want to leave. Are you going to get my wrap, or should I?"

The short drive to his condo was made in complete silence. "Are you planning to share with me what I did to upset you?" he asked after following her into his foyer.

"If you haven't figured it out on your own, there's really no point." She hung her wrap in the closet and walked towards the family room.

"I have no idea what I did. Don't be like this."

Lia stopped before the large windows overlooking Pennsylvania Avenue, her arms crossed over her chest, her back to him as she stared at the street below. "How do you want me to be? Do you want me to be okay with the fact that my fiancé—the man who's supposed to love me more than anyone else in the world—shook hands with and chatted about the price of a sculpture with the man responsible for prostituting me?" She turned to face him, more hurt now than angry.

"Lia," he began softly, "I wasn't—"

"And I guess you also want me to be okay with the fact you did everything in your power not to admit to your beautiful ex-girlfriend that I was your fiancée?"

"You don't understand."

"You're right, so why don't you try to help me? Help me understand why you didn't want her to know I'm your fiancée. Are you embarrassed of me because I'm not as beautiful as she is?"

"That's absurd. No one is more beautiful than you." He reached for her.

"Don't." She put up her hands as she took a step backwards.

"Don't what?" He frowned. "Don't touch you? I love you."

"It didn't feel like it back there."

He moved his hands to his hips, his eyes not leaving hers. "You're right—I didn't want her to find out about us while I was standing there with you. I didn't want to cause her more pain than I already have. When I ended the relationship, she was hurt. And I meant to call her and tell her about the engagement before someone else did, but I hadn't gotten around to it, and then we ran into her and I didn't know how she'd take it—"

"She's engaged to someone else." Lia crossed her arms over her chest.

"I'd already introduced you when I found that out."

"You could have told her. You had a perfect opportunity when she asked how long we've been dating."

"Please don't read anything into this. I dated Kathy for over a year, and she was torn up when I ended it with her. She thought I was going to marry her, and the truth is, when I saw her today, I didn't want to tell her in front of you. I knew it would hurt her."

"And what about me? Were you concerned with hurting me?"

"I'm marrying you." He lifted her left hand, looking pointedly at her engagement ring. "I would think that would be enough validation of my feelings."

"So you didn't have any regrets when you saw her? Any lingering feelings?"

"No, Lia. No regrets. No lingering feelings. I'm in love with you. Only you. And as far as this thing with Stan Hall went, I wasn't chatting with the guy. I knew exactly who he was and what he'd done to you, but I was trying to figure out why I recognized him. And then how he could afford a sculpture worth more than he makes in a year. Plus, I didn't want him to know I knew what he did. I still plan to expose him."

"I don't understand." Lia frowned. "How could he not know you know? You must have sent Zurtech a letter when they asked me to pay back the six thousand. What reason did you give them for not paying it back?" He dropped his eyes and she instantly knew he'd sent them the money. "You paid them the six thousand?"

"Yes."

"Why?" She was completely confused. "Why would you do that? I told you under no circumstances would I pay them back. I said they'd have to sue me to get the money, and you agreed. What changed?"

He dragged a hand down his face, pausing with it on his mouth. "I didn't want them to know we were investigating them. I had a detective looking into their operation, trying to prove our case, and if they knew I was representing you, they may have started covering things up."

Now she was even more confused. "But you said there wasn't a case. You told me there wasn't enough evidence."

"Right." He nodded. "And I hired a detective to, hopefully, find some."

"And what happened with this detective? Did he find anything?"

"No. Unfortunately, he couldn't find any more proof so I called off the investigation."

"I'm still not sure we shouldn't have called the police," she said. "I mean, at least that way Stan Hall would know he was under investigation and he might have thought twice before exploiting more innocent women."

"And you would have been humiliated in the process. Calling the police would have been a terrible idea. You would have been the only one hurt."

WHEN I SAW YOU

"I was already hurt. Maybe I could have spared another woman the same humiliation." She hated knowing Eric Nettles was still out there, taking advantage of innocent women.

"Most of those women were willing participants like Claudia. You were the anomaly."

"I don't know if that's true," Lia said, shaking her head. "I wish I had never let you talk me out of going to the police, because I guarantee if I had gone to the police last year when I wanted to, he wouldn't have come up to us tonight, and for that reason alone it would have been worth the embarrassment of having to tell my story."

"You did not want to put yourself through that. And I promise you, Stan Hall will get his."

"How? How is he going to get his? You said there was no proof."

"It'll catch up to him," he said after a long pause. "Everything does eventually."

"Yeah, well." She shook her head. "I'm not going to hold my breath."

Two days later, Joseph met Kathy for dinner at a Thai restaurant in Alexandria, Virginia. After several minutes of superficial conversation, he turned the conversation to Stan Hall.

"How do you know the guy from Zurtech?"

"Stan? I've known him for a couple of years. He comes into my gallery. He has an extensive collection of his own. Why do you ask?"

"I don't know. It seems kind of odd to me a man that works in marketing at Zurtech can afford to spend four hundred thousand on a sculpture."

"Oh, that's not his only job. He owns Tia Tacos. He and his brother, actually." She glanced at her watch. "We've been here exactly twenty-eight minutes and neither of us has mentioned the fact that the other's engaged. Pretty weird, huh?"

"I don't know." Joseph looked down at the scotch in his glass before meeting her eyes. "Phil's a great guy. I'm sure he'll make you happy."

"He is, and he will. I hope I can make him happy too."

"You're an extraordinary woman. I'm sure you won't have any problem making him happy."

"I couldn't make you happy."

"You made me happy for a long time."

She turned her lips up in a halfhearted attempt at a smile. "We had some great times together."

"We did." He put his elbows on the table as he leaned forward. "I'm sorry for not calling and letting you know about the engagement. I know I should have, and I meant to."

"Joseph." She touched his hand. "It's okay, really. I've moved on and I'm happy. I love him very much and he loves me. I always had insecurities with you. With him it's different—it feels right. Do you know what I mean?"

"I think so. I want you to be happy."

"I know you do." She sighed. "Is she the one? The one you can finally open up to? Share your fears, your dreams, your life?"

"Yes. She is the one," he answered.

"I hate her," she teased. "Actually, I'm sure half the women in the city do. What makes this Lia Merrick so special? Why is she the one?"

"It's hard to explain. But the moment I saw her, before I even knew her name, I knew she was the woman I was going to marry. I felt it."

Her eyes widened. "I think I really do hate her. It was really love at first sight?"

He chuckled. "Yes. And then I had to convince her. Fortunately, it worked out."

"I'm sure it didn't take much convincing."

"It took four months to get her to agree to a date."

Kathy's eyes widened again. "That must have been a first for you. How did that make you feel?"

"Determined."

— —

Joseph closed the Zurtech file and leaned back in his chair, his eyes staring unfocused at his computer screen. He glanced at his watch. It was almost midnight. He picked up his cell phone and quickly sent Lia a text. Within seconds, his phone was ringing.

"You're up late," he said.

"I was dozing. Your text woke me. I'm on the couch."

"I need to ask you something, and I need you to be one hundred percent confident in your response."

"Okay?"

"Did you ever have sex with Eric Nettles in the Zurtech house?"

"What? No! Of course not. I can't believe you would ask me that."

"I'm sorry, but I needed to know. I didn't tell you this earlier because I didn't see the relevance, but the bedrooms were being video recorded."

"Video recorded?" Lia gasped. "Why?"

"I'm not sure exactly, but before we delve deeper, I wanted to make sure there was no possibility you were on any of the videos. I'm sorry."

"Are you opening the investigation again?"

"I think so. It's late—let's talk tomorrow."

As soon as he ended the call, Joseph was calling Sam Malone. "Good, you're up. I need you to find out if Stan Hall is on Tia Tacos' payroll. I think you may have missed something." He set down his phone and opened the Zurtech file, flipping through the various pages until he came to the client sheets for Alan West. His eyes scanned the information and then he was again sitting back in his chair, rubbing his chin as he stared up at the ceiling. After several minutes, he sat up and leaned over his computer, typing "money laundering" in his Internet search engine.

—⁓   ⁓

"Are we ready?" Joseph sat down at the conference table in Tony's office the following afternoon, ten minutes early for a 4:00 p.m. meeting with a new client.

Tony looked up from the open file on his desk. "You tell me."

"Mr. Craig?" Tony's secretary poked her head into the office. "Sam Malone is here to see you. He doesn't have an appointment, but—"

"Start the meeting without me, Tony." Joseph was out of his chair and headed towards the door.

Kevin Stuart stepped out of his office just as Joseph passed. "Joseph, can we talk for a few minutes before the meeting?"

"No." Joseph didn't look at him or slow his pace. "You're going to have to start without me. Something's come up."

"What?" Kevin practically ran to keep up with him. "The only reason we're having this meeting at four is because you couldn't make it at any other time."

"And now I can't make it at four." Joseph rounded the corner and moved into his reception area. "Sam, how are you?"

The detective slowly stood up. "Good." He shook Joseph's hand, and then his eyes shifted to Kevin, who had moved up behind them.

"Let's go into my office." Joseph gestured towards the open door. "Hold my calls," he told his secretary as he followed Malone.

"Joseph!" Kevin was on his heels. "What is going on?"

"Nothing that concerns you. I'll be there as soon as I can." He closed the door in his face before turning to Malone. "What did you find out?"

"Stan Hall is on the board of directors for Tia Tacos and acts as an advisor."

"An advisor?" Joseph repeated as he dropped down behind his desk. "I'm assuming he's a paid advisor?"

"Yes." Malone remained standing. "He was paid seven million dollars last year for his advising, according to my contact at the IRS."

"Seven million! Jesus, Sam, how could you miss this?"

"I was concerned with Zurtech. And he wasn't an owner. I knew his brother was the sole owner."

"You told me when he met his wife, for Christ's sake! Jesus, Sam. This is something you should have known in the first fucking week."

"Probably," Malone reluctantly agreed.

"Sit down." Joseph leaned back in his chair. "I think your blackmail theory was right."

"I thought you said the clients would never come back if they were being blackmailed?"

"Right—I think he was blackmailing very specific clients. And I'm sure once they were blackmailed, these clients didn't come back." He linked his hands behind his head as he met Malone's eyes. "None of this has to do with marketing. Someone who is already worth millions of dollars—hell, I know he's worth that in art alone—someone worth millions isn't going to risk their entire reputation, or freedom for that matter, by prostituting his female employees to increase his sales numbers. It never made sense."

"I agree. Blackmail makes more sense."

"I read something interesting online last night," Joseph continued. "The Mafia used to own a lot of movie theaters because it was a cash business, and the number of movie tickets sold couldn't be verified. This was back before computers. They would claim to sell three, four, even five times more tickets than they actually did and launder their illegal cash through the theater."

Malone nodded, a slight smile coming to his face. "And a food truck is like a movie theater. A mostly cash business, with no real proof about how much food is being sold."

"Exactly," Joseph said. "Stan Hall is probably blackmailing clients and funneling money through his brother's business."

Malone stood up and began to pace back and forth in front of the desk. "I'm going to need to put a tail on Rodriguez again—and probably get into his house, if you want proof."

"Whatever it takes. Hire as many people as you need. I want you to find the proof. Just don't get caught."

After Malone left his office, Joseph's eyes focused on his small desk calendar. It was April twenty-ninth. He reached into side drawer, took out a *Fortune* magazine and looked at the cover. A picture of Richard Eastman was looking back at him. He smiled and tapped it lightly on his desk.

Sorry I'm late," Joseph said as he entered Tony's office a few minutes later. He shook hands with the potential clients and within minutes was running the meeting. An hour later, as the elevator doors closed on the clients, he turned to Tony and Kevin. "They were sold. They'll be calling by tomorrow morning."

"If they do, it's no thanks to you." Kevin glared at him. "I'm tired of my schedule having to adapt to yours! You seem to think this entire firm revolves around you."

"I don't have the time or energy for you right now. I have hours of work left before I can call it a night, and I'm not going to waste any of them on you." He turned to walk off.

"You're a senior partner in this firm and you're notoriously late for meetings, some that you're supposed to run. I'm tired of covering for you."

"Then don't." Joseph turned back to him. "Don't cover for me. It's funny that you're the only one who ever complains about me, Kevin. I don't hear my clients complaining, and that's what's ultimately important, isn't it?"

"No. What's ultimately important is the reputation of this firm, and you've jeopardized it more than once with your frat-boy behavior."

"Fuck you! You are such a Goddamn hypocrite. You have no problem taking your share of the money I bring in to this firm, so don't start with that holier-than-thou attitude. I've had about as much of your shit as I'm willing to take. And I don't need it! I work my ass off and bring in a hell of a lot of money and business, and you'd better start remembering that and start treating me with some respect!"

"Respect?" Kevin sneered. "That would take an Oscar-winning performance, and—"

"Enough!" Tony's eyes flew between them.

"Then tell him to get off my back!" Joseph yelled.

"Let's take this into my office," Tony bit out. "I think we've given everyone enough to gossip about for one day."

Moments later, Tony slammed the door to his office and turned angrily on his partners. "This has got to stop," he said, his eyes darting from Joseph to Kevin. "I am so fucking tired of listening to the bickering between the two of you. I have more important things to do than play the mediator to my partners. If you can't figure out how to make this work then we're going to have to figure out how to dissolve this partnership, because it's gotten to the point where it's starting to affect the professional-ism of this office. For years I was the only one who knew the two of you couldn't stand each other. Now every person at this firm knows, and they're starting to talk."

18

wo weeks later, associates of Sam Malone broke into the
house of Marcos Rodriguez. Surveillance had revealed
Rodriguez worked out at a nearby gym for an hour and
a half at the same time five days a week. It took exactly seven
minutes to locate a box of thumb drives, which was in a storage
area off the basement, and a laptop computer, which was in an
upstairs bedroom.

At the exact same time, eleven miles away, another associate
was driving a dark van with the logo of a major computer manu-
facturer into the driveway of Stan Hall's house. Surveillance had
revealed Mrs. Hall took her daughter to a biweekly gymnastics
class, leaving a ten-year-old boy alone in the house for a brief
time after school. "Yeah?" The young boy opened the front door
of the house in response to the doorbell.

"Is this the Hall residence?" A man with a computer company logo on the breast of his shirt stood on the porch.

The boy nodded. "Yes."

The man looked down at the clipboard in his hand. "I have a work order on Mr. Hall's computer, if you can show me where it is."

The boy stood back to let him enter before leading him to his father's study. "It's right on his desk."

Thirty minutes later, the man left the house with copies of hundreds of files.

— —

"Finally." Lia was curled up beneath a blanket on the couch in Joseph's family room when he arrived home after midnight the following Friday.

"I'm sorry." He loosened his tie as he lowered himself onto the couch beside her feet. "Did you eat?"

"It's almost twelve thirty in the morning. I ordered pizza hours ago. It's in the refrigerator if you want some."

"In a minute. There's something I need to tell you, and I think it'll probably come as quite a shock."

"Does this have to do with where you were tonight?" She pushed back the blanket and sat up beside him.

"Yes. I was meeting with a private detective about Zurtech."

"And?" she prompted, her heart rate accelerating.

"And Stan Hall has been running a blackmail scheme. He was recording the sex and blackmailing the CEOs of some fairly large corporations."

"Oh my God." Lia brought a hand up to cover her mouth. "Eric was being blackmailed?"

"No." Joseph shook his head. "Hall was blackmailing specific clients—clients meeting a defined profile. They were married with children and had stellar reputations. He was blackmailing clients who had everything to lose and could easily afford to pay."

"How do you know? I mean, how did he find out?"

"I'm not sure exactly how my detective got the information, but I have copies of the blackmail letters with the names and addresses of the men being blackmailed, the amount of money demanded and the PO boxes where the payment was to be sent, which changed with each letter. I also have hundreds of videos that have been made over the past few years."

"He's disgusting. He was using those women so he could blackmail clients? It didn't have anything to do with the sales? I mean, that wasn't what was motivating him?"

"No. That was a bonus. If he received the money he asked for over the last three years, which is as far back as the letters go, he collected over twenty-six million dollars."

"Twenty-six million dollars," she repeated. She couldn't believe it.

"He blackmailed five men. It started with Alan West—a family man who preaches family values. I think those detailed client files were used by Hall to decide who had the most to lose."

Lia combed her fingers back through her hair, trying to absorb the information. "So where were you all this time, at the police station?"

"No. I was going through the evidence."

"When are you going to the police, tomorrow?"

"I'm not taking the information to the police. I don't want my name or your name associated with this case."

"How can they not be? We were involved. You have the evidence."

"That's right. I do. And I'm not taking it to the police."

"Then I'm confused. What was the whole purpose of uncovering this information if it wasn't to go to the police? If you don't want our names associated, what are you going to do with the information?"

"I'm going to send my evidence to the *Washington Post*."

"The *Washington Post*? Why?"

"So I can expose Hall and Zurtech for what they made you and countless other women endure. I want him to turn on the television or go online and see himself as headline news. In that brief moment, he'll know he's been destroyed."

"But wouldn't going to the police do the same thing? I mean, wouldn't it end up in the paper anyway?"

"Eventually, but then we'd be involved and they'd want to know where we got the information, and they'd want to talk to you. I don't want you to have to go through any of that."

"But aren't I part of the proof? My story?"

"I don't need it. All I need to provide are the videos, blackmail letters, client files and some emails from Claudia. I have proof that he's been using female employees from Zurtech in a sexual blackmail scheme. That's enough. The police will easily be able to unravel the rest." He came to his feet. "I'm going to heat up the pizza and then we'll talk some more."

"But what about Eric?" She gripped his hand. "Why did Stan let him get off scot-free? I mean, why would he do that?"

"So he'd spread the word. It's common knowledge Zurtech provides this...this—"

"Service?" She felt sick. "You're telling me that people know this is going on and no one has done anything to stop it?"

"It's considered one of the perks of doing business with Hall. And considering ninety percent aren't being blackmailed, no one's complaining."

"That's disgusting."

"It is, but don't worry," he said, squeezing her shoulder. "When this story breaks, Hall isn't the only one who's going to be exposed."

— ~

Joseph met with Sam Malone the following Thursday evening to finalize the contents of the package that would be delivered to Richard Haze, a Pulitzer Prize—winning investigative journalist on staff at the *Post*, after 4:00 p.m. Friday.

After a morning meeting on Friday, he closed himself in his office with strict instructions to his secretary not to let him be disturbed.

At 2:15 p.m., Kevin Stuart, who moments earlier assured the secretary he could indeed disturb her boss, strolled into his office. "Did you get my email this morning? The Media Group needs to meet with you in twenty minutes," Kevin said, referring to one of their clients.

Joseph didn't look up from his computer. "I'm not meeting with anyone today. I sent an email out Monday morning saying I wouldn't be available for anything after noon today."

"Something's come up they need to discuss with you today." Kevin approached the side of his desk. "What in the hell?" He squinted at the computer screen. "You're playing with your stock portfolio."

"That's right." Joseph minimized the window. "If you're having the meeting without me, that's fine. But it's your choice— I gave you plenty of notice that I would be unable to attend."

"And this is why?" Kevin gestured towards the computer. "So you can fool with the stock market?"

"Go away."

"You're a Goddamn partner. What kind of example do you think you're setting for the associates when you'd rather play around with your stocks than attend meetings?"

"I don't care what you or anyone else at this firm thinks about me. I told you four days ago I wasn't available this afternoon. If you scheduled a meeting, that's your problem." He lifted his eyes. "Now please. I am busy. I'd appreciate if you would leave."

"You're unbelievable!"

Five minutes later, a light knock preceded Tony's entrance. Joseph lifted his gaze, cursing softly under his breath. "Is Sonya out there?" he asked, referring to his secretary.

"Yes, and she told me you didn't want to be disturbed."

"That's right," Joseph said shortly. "I am working on a deadline here. I sent an email Monday telling everyone I wouldn't be available after noon today. And I don't have time for this right now."

"Deadline for what? What case are you working on?" Tony lowered himself into one of the chairs in front of Joseph's desk.

"You know what I'm working on. I'm sure Kevin ran to your office as soon as he left mine."

"So you're working on your stock portfolio."

"Yes." Joseph gave an exaggerated nod. "I'm working on my stocks, and yes," he continued, holding up a hand before Tony could say more, "they are more important than any client, so I'd appreciate it if you'd leave me alone." He dropped his gaze back to his computer. "Come back when the market closes and I'll be happy to talk to you then."

"So, what? Now you'd rather be a stock broker than a lawyer?"

"At this moment, yes. At four, no." Joseph met his friend's eyes. "This is important, Tony. I'm working with some serious money and I can't afford to be distracted."

Tony crossed his arms over his chest. "Funny you should choose the word distracted because that's what you seem to be. This case is worth a lot of money to this firm. And you seem to be putting your personal finances in front of the finances of this firm."

"Are they worth fifty million dollars to us?" Joseph asked with an intensity usually reserved for the courtroom. "Because that's the amount of money I'm playing with right here." He gestured with a thumb towards his computer.

"You think you're going to make fifty million dollars on the stock market today?" Tony asked. "Are you listening to yourself?"

"Yes, I am listening to myself, but apparently no one else is. I am not playing here. I am working with fifty million, fifty million real dollars, fifty million of my own money." He put his hands on his desk and pushed himself up. "And I don't want to lose it. I don't want to screw up what I'm working with, so please let me finish what I'm doing!"

Tony stared at him. "You have fifty million dollars in the stock market?"

"No. I have about five hundred million dollars in the stock market. And if you leave me alone like I'm asking, I think I can make a lot more."

Tony continued to stare at him, his expression unreadable.

"Now will you leave me alone?" Joseph asked. "You can ask me anything you want at four."

"Well?" Kevin asked as soon as Tony closed the door to Joseph's office. "They'll be here in ten minutes. Is he coming out?"

Tony shook his head. "No. Collins is going to have to handle it himself," he said, naming the junior partner working with Joseph on the case. "Just tell them Joseph can't make it."

"Because he's playing around with his fucking stock portfolio?" Kevin whispered as he followed Tony down the hall towards his office. "He's not going to meet with one of our most impor-tant clients because he's too busy trading stocks?"

"Apparently." Tony walked into his office.

"And you don't have a problem with this?"

"I don't think it really matters whether or not I have a prob-lem." He sat down behind his desk. "He's an equal partner in this firm. This is his client we're talking about. And he says he's too busy to meet with him."

"But he's not even working! Not on a case."

"Look. I don't want to argue with you. I agree with you, but Joe has a point. He sent us an email Monday saying he wouldn't be available. If he wasn't in the office, you would have just told Collins to take the case."

"But he *is* here. He's sitting at his desk."

"Joe bills more hours than either of us. I really don't think we're in a position here to say much."

"No." Kevin shook his head as he began to pace back and forth in front of Tony's desk. "He *used* to bill more than either of us. For the past few months he's been behind, and it's not be-cause we're suddenly billing more hours."

Tony frowned. "I guess that's a result of Lia. He—"

"This has nothing to do with Lia. He's still here sixteen hours a day. He's just more interested in his other investments than the health of this firm."

"Okay. Okay." Tony held up his hands. "So he isn't billing as many hours. He still works a hell of a lot and brings in clients, and he's still the best trial attorney I've ever seen."

"He's changing, Tony. He doesn't put the needs of this firm first anymore."

"So what's your point? You want to dissolve the partnership?"

"I don't know." Kevin stopped pacing. "He isn't a hundred per-cent anymore. I do not like the idea of dissolving this partnership, but I want him to shape up. He isn't putting this firm before his personal life. I don't want him to blow off meetings, or come late to meetings, or leave meetings because Sam Malone or Lia or his Goddamn partner from one of his companies calls."

"He doesn't need to work eighty hours a week anymore. You want him to act like he did when we were starting up, and I don't see that happening."

"So, what? You're not going to say anything to him? You're just going to let this continue?"

"That's right. And be honest, Kevin. No one's complaining—not one client. I'd advise you to stop pushing him unless you want his name off the placard in the lobby."

"I would never be so lucky. You think he's going to walk out? Just quit? He's not that stupid. He likes the respectability of being connected to this firm. And I'm sure he's become accustomed to these nice paychecks. If he went out on his own, it would take him a long time to get back to this level."

"Don't you get it, Kevin? He doesn't need this firm anymore. He's working here because he likes to practice law. He doesn't need the money."

"Neither do I, and I never have, but you don't see me blowing off meetings."

"Joe has gotten to the point where he's making a lot more money on his investments than he is working for this firm."

"What are you talking about?"

"He's in his office right now playing with fifty million of his own money. That's right," he continued when Kevin looked at him in disbelief, "fifty million."

Kevin quickly composed himself. "So what?"

"So, maybe you need to decide what's more important to you—having him around the way he is or not having him at all. I, personally, don't want to see him leave."

"If he can't start putting the firm's needs ahead of his personal investments, he's making his own decision. It's only a matter of time before his clients start to notice. And for the kind of money he charges, they're not going to put up with it."

Joseph came into Tony's office a few minutes past 4:00 p.m. and, after pouring himself a glass of scotch, dropped down into one of the chairs in front of Tony's desk. "I apologize if I was short with you earlier."

"It's okay." Tony turned down his mouth and shrugged. "You had a lot of money on the line. It's understandable."

"Yeah." Joseph blew out a stream of air as he crossed one of his legs over the other. "About the money. I, uh. I didn't mean to tell you that way. It just came out."

"It's none of my business. I admit I was a little shocked, but it's none of my business."

"I'm making it your business. I've made some smart investments over the years and I've managed to accrue some money."

Tony laughed. "I'd call five hundred million a sizeable fortune."

"Actually, it's more like eight hundred million."

Tony stared at him. "This money is from investments?"

"Yes. Most of it is from the Angel investments, but also stocks and real estate."

"Jesus, Joe. This is hard to take in. How come you never mentioned it before?"

"I was never pissed off, I guess. I tried to get you to invest."

"Did you really need to say that? I mean..." He laughed. "I can't fucking believe it. You have eight hundred million? Since when?"

"I've been accruing it since college."

"Why didn't you tell me how much money you were making? Maybe then I would have taken more of your advice."

"You've always been conservative with your investments. I was willing to lose it all."

"What were you investing in today that was so important?"

"Nothing in particular. A number of different companies I've been following."

"Do you manage this money yourself?"

"Yes."

Tony linked his hands behind his head, his eyes continuing to study his friend. "You've impressed the hell out of me, Craig."

Joseph shrugged. "I'm the same person I was this morning."

"Not quite."

— —

Joseph was sitting behind his desk in his study at 4:30 Monday morning, his eyes scanning articles in the *Washington Post*.

"Fuck." He reached for his cell phone. "Sam, it's Joseph Craig. I want you to send the same information to the *New York Times*, CNN, NBC, CBS, FOX and ABC. Call and let me know you received this message." He set his phone back on his desk, his eyes returning to the computer.

Fourteen hours later, Joseph was in his family room watching the evening news, when his front door opened. "What in the hell?" He stood up, his eyes moving to the foyer.

"Joseph?" Lia called. "Are you home?"

"What are you doing here?"

"I was going to surprise you and make dinner." Her arms were full of bags. "I didn't expect you home for a couple more hours. Aren't you happy to see me?"

"Of course." He removed the bags from her arms and followed her to the kitchen. "Where's Taylor?"

"With my mom. There's no school tomorrow, so she's going to keep her overnight. Why are you home so early?"

"I don't know. I felt like coming home early." He set the bags on the island in the kitchen. "What are you making?"

"Shrimp scampi over linguini and a salad."

"Sounds good. I was watching the news." He gestured with his hand towards the family room. "Do you mind?"

"No, of course not, go ahead." She watched him cross towards the family room. He was still preoccupied with the Zurtech information, she realized. He'd expected something to come out over the weekend and barely left his computer. Now it was Monday, and he was even more distracted.

Twenty minutes later, the salad made and scampi warming on the stove, Lia walked out into the family room carrying two glasses of wine. "Wine?" She sat down next to him on the couch and set the wine glasses on the coffee table.

"Hmm?" He turned away from the television. "Did you say something?"

"Yes, I asked if you wanted wine." She looked pointedly at the glass she'd set in front of him.

"Sure. Thank you." His eyes returned to the television as he raised the glass to his lips.

"How was your day?"

"Hmm?" He glanced away from the television momentarily before immediately returning his attention to CNN.

"I asked how your day was."

"Fine." He picked up the remote and began to flick between channels.

"What are you trying to find?"

"Hmm?"

"Joseph, do you want me to leave?"

"No, of course not." His eyes didn't leave the television screen.

"You're waiting for news about Zurtech, aren't you?" She'd promised herself not to bring it up, but she couldn't stop herself.

"No, I'm watching the news."

"Joseph." She took the remote from his hand. "You're not watching the news. You're consuming the television." She pushed the off button.

"Hey!" He reached for the remote, his brows pulled together in a frown. "Turn it back on."

"No." She shook her head as she held the remote out of his reach. "You're so obsessed with Zurtech and Stan Hall, you can't even give me a minute of attention. It's ridiculous. I mean, I'm the one who should be obsessed with it. Not you."

"I was watching the news." He threw his hand towards the television. "Fine. Keep it off." He crossed his arms over his chest and leaned back on the couch.

"Joseph, will you please talk to me? Why is this suddenly so important to you? Until we ran into Stan Hall, you hadn't even mentioned it in at least six months."

"I've invested a lot of my own time and money in this case, and I want to see it completed. I want to know it wasn't all for naught. I want the information released. Is that so difficult to understand?"

She was getting on his nerves, Lia realized as she met his eyes. For the first time in their relationship, he wasn't thrilled to see her and certainly didn't seem to want her in his house. "I'm leaving."

"What?"

"I said I'm leaving." She was off the couch and headed towards the foyer. "And don't pretend that's not what you want. It's all over your face."

He cursed softly under his breath before following her to the door. "Don't go." He reached out and took hold of the strap of her purse as she opened the front door. "I don't want you to leave."

"Yes, you do." She glanced back over her shoulder. "I don't understand this. Is this about revenge or something?" His preoccupation with Zurtech reminded her of the time he was so preoccupied with Ned's time records.

"Close the door." He pulled back on her purse until she took a couple of steps backwards. "I'll push the article from my mind and we'll have a nice, quiet dinner—television free. I promise. I just want them to pay for what they did to you."

Joseph was wiping down the counters when the phone began to ring an hour later. He tossed the sponge in the sink before picking up his cell phone and looking at the display. "Turn on the television," Tony's voice said over the line. "ABC is reporting Zurtech was taking videos of female employees having sex with clients in order to run a blackmail scheme."

By midday Tuesday, Joseph was up by over two hundred and fifty million, and on Wednesday he cashed in, completely disassociating himself from the unfolding scandal.

After working tirelessly from the day he found the letter from Richard Eastman in his mother's closet twenty years earlier, he was close to the culmination of his plan.

"He's behind this Zurtech stuff," Kevin said Thursday afternoon. He had just dropped down in a chair in front of Tony's desk. "I'd bet a month's salary on it."

"Come on." Tony frowned. "What could possibly give you that impression?"

"It's obvious. He was preoccupied for days, and *boom*." He threw up his arms. "Suddenly he's on top of the world. You think it's a coincidence that his entire disposition changed with the release of that story?"

"Yes. I do. I mean, let's be realistic, Kevin. Why would Joseph be behind this? What is his motivation?"

Kevin raised his eyebrows. "Money. Nothing else motivates the guy. Oh," he continued, raising his index finger, "and as an added bonus, he gets revenge for his fiancée."

"I'll give you the revenge card, but you're going to have to work a little harder to prove the money theory."

"Something on the stock market."

"Right." Tony laughed. "He bought stock in Zurtech and then released the information so he could watch it tumble. Last I heard, they were down twenty-five percent. He's not going to make a whole lot of money there."

"I don't know. Maybe he invested in one of their competitors, thinking their stock would go up as Zurtech's went down."

"You're reaching, Kevin."

"I don't know what he did, but I'm sure he did something. There was a reason he initially called those women into this office after the two of you decided we weren't going to take the case."

"Not this again." Tony glanced at his watch. "I've got a meeting in thirty minutes, and I don't have time to sit here and listen to you throw out wild accusations about our partner."

"I know I'm right," Kevin said. "And if he used this firm to gather information for his own financial gain, we could all be in trouble."

"Enough!" Tony stood up and buckled his briefcase. "I was serious the other day. I've had enough of the two of you, and I don't want to sit around and discuss what-ifs about Joe. It's a waste of both our time. If you have proof—actual evidence to back up your claims—then come talk to me. I've got to go."

19

ony's Friday started out normal enough. He left his house at 5:00 a.m., stopped at the gym to work out and was sitting behind his desk with a large mug of coffee by 7:00 a.m.

He opened his appointment book and began to scribble himself a note, but halfway through the message, his pen ran out of ink. He opened the left lower drawer of his desk and began rummaging through its contents in search of ink refills. When he pulled out a stack of manila folders, half of them spilled to the floor. Without the blunder, his day may have gone differently. As he knelt down beside his desk to put the papers back in their files, he picked up an invoice that had slipped out of one of the folders.

He frowned as he looked at it. It was over a year old and from Malone Investigations for surveillance work at an address in Reston. His eyes centered in on the address and then moved to the sticky note, which read *Give to Joe*.

He left his office, invoice in hand, and crossed to Joseph's office. "Is he in?" He stopped at the secretary's desk.

"He's in court today."

Moments later, he was in the office of the firm accountants. "What account was this charged to?" He held out the invoice to the lead accountant.

"This is over fifteen months old," the man said, looking up from the invoice.

"I know the date," Tony said shortly. "Can you plug in the name or invoice number or something to let me know what client it was charged to?"

"Sure." He set the invoice off to the side of his desk, his eyes returning to the spreadsheet on the computer screen. "I'll let you know when—"

"Now." He put his hand on the sheet and slid it back towards the accountant. "I need to know now."

Within a minute, he held the sheet out to Tony. "It wasn't charged to a client. Mr. Craig paid it himself. He said it was personal business."

"Personal business?"

"That's right." The accountant nodded. "I remember, because I'd charged it to another client, and he told me to transfer the charges to him. He wrote out a personal check. See?" He pointed to the monitor where, next to the charge, was a note reading, *Paid—J. Craig by personal check.*

⁓ ⁓

Tony met John Bianchi for a lunch meeting to discuss the mechanics involved in setting up a trust for his son. When the business concluded, John turned the conversation personal. "I made a killing on the stock market this week, thanks to Joe's advice."

"Is that so?"

"As soon as I heard the news break on Monday night regarding Zurtech, I put a call in to my stock broker and had him sell three hundred shares short. By yesterday, I'd made over thirty thousand dollars—"

"Joe told you to sell Zurtech stock short?" Tony sat up straighter in his chair.

"Not specifically. I had lunch with him a few months ago, and he gave me a short course on investment strategies. He told me you could make as much money when a company is losing value as you can when it's gaining. He explained the whole 'selling short' strategy to me. I took his advice. I knew Zurtech wouldn't be going up this week, so I did what he said and made a bundle. He probably did too."

"Probably," Tony said.

—～—

When Joseph walked into his office at 5:30 p.m., Tony was sitting behind his desk, a highball glass full of scotch cupped in his right hand. "Hello." Joseph hesitated briefly before setting his briefcase next to the door. "Are you waiting for me?"

"Yes." Tony made no move to vacate the chair. "Close the door."

Joseph pushed the door closed before crossing the room and lowering himself into one of his club chairs. "What's up?"

"I don't know." Tony met his eyes. "I was hoping maybe you could tell me."

Joseph leaned forward, resting his elbows on his knees and linking his hands. "I think you need to tell me what's on your mind. You're the one sitting in my chair, and I'm assuming there's a reason."

"I want to know what your involvement is in this Zurtech story."

"What?" Joseph sat up. "How could I possibly have any involvement with that?"

"I don't know. That's why I'm asking." The set of Tony's jaw was the only indication he was angry.

"I'd expect this from Kevin, but not from you. I didn't have any involvement." He was out of his chair and crossing to the bar.

"Is this the first time?"

"I have no clue what you're talking about. Did Kevin put you up to this?"

"I figured it out myself."

"Figured what out?" Joseph asked shortly.

"You're going to stand there and lie to me? Like I'm just anybody?"

"Well, you're sitting there accusing me of who knows what, like I'm just anybody."

"I know you met with Lia and the other woman after this firm and, in particular, you and I decided we shouldn't take the case. I know you paid to have surveillance on the house at 52561 Orange Avenue in Reston and I know you came to a meeting forty minutes late a few weeks ago because Malone stopped by the office. Who, as far as I can tell, isn't involved in any of your cases with this firm." He stood and walked around the desk, stopping just feet in front of Joseph. "Don't lie to me, Joe. I want to know what you were doing."

"This has nothing to do with you or this firm. And I have a problem with you coming into my office, sitting behind my desk and acting like you're sitting in judgment over me. Zurtech and my involvement in it, or lack thereof, is none of your business."

"That's where you're wrong. The Zurtech case was brought to your attention because of your involvement in this firm."

"So?" Joseph crossed his arms tightly over his chest.

"So, you used insider information for your own gain."

"And how did I use it for my own gain? Even if I am responsible for leaking that information to the media, which I'm not admitting, how does that benefit me?"

Tony stared into his friend's eyes. "I've been defending you to Kevin for years. And he was right. You're standing there, looking me in the eyes, and lying to me."

"And you stand there in judgment over me, accusing me of God knows what!"

"Damn it, Joe! You better answer my questions, or so help me, I'll turn you in to the SEC and the bar association."

Joseph took a step backwards, his cheeks turning red. "What are you talking about?"

"You!" Tony closed the distance separating them, their faces inches apart. "You betrayed this firm and me."

"What are you talking—"

"Stop fucking lying to me," Tony growled. "Don't you get it? I know what you did. You gathered the evidence and then, last Friday, while you were holed up in this office too busy with your portfolio to deal with firm business, you sold stock of Zurtech. Then you leaked the information you gathered to the media and waited to cash in."

"Wow." Joseph smiled slightly as he shook his head. "You think you've got this figured out, don't you?" He turned from Tony and walked across the office.

"Yes. I do." Tony's gaze followed his movement to the window. "How many times, Joseph? How many times have you used information from our clients—insider information—to line your own pockets?"

"I'm not even going to dignify that question with a response."

"You'd better, because I'm close to turning you in to the SEC."

"Really?" Joseph turned from the window, his eyebrows raised, his jaw clenched.

"Yes." Tony gave an exaggerated nod of his head. "Did you give any thought to the other people at this firm when you decided to break the law?" His face was red and his lips were turned down. "Did you consider that you were jeopardizing this entire practice?"

"I think you're being a bit melodramatic."

"Damn it, this is serious! You used insider information to make a profit on the market—information you were privy to because of your association with this firm. If the SEC starts investigating, they'll figure it out and then we'll be no better than Zurtech. No one in the city will hire us."

"They weren't clients of this firm. The records aren't even here. There's absolutely no proof."

"Except for the word of the women that came in here seeking our service! Jesus, does Lia have any idea what you did?"

"You're blowing this whole thing out of proportion." Joseph crossed the room to stand in front of Tony. "I told them there was no case. That a jury would not award them any money. And that was the truth. Then I conducted an investigation of my own, an investigation that cost me over a hundred and twenty-five thousand dollars."

"Stop pretending that what you did wasn't illegal," Tony said through clenched teeth. "You broke the law. You broke the law using that computer." He pointed to the computer on Joseph's desk. "In this office."

"The information was available to the general public. Anyone could have uncovered this information if they watched the house."

"Anyone who knew to watch the house! Anyone who attended the staff meeting where we discussed the case—"

"That's not—"

"Save it! We both know the law and the truth."

Joseph sighed. "I'll stop arguing with you about it, but it doesn't mean I agree."

Tony glared at him for several silent moments. "You may have almost a billion dollars, and it may be worth jeopardizing the reputation of this entire firm so you can make whatever the hell you made, but what about the rest of us? Huh?" He took a couple steps forward until he was inches from Joseph. "I've put everything I have into this place. Everything! And I need my draw. I count on it, as do the other partners who work their asses off for this place! And then there's you," he spit out, poking Joseph in the center of the chest. "You used this firm. You used me. Hell, you even used Lia to make a quick buck." As he spoke, getting angrier at each word, he moved still closer to Joseph, who backed up until his thighs came into contact with his desk. "And all I want to know now is why. Eight hundred million isn't enough? How much is going to be enough? And how many of our clients did you use? How many times over the past six years have you used insider information?"

"None!" Joseph stepped sideways to remove himself from the small space between Tony and his desk. "I've never used information gained from our clients to make stock picks."

Tony turned to face him. "You just did."

"No." Joseph shook his head. "We're not in total agreement over that point, but I assure you, I've never used information gained from our clients to make money on the market."

"Of course we may not be in total agreement on that point."

"Tony, come on," Joseph said. "I have a record of every stock I've ever purchased. If you don't believe me, you can—"

"I want you out of here. I want to dissolve this partnership. I can't—I *won't* work with someone I don't trust."

Joseph's eyes opened wider. "Tony?" He reached out, but Tony moved back before he could touch him. "You can't mean this. We've been friends for—"

"You're not *my friend*. *My friend* wouldn't jeopardize this firm for his own personal gain. My *friend* wouldn't look me in the eyes and lie to me. The person I thought was my friend is the person Kevin Stuart has been describing for years, only I didn't believe—didn't *want* to believe the truth. I don't know you, Joseph." He pushed past him and walked towards the door.

"Tony! Don't walk out of here!"

"We're done."

"What's going on in there?" Kevin asked as Tony passed him, coming out of the office. "What in the hell is all the yelling about?"

"Nothing," Tony snapped, continuing down the hall.

"Hi." A light knock on Joseph's office door preceded Lia's entrance thirty minutes later. "Are you sleeping?" she asked when she saw him stretched out on the couch.

"No." Joseph pushed himself up on his elbows. "I was just resting."

"Long day?"

"Yeah. Are you ready to go?" He threw his legs over the side of the couch and sat up, running a hand through his already tousled hair.

"Yes. I'm starved. I missed lunch." She followed him towards his desk and watched as he sorted through a stack of messages. "I ran into Tony downstairs."

"Oh?"

"He almost walked right past me without saying a word. I think he would have if I hadn't stepped in front of him. He seemed upset."

"What makes you say that?"

"He barely acknowledged me. He said hello and that was it. He never even stopped walking."

"He was probably distracted about a case."

"I guess. Are you ready?"

He placed the messages back on his desk. "Yes, let's go."

"Did you see the paper today?" Lia asked as they entered Joseph's condo hours later, recalling something she'd heard earlier on the radio. "It looks like Stan Hall's brother will be indicted on charges of conspiracy to commit money laundering or something like that."

"Extortion and money laundering," Joseph said as they walked into the family room. "And yes, I saw the paper. It should be around here somewhere. I read it before going off to court this morning." He glanced around the spotless room. "It must be in the kitchen or study."

"It's amazing how quickly everything's unraveling." Lia sat down on the couch, curling her legs up beneath her.

In the days since the media began reporting the Zurtech story, Stan Hall had resigned, several CEOs had admitted to being blackmailed, several female Zurtech employees already had law-yers filing motions against Zurtech, and a financial officer of Tia Tacos had come forward to say he personally saw Stan Hall bring large sums of cash to the office for deposit into Tia Tacos' bank accounts. He said that when he asked Mike Hall, Stan's brother, where the money came from, he was told it came from trucks, but he knew it wasn't the truth. When the story broke, he immediately called the police, not wanting anyone to think he was involved in money laundering.

As the nation and the world watched, seemingly mesmerized by the soap opera like plot, the story of the blackmail scheme slowly unfolded, reading more like a fiction novel than an ac-tual news story as new details made the front pages of papers worldwide.

"Eric Nettles made today's paper," Joseph said as he joined her on the couch. "Someone in the FBI leaked out the names of the men on the tapes."

Lia sprang up. "I want to see it."

Joseph's lips turned up. "I thought you didn't want revenge."

"I don't. But if he's in the paper being exposed for the jerk he is, I can't help but take enjoyment in that fact. Where did you say the paper was?"

"In the kitchen or my study. I'm going to take a shower while you get your enjoyment, okay?"

"Maybe I'll meet you there." A few minutes later she closed the front section of the newspaper and set it on Joseph's desk. She'd never considered herself vindictive, but knowing Eric Nettles didn't get off scot-free—that he'd actually experienced a degree of humiliation like many of his victims—felt, well, good.

She was about to leave Joseph's office and join him in the shower when she noticed a few sheets of paper on the floor to the left of the desk. She reached down and picked them up, her eyes automatically scanning the contents of the top sheet. It was a confirmation report from his brokerage firm, detailing stock activity from the week prior.

She placed it on the center of his desk and pushed back her chair, intending to leave the room, when she reached out and picked up the sheet again, her unconscious mind catching something on the first glance that her conscious mind missed. Zurtech! He'd conducted some type of transaction with Zurtech stock. Either buying or selling, but with her limited knowledge of the stock market and even more limited experience interpreting broker transaction reports, she couldn't figure out what he'd done.

She'd ask him, she decided, standing up. And then, as she walked towards the door, she noticed the secret panel leading to his hidden room of files was open.

"I thought you were going to join me," Joseph said when he came out of his bathroom, freshly showered with a towel wrapped loosely around his waist.

"What did you do?" Lia's voice was barely a whisper as her eyes met his. "Were you using me all along?"

"Don't be ridiculous. Tony's upset, you can't listen to him."

"Tony? Was he involved in this too?"

"What are we talking about here?" He lowered himself beside her on the bed, his narrowed eyes meeting hers.

"I'm talking about what you did."

"What I did? Why don't you tell me what you think I did?"

"I..." She couldn't believe it. She felt completely numb.

"You what?" Joseph took her hand. "Tell me what's going on."

"I went through the Zurtech file. I know everything." Her eyes met his. "Everything."

"Lia, you don't understand."

"You're right." A few tears escaped her eyes. "I don't understand how someone can use someone else's pain, someone else's humiliation, for their own financial gain."

"I didn't—"

"Yes, you did. It's in the file. And it's dated. Back in December, after your meeting with Claudia, before we ever even met, you have notes about how far you thought the stock would fall when the news was released. You—you planned this before you ever met me."

"That's right." Joseph gripped her upper arms and turned her to face him. "I planned it before I ever met you, but I fell in love with you. I am in love with you."

"What does that have to do with anything?" She frowned through her tears.

"A lot. I didn't know I was going to fall in love with you when I came up with the plan."

"So?"

"So I never used you."

"Oh, okay. So it's okay to use innocent women as long as you're not in love with them, and if you are in love with them it's not using them because you are in love with them?" She was infuriated with the sheer absurdity of his argument. "Are you even listening to yourself?"

"Yes, but you're obviously not. My plan was not to use innocent women. Claudia was a prostitute. There was no way in hell a jury was going to award her one cent. And if she went to the police, Hall's operation was so clever they wouldn't have been able to prove anything. It would have ended up in the news—like it is now, except your name would have been attached to it. And Hall would have covered everything up and nothing would have happened. Your reputation would be soiled, and he would have gotten away with it."

"Oh, so you were doing us a favor by exposing the operation and making yourself a huge profit on the stock market in the process."

"That's right. I exposed Zurtech and Stan Hall for what they were, exactly like you wanted. And instead of receiving payment from you and the other women involved, I extracted my own."

Lia stared at him in silence, trying to understand how he could believe there was nothing wrong with what he'd done. "How much?"

"How much what?"

"How much money did you make? How much pay did you manage to extract?"

"I only made about twenty million from Zurtech."

"But that wasn't all you made, was it? You were making money on other companies too, right?" She hadn't read it in the file, but she recognized the names of other companies on the transaction report in his office.

"My investments were risky and speculative. I sold short in the hopes that some of the CEOs would be mentioned, and I also bought heavily in a small electronics company that had been competing with Zurtech for a large contract. I was hoping they'd get the contract because of Zurtech's negative publicity, and I was right."

"So, how much?" Lia repeated. "How much money did you make?"

"I don't know exactly. I haven't computed everything. And I still own over twenty-five percent of this electronics company, so

I wouldn't be able to cash it in, even if I wanted to, without seriously bringing down the value of the stock."

"Approximately, Joseph. How much?"

"Three hundred million." He continued meeting her eyes. "Approximately."

She felt like the wind was sucked out of her lungs, never having imagined the amount could be so high. No wonder he'd been so upset when the story wasn't immediately released. "And here I thought you were trying to get back at the men who humiliated your fiancée. How naïve you must have thought me."

"I was. That was a big part of—"

"Stop lying to me. Hasn't there already been enough of that?"

"I'm not lying."

"Yes, you are." She stood and walked towards the bedroom door.

"Where are you going? Lia, don't be this way. Don't make a bigger deal out of this than it is."

"I'm not, Joseph." She turned back to him. "I don't know who you are anymore. The person I thought you were wouldn't be capable of something like this." She turned and left the room.

"Wait!" Joseph followed her down the stairs and into the family room. "Lia, please, let me explain."

"Explain what?" She picked up her purse. "How money is more important to you than me?"

"That isn't true." He touched her arm. "Don't leave. Let's talk this out."

"There's nothing left to say. The file speaks for itself."

"Lia, this has nothing to do with you. I swear, I never would have done this if I knew you'd interpret it this way. Please, please sit down and let me explain."

She knew she should leave, because there was no way he could make her understand, but she wanted to believe him. To believe he was the man she thought he was, because anything less meant it was over, and that thought was beyond comprehension.

She let him pull her down onto the couch beside him and did her best not to cry as she looked at his handsome face, strands of wet hair falling over his forehead. He was still naked except for the towel at his waist, and her eyes moved to the large expanse of his chest. She wanted to touch him, suddenly needing to feel the reassurance of his touch. Or maybe she knew it might be over, and she wanted to make love to him one more time before letting the realization sink in. Because she loved him—at least the man she thought him to be. And if that wasn't who he was, she surely could wait another few hours to find out.

"Just listen to me for a second."

"I don't want to talk," she whispered. "I want to go to bed." She didn't want to leave him tonight, and she was afraid if he explained, she'd have to.

It took him a few moments to change gears and comprehend what she was saying. "I thought you wanted to talk."

"We can talk later." She touched his leg. "I want to go to bed."

"Why?" He frowned.

"Make love to me, Joseph."

It was bright outside when Joseph awoke. "Lia?"

"I'm here." Her light voice came from the leather couch across the room, where she was sitting fully clothed, her knees drawn up against her chest, her arms wrapped tightly around her legs.

"Come here." He patted the bed.

"No. I'm ready to talk now."

"We can talk in bed."

"No, Joseph."

"May I at least have a cup of coffee first?"

"The kitchen's probably a better place to talk anyway."

"You betrayed me," she said when they were sitting across from each other in his kitchen. "After what I've been through with Ned and Eric, I thought you understood how important honesty was to me." She'd been up for hours, and she knew there was nothing he could say to undo the truth. He had lied and manipulated her so he could make money. It was like some kind of nightmare she was never going to wake up from.

"I didn't exactly lie to you."

"Yes, you did. You've been lying to me since the first time we met. You told me we might have a case and the whole time you knew we didn't. You wanted to gather the information necessary to carry out your already well-conceived plan—damaging Zurtech's reputation and therefore their stock price."

"No." He shook his head. "I told you from the beginning you shouldn't go to court. That Zurtech's attorneys would destroy your reputation. I said that from the beginning."

"Okay, maybe." She couldn't recall their discussion as clearly as he obviously could. "But I distinctly remember you saying that they might settle—that I might receive money."

"Right. And do you recall what you said?" When she didn't respond after several seconds, he continued. "You said you didn't care about compensation. You wanted them to pay for what they'd done to you. You wanted Zurtech and Stan Hall to be exposed, and that's what I did, Lia. I exposed them."

"But I wanted to go to the police. That's how I wanted them exposed. I wanted the police to start investigating."

"Going to the police was not the answer. It may have exposed Hall, but it would have hurt you too. As your lawyer and friend, I had to advise you against that."

"Maybe that's true. Maybe I should never have gone to the police, but your motivation for telling me not to go had nothing to do with my reputation or well-being. You wanted to gather more information on your own and—and time the release of the information. The truth is you lied to me."

"How did I lie to you?" He brought his eyebrows together. "I may not have told you everything I was doing, everything I was thinking, but I didn't lie to you."

"Yes, you did! You represented yourself under false pretenses. I thought you were my lawyer. Claudia thought you were her lawyer. But you were using us to get information."

"Look." He reached across the table and covered one of her hands. "You wanted them to pay for what they did to you."

"Forget it—"

"No, no." He gripped her hand when she attempted to pull it back. "Did you or did—"

"Forget it," she repeated, louder this time, but there was no quieting Joseph, who continued to talk over her interruption.

"Did you or did you not tell me all you were interested in was having the operation exposed?"

"Fine." Lia sighed. "Fine, whatever you say. You were trained at the top law school in the country. I don't have a chance to win in an argument with you, regardless of whether or not I'm right. You're twisting everything I say to fit your argument."

"No, I'm not. I'm trying to point out that you got exactly what you wanted."

"And you certainly got what you wanted too, didn't you, Joseph?"

"Yes, I did."

She felt defeated, numb, like she'd been in a physical fight, and there he sat, completely calm, as if he really believed there was nothing wrong with what he'd done. "Was it worth it?"

"Worth what?"

"Hurting me. Breaking the law. I mean, isn't what you did considered insider trading?"

His lips turned up. "Technically, I suppose. Are you planning to turn me in?"

"This isn't funny, Joseph."

"It certainly wouldn't be if you decided to turn me in."

"This is serious. I feel like you've betrayed me." She laid her hand on her chest as she pleaded with her eyes for some level of understanding.

"But I didn't. I can't help what you think or feel. All I know is my own motivation. And it certainly wasn't to betray you."

She dropped her face into her hands for several seconds before once again lifting her head and meeting his eyes. "I know it wasn't to betray me. It was to make a bunch of money—"

"And to expose Hall and Zurtech for what they did to you."

"That may have been an outcome, but that wasn't your motivation. Your motivation was to make the money."

"My motivation for taking any case is to make money. But I guess because I fell in love with you, I was expected to handle the case pro bono?" He finished the coffee in his mug and pushed back his chair. "You want some more?" he asked, reaching for her empty cup.

"No." She shook her head. "I'm going to leave."

"Leave?" Joseph slowly sat back down. "Where are you going to go?"

"Home." She suddenly felt close to tears, but she was determined not to cry. "You betrayed my trust. You can pretend you didn't because I ultimately got what I wanted, but it doesn't change the fact that you weren't honest with me. That your overriding motivation was to make money."

"So you're leaving?"

"I can't trust you."

"You aren't serious. You're leaving because of a little misunderstanding?"

"It's not a misunderstanding. We have completely different ethics. To me, lying by omission is the same as lying. I mean, in your world, I guess Ned didn't betray me when he started sleeping with Candice."

"In my world?"

"Right. Because he never told me he wasn't sleeping with her, so he wasn't really being dishonest."

"What are you saying?"

"That as your fiancée, the woman you're supposed to love more than anyone else in the world, there shouldn't be any omission. We've been together over a year, and if there wasn't anything wrong with what you were doing, why didn't you ever mention it to me?"

"Because it didn't have anything to do with you. I wasn't stealing money from you. I wasn't doing anything to you. It was none of your business."

Lia's mouth dropped open and she could feel her face heating up. "None of my business! If it weren't for me, you wouldn't have made that money."

"No, if it weren't for *me*, I wouldn't have made that money. I spent over a hundred thousand dollars on the investigation.

Without the information I uncovered, nothing would have happened. Neither of us would have gotten what we wanted."

"Oh, I see." Lia stood up and glared down at him. "Now I'm supposed to be grateful to you?"

"No." He reached out for her arm, but she stepped back before he could touch her. "You don't have to be grateful, but I think you're blowing this completely out of proportion. This isn't a big deal."

"But why?" Lia met his eyes. "Why would you be so desperate to make money?"

"Because of Eastman. I want to meet him before he dies."

Of course, Lia thought as she slowly lowered herself back into her chair. How could she not have realized it sooner? His whole purpose for being was to make the *Forbes* list so he could meet his father, and that obsession resulted in him not only betraying her, but also betraying his ethics and probably his partners too. "But you broke the law. I mean, you used information from a client who came to your firm to manipulate the stock market. If it came out, your whole firm would suffer."

"It's not going to come out. I covered myself. Most of my money was made through the small electronics firm. The SEC would have a hard time proving insider trading there."

"But why would you even take the chance?" Lia was trying her best to understand. "Just the hint of an investigation would hurt your law firm."

"I needed to finish this." He gripped her hand. "I'm going to make the list this year. He's going to see how successful I am."

"But what about the rest of us, Joseph? Is this why Tony seemed so distracted when I ran in to him yesterday? Does he know what you did?" His lack of response was all the answer she needed. She could feel herself getting angry all over again at the ludicrousness of his motivation. Here he was, hands down the most intelligent person she'd ever know, more concerned with what a stranger thought of him than his fiancée and best friend.

"You don't understand."

"You're right, I don't. Because from where I'm sitting, it seems you care more about impressing a man you don't even know than being loyal to the woman you want to spend the rest of your life with."

"One has nothing to do with the other. I've been working towards this goal my entire life, and I've finally reached it. You should be happy for me."

"I'm happy it's over, if it really is. What happens if he makes the list too? Does that mean you'll have to do whatever it takes to make more money for another year?"

"That's not going to happen."

"But what if it does?"

"It won't. It's over."

Lia sighed as she pulled her hand back and once again stood up. "You're thinking is so warped."

"You don't understand."

"You're right."

"Well, at least we can agree on that. We should probably drop it because this isn't a big deal."

"And that is the problem," Lia said, pointing at him. "The fact that you don't realize what a big deal it is shows how different we really are. I can't spend my life with someone who thinks what you did was okay. I can't."

"So, what?" Joseph laughed. "Now you're breaking up with me over this?"

"I don't know." Lia's voice caught as she met his eyes. "I don't know. I need to think. I have to go."

"Lia!" Joseph was out of his chair and following her into the family room, taking hold of her arm and forcing her to stop. "Look at me!" He gripped her upper arms and turned her to face him. "Remember me? I'm the man you made love with last night. How can you even imply that you're not sure about us? I love you. You love me."

"I don't know if that's enough."

His eyes opened wider. "You don't know if that's enough?"

She dropped her gaze, refusing to let the pain so evident in his eyes sway her from what she knew she had to do. She remembered the pain in her father's eyes when he told her he was leaving the family and then in Ned's eyes the first time he told her he was leaving. It certainly didn't mean they were better people than she thought they were. It just meant at those moments, they were feeling pain. "You lied to me, Joseph. And you used me." When she pulled back, he let her go, dropping his hands to his sides.

"I'm sorry you see it that way, because I love you more than anything in this world. And I would never do anything to intentionally hurt you."

"And you really don't see anything wrong with what you did?"

"No." He shook his head. "I don't, but it obviously hurt you, and that certainly wasn't my intention."

"What was your intention? To impress a man you don't even know, without thought to how I would feel? You betrayed me, Joseph. You betrayed me to better a man you don't even know."

He scraped a weary hand down his face as he closed his eyes. "Why can't you understand?"

"I do understand. You're the one that doesn't understand. You put money before my feelings."

"You're thinking of this wrong."

She held up her hands. "I need to get out of here. I can't bear another minute of this."

"Lia—"

"No. Please, don't say another word." And with that she left.

— ~

Lia glanced at her cell phone. It was almost 11:00 p.m., and she hadn't heard a word from Joseph since leaving his condominium that morning. She'd cried the whole drive back to the townhouse, unable to reconcile how the man who claimed to love her could put his desire for revenge before all else. She couldn't believe it, and yet it was the truth. He was more concerned with impressing his biological father than protecting the woman he professed to love.

When she'd arrived home ten hours earlier she was convinced the relationship was over, that Joseph was the same as her father and Ned—someone who couldn't be trusted. But as the day progressed, little cracks began developing in her resolve. Her mind kept conjuring up images of him running to the hospital when Taylor was sick, images of him pulling her fully clothed into the shower, images of him threatening Ned for disrespecting her, and finally a recurring image of him bending down on one knee and asking her to be his wife.

As hard as her mind tried to tell her otherwise, she couldn't believe he was like her father and Ned. She knew he'd betrayed her, but it was more the betrayal of a fourteen-year-old boy than the man he was today. He'd made a vow to himself as a boy and apparently never reexamined it as a man. It was true he'd let it consume a large portion of his energy, but he was still the most amazing man she had ever known.

Part of her feared she was rationalizing his behavior because she didn't have the strength to let him go, but the truth was she didn't have the strength to let him go. She knew choosing to end her relationship with Joseph would be something she would regret every day for the rest of her life.

She picked up her empty wine glass and was on her way to the kitchen when she heard the doorbell. She closed her eyes, giving a silent prayer of thanks, and then was setting down her glass and making her way to the front door.

Moments later, she pulled open the door, her eyes meeting Joseph's. He looked as bad as she felt. He was dressed uncharacteristically casually, in worn jeans and a Harvard T-shirt, his hair uncombed, his eyes red, but he was the most beautiful man she had ever seen.

"I'll give it away," he said deeply, his eyes meeting hers. "I'll give every dollar I have away if it means keeping you."

"Joseph." Lia shook her head.

"I will." He was in the house, his hands moving to the sides of her face. "None of it means anything to me if I can't share it with you."

"I love you," she said softly, tears coming to her eyes. "I could never leave you."

"Thank God." He kissed her forehead as he pulled her into his arms. "Thank God."

~ ~

As Tony approached the reception area in front of his office Monday morning, Joseph stood to greet him.

"I was beginning to think you weren't going to show."

"I'm a few minutes late." Tony glanced at his watch. He'd left a message for Joseph saying he wanted to meet with him at 10:00 a.m.

"Good morning, Jennifer." Tony turned his attention to his secretary. "Would you hold my calls?" He preceded Joseph into his office. "Have a seat."

"I know you're upset," Joseph began as soon as they were seated, "but I think I can explain this so you'll understand."

"I'm listening."

It took Joseph exactly twelve minutes to explain why he had risked his reputation and the reputation of the firm in order to make a virtual killing on the stock market. By the time he finished, Tony's anger had returned.

"Let me get this straight." There was a smile of disbelief on his face. "All of this, all your investments. You did it so you could make the *Forbes* list and meet Eastman?"

"Yes."

"How much did you make?"

"About three hundred million."

"So you think you have the money now?" If he was surprised by the amount, his face didn't register it.

Again, Joseph nodded, but this time more hesitantly. "Yes. I think I do."

"Congratulations," Tony said after several seconds of silence. "You accomplished everything you set out to and, if I'm as lucky as you've been, you won't bring this firm down in the process. Not that it would matter to you, especially if the fines weren't large enough to cut too severely into your net worth."

"Nothing's going to—"

"Is there anything else?" Tony interrupted coldly. "Because I met with Kevin over the weekend and..." He paused as he leaned over and picked up his briefcase. "We came up with the terms for your departure."

Joseph laughed. "What are you talking about?"

Tony opened the briefcase and pulled out a folder, opening it quickly before holding it out. "Here. Why don't you go through this over the next day or so? I wrote it myself. It's fairly straight-forward and, under the circumstances, more than generous."

Joseph frowned. "Did you listen to what—"

"Every word. And like I said, congratulations on accomplishing everything you set out to. I'm sure Eastman will be duly impressed. And now I'd like you to disassociate yourself from this firm."

"I don't want to disassociate myself from this firm."

"Well." Tony cocked his head to the side. "Then I guess you should have handled yourself in a way that would have benefited all of us and not only yourself."

"Tony, this was it." He held up the index finger of his right hand. "One time, just one time. You can go through my files. Before Zurtech, I never—"

"It doesn't matter. It's too late, Joe. I don't trust you, and I told you Friday I won't work with someone I don't trust."

Joseph gripped the folder in his hand, making no move to look at the contents inside. "You told Kevin about this?"

"No." Tony lowered his eyes to his hands and studied his fingernails. "I told him you were leaving."

Joseph's face turned red. "Our friendship means so little to you?"

"Our friendship was important to me, and you took advantage of it. Kevin tried to warn me about you for years—about your insatiable appetite for money—but I wouldn't listen because you were my friend, and I didn't believe you were capable of doing something to jeopardize what we'd worked so hard to create. I trusted you. But I was wrong, because your obsession with making the *Forbes* list was apparently more important to you than anything else."

"I'm ready to be a full-time partner again. This is what I love to do."

"Well you're going to have to do it elsewhere, because I can't work with you." His jaw was set as he looked at Joseph.

"So, that's it."

"Yes, that's it."

Joseph looked down at his hands, which were shaking. "Kevin must be overjoyed."

"This isn't about Kevin. You brought this on yourself."

"Okay." He nodded as he stood up. "I guess I'll go read this." He held up the file. He crossed to the door, stopping with his hand on the knob. "Besides Lia, you're the only person I've ever told about Eastman, and I thought you understood." He looked back over his shoulder. "You know what he did to me. You know. How can you not understand what I did?"

"I know what he did. And I know how deeply you feel about him, Joe, but that can't begin to justify what you did. You betrayed the trust of every person at this firm, and you put us in jeopardy."

"I'm sorry you feel that way," Joseph said before leaving the room.

"I'm sorry too, Joe," Tony said to the empty room.

～ ～

Two weeks later, Joseph lay on his bed fully clothed, waiting for Lia to arrive for dinner, the music of Copland's *Fanfare to the*

Common Man blaring through the stereo speakers as he stared up at the skylights above his bed. He'd been in the same position for over an hour.

He was worth over a billion dollars. Joseph Craig, the illegitimate son of a maid, in a matter of twenty years, went from owning only clothes and a few pieces of furniture to having a net worth of over a billion dollars. He was positioned to make the *Forbes* list of richest Americans. He had more money than the biological father who'd never acknowledged him. He'd realized his lifetime goal.

In the process, he'd broken the law, compromised his own principals, betrayed his fiancée and lost his best friend, a friend who served as the most stable influence of his adult life. He'd lost the respect of a man he held more esteem for than any other—a man who'd taken him into his home and made him part of his family, a man he thought of more as a brother than a friend.

"Joseph? Are you here?"

Joseph pushed a button on the remote, silencing the stereo. His gaze found Lia, who came through the doorway. "I love you," he said as he pushed himself to a sitting position. "I love you more than I ever imagined possible." He threw his feet over the side of the bed and stood up, crossing the room and meeting her at the door. "And I'm determined to get that sparkle to come back to your eyes when you look at me."

"Sparkle?"

"The one that used to come to your eyes when you saw me." He pulled her slowly towards him, his eyes never leaving hers. "I love you," he said again before dropping his mouth over hers.

"Wow," Lia said softly, when he lifted his head. "What's gotten into you?"

"Sense." He kissed her forehead. "I have a phone call to make, and then I'll be ready to go."

20

ive months later, Lia was sitting opposite Joseph at the kitchen table in their Georgetown home, nibbling on a toasted bagel and reading the Sunday Style section of the *Washington Post*, when she saw a picture of Joseph.

Washington's own Joseph Craig reportedly missed being included in the Forbes 400 richest Americans list by $50 million. But don't feel too sorry for the ex–senior partner at Prossi, Stuart & Craig and current professor at Georgetown Law School—he is worth $950 million, according to sources. The magazine, which will hit newsstands in about two weeks, reports Craig kept himself from contention by quietly giving away $380 million to several charities benefiting abused women and children. He originally gave a donation of $300 million, but apparently gave another $80 million away when he learned he still had enough to make the list...Go figure.

Lia lifted her eyes from the article. "Joseph?"

"Yes?" His brown eyes met hers.

"I love you."

— —

A little over twenty-four hours later, Tony opened the door to a classroom at Georgetown University and, ignoring the curious stares from the twenty or so students in attendance, took a seat in the back row.

Joseph, who was standing at the front of the classroom, hesitated, clearly surprised by the identity of his visitor. "I'm sure most of you recognize our distinguished guest in the back row, my former law partner, Tony Prossi. Now that I'm no longer practicing, I'd say he's hands down the best trial attorney in the country, so this is indeed an honor and, if we're lucky, he'll join in on our discussion today."

Forty-five minutes later, after the last student filed out of the classroom, Joseph found himself alone with his ex-friend and partner. "You're good at this," Tony said, filling the silence as he walked towards Joseph, who was still standing at the front of the room.

"It's an interesting change. I like teaching."

"I read you signed on with CNN."

Joseph had recently been hired to serve as their on-air legal analyst. "They've been trying to get me for a couple years and now I finally have the time." He pushed his hands into his pockets. "I guess you saw the article in the *Post* yesterday."

"I had no idea."

"Well, it was supposed to remain confidential," Joseph said. "I gave the money away with the agreement they wouldn't release my name. I'm not sure what happened."

"Well, I'm glad they did. It was a noble thing to do."

"It was the right thing to do. The money wasn't rightfully mine."

"Eighty million of it was," Tony said.

"Yeah, well. I didn't want to make the list."

Tony nodded, his eyes searching as they looked into Joseph's. "So, did you meet him? Did you meet Eastman?"

Joseph shook his head. "No. I gave the man twenty years of my life. I think that's enough."

"You know it was always his loss."

Joseph shrugged. "It doesn't matter. All that matters is how I conduct myself. What kind of man, what kind of father I am."

"Is Lia pregnant?"

"She is." Joseph smiled.

"Congratulations. That's great, Joe! You didn't waste any time. You haven't been married long. I heard you eloped."

"A few months. We went to Bermuda—just the two of us."

"Congratulations."

"Thanks." He turned away then and began to gather his papers.

"How's Lia? I hear she's still working for Nick."

Joseph finished packing his briefcase and then pulled up a chair in front of Tony's and sat down. "Lia is the one person in this world I can't imagine being without. Lia is amazing and she's stayed amazing through this whole thing."

"You seem happy."

"I am—most of the time." He hesitated, continuing to meet Tony's eyes. "I'm sorry for...for everything. I should never have risked the firm."

Tony shook his head. "It's the past. Nothing came of it."

"But it could have, and I want you to know I'm sorry. You deserved more from me. I let you down. I let myself down. And I'm sorry."

"You're forgiven," Tony said as he pushed back his chair. "Do you have time for lunch?"

"Definitely." Joseph smiled. "My treat."

Also by Laura Branchflower

A Sense of Belonging

A White Picket Fence

Made in the USA
San Bernardino, CA
02 June 2018